PROTECTED
MERCILESS FEW MC

S. COURTNEY

Chapter One
Asher aka Wicked

PROTECTED
THE MERCILESS FEW MC: DEVIL'S IGNITED
Williamstown, Mass.

You know what they say, why have an ol' lady when you can have two willing and ready girls that get on their knees at the snap of your fingers?

Am I right?!

Trust me, if you saw me, you wouldn't pass up the opportunity to be a notch on my belt.

And plenty of girls have had the opportunity, but only top tier trim makes the cut.

sigh

Who am I kidding?! That macho bravado schtick is more Demon's territory.

I really thought I could pull it off, and I made some pretty dumb decisions, dismissed emotions, and learned some harsh lessons.

It forced me to grow up.

I don't want to sound like I'm making excuses, but I was simply imitating the behavior I saw around me. Looking back, I now understand that my brothers were vulgar and sexist. Stupidly, I looked up to them and wanted to be like them.

Before I knew it wasn't a good thing.

Every night, I would practice repeating those smooth player lines that always bagged them the girls. It wasn't until high school I used them with confidence. By then, it was only Diego and I. He was in his senior year and me in my freshman year.

Bernard and Terrence, the oldest Benedict brothers, had made us popular by association.

I was the youngest Benedict and fresh meat for the ladies. I knew with a flash of my smile I could make any girl weak in the knees, regardless of age.

I acted like a bad boy, but I did great in school. I wasn't stupid! Both my parents had respectable professions - my father was a retired Sergeant Major in the Marines and my mother a nurse practitioner. I knew better than to slack off in my studies. Punishment from dad would be brutal!

Terrence stupidly tested the waters when he went to the movies with his girl of the month and their friends instead of studying for the mid-term. His final midterm before graduation. He said this movie was the blockbuster of our time!

He barely passed with a C minus, which we all knew was unacceptable. Dad asked about what he did to prepare the days leading up to it. Dad had the house phone in his hand when he said he was going to call the parents of all the kids to find out if he didn't answer. Terrance finally had to confess he went to the double feature the night before instead of that all-night study session mom and dad said he could go to.

My dad was red hot and had him write a note to the teacher apologizing for not being fully prepared. Then he had to beg for a retest. The teacher agreed and gave him two days to prepare. He got lucky that Mr. Henderson was one of dad's military buddies.

After the humiliating apology, dad had him doing wall sits while reading the required chapters aloud. He had to do it for ten minutes straight and got a five-minute break in-between. My dad would immediately quiz him on what he just recited and if he got it wrong, he'd have to do a one minute plank!

And we all know exercise and punishment minutes are twice as long as actual minutes.

No, I never wanted that, so I dedicated myself to studying and just pretended to be a bad boy. But there was one element that was authentic: It was my dream to graduate and eventually have enough money to buy a motorcycle. While others were hoping for fancy sports cars or wishing to avoid inheriting their family's old and worn-out car, I was daydreaming about the freedom of riding on two wheels, my boots in the breeze.

Plus, ladies love a bad ass biker boy. It was a guaranteed chicken magnet, not that I needed any help.

Unfortunately, my dream came with fear because we knew how much dad harped on having a plan for your life. "Don't spend your youth lollygagging," He'd say, while pointing with authority. "build your future to be successful men! Do not embarrass me!"

The oldest children faced the most pressure as my dad forced them to choose between college and military service. There were no other options.

Terrence attended the University of Massachusetts, although it took him two years to decide on his degree program. Eventually, he settled on sports medicine. I believe he pursued a field that would please dad because he was tired of his constant input.

Bernard, being the oldest and model child, followed dad's footsteps into the Marines.

I think he's still stationed at Hawaii Kaneohe Bay, also

known as K-Bay. The sight of the graduation ceremony was awe-inspiring, with vibrant flags fluttering in the breeze. The speeches filled the air with messages of hope and purpose. Pride and anticipation filled the atmosphere. The deafening roar of the F-18 flyover resonated through the hearts of all in attendance.

My once cocky and arrogant brother, who dated the most beautiful and popular girls, stood before me as a man's man. His uniform, pressed to perfection, he stands tall, radiating confidence. The sun bounced off his neatly arranged ribbons, each one telling a story of his recent triumphs. One can't help but feel a sense of admiration and respect in the presence of such an impeccable presentation. I noticed Bernard had more ribbons than Dad did at his graduation. Wonder if he would notice, too? Would it spark adoration or hostility?

"You look good, big bro! Like those old pics of dad in his uniform. Guess you'll get all responsible now, settle down and all that?"

He laughed as he clapped my back, turning us away from everyone's view. "Are you kidding? I get way more ass now, especially the officer's wives who like to treat themselves to a little enlisted dessert. Plus the adrenaline of watching them watch me graduate while they sit next to their stiff, dry ass husbands. They might yell and have authority over me, but I'm the one banging their wives out! Hopefully, they never scream my name out. Don't want to end up in the brig." He nudged me while laughing. "I may never settle down! But that's between us, little brother. Dad would have a fit."

"Why, if he knew you were a side piece? Oh, definitely!" I burst out laughing, but his punch to my arm quieted me quickly. "Shhh! And I'm not a side chick. I got plenty of fellow enlisted babes I've conquered and plan on adding to my list. I may live dad's dream but I'm enjoying it my way!"

"Congratulations, I think?"

And then there were two Benedict brothers left in the nest.

4

I knew I didn't want to follow in anyone's footsteps. I had been my whole life, stepping on the worn path of my brothers. I had been treading the same worn path of my brothers. But now, I was determined to veer off course and forge my own path.

Diego had a similar idea, but the big revelation didn't come until he was an ocean away in London. He secured a role at a playhouse renowned for its prestigious reputation, although he harbored doubts about dad's approval. He told mom and being the caring, understanding and supportive matriarch she was, she gave him her blessing and said she would tell him.

I think mom was tired of dad trying to mold us into his exact image and ruling by force instead of love.

It went exactly as I expected. I was listening from the hallway near the steps. His voice boomed throughout the house. "Why didn't he tell me, Diane?!"

"This! Tobias, you expect all of them to be carbon copies, but did you even think that they may have taken on some of my traits? They're not robots! Diego has always loved arts and theater. It's HIS dream and so help me, Tobias, we are going to be supportive no matter what our boys decide. We raised them right, and I won't hear another word about it! Now go wash up for dinner!"

I peeked to see my 5' 6" mom standing up to her 6 foot tall husband. His anger vanquished, especially when she placed her hands on his chest. He took one hand and kissed it.

"No matter what, you have raised them right, Tobias."

And now there was only me, and I knew my decision would never make sense to them. I would bite the bullet and tell them after I did some scouting and bought my bike.

My obsession with motorcycles began when my brothers rented *The Last Riders*, and I watched from the stairs because of the film's R rating and also because it was 11 at night. From there I watched every motorcycle movie I could find, from the

50s classic *The Wild One* to the modern day *Biker Boyz. Easy Rider* was my go to, I knew it line for line.

I was going to be a biker boy, and I found the perfect club nearby. About an hour and some change north of Williamstown in Briarswood. It wasn't the typical club filled with only chaos and mayhem. They came with a purpose, to protect children from dangerous individuals and situations.

And that brought up painful memories that were not my own.

My 4th grade friend Franklin was one of those kids, and I remember it vividly. He would always come to school with bruises, which he would hide under his jacket, regardless of the weather. The only time he would take off his jacket was when he was at my house, and he spent a lot of time there. My home became his safe haven. Even though he never opened up to my parents, he confided in me about all of his abuse.

It was his mother abusing him at the discretion of her husband. Saying she needed to beat him when he disobeyed them. He wasn't even his dad, just some lazy, jobless, worthless loser she married. I only needed one interaction with him to know I'd knock his teeth out if he touched me. Or I'd tell my dad.

One night, Franklin admitted he was at an unfortunate breaking point and needed to get out or he was going to hurt himself. He was tired of feeling pain instead of love. He saw no other way out.

Here he was, nine years old, contemplating suicide.

I remember choking back the angry tears and bile as I devised a plan because even though I knew I'd lose a friend; I wanted him to be alive and happy. He deserved everything I got from my parents. Of course, they loved having him around and I saw how it would brighten his outlook, but only temporarily

Then one day it happened. I could tell he endured a

vicious beating because he limped to his locker, wincing in pain, barely able to hold back the tears.

I had seen enough!

I took him to the principal and convinced him to tell Mr. Sams everything, including how he feared for his life. The black and blue bruises all over his arms and sides told the tale better than his words.

Enraged, Principal Sams called the police and child protective services. He knelt in front of Franklin. "You're going to be safe from now on. I'll make sure of it. And I applaud you, Asher, for being brave for your friend. You may have saved his life."

Though I was brave, the darkest parts of me wanted to burn his house down with his so-called parents in it. To make them suffer as they did to their own child. I couldn't understand how they could do that.

That was the last time I saw Franklin. He hugged me as hard as his bruised body could endure and thanked me. I said he deserved better, and he nodded. I saw a bit of hope in his eyes.

A week later, Principal Sams called me in and told me a wonderful, loving family from Pennsylvania adopted him. And you know what? That's all I could ask for.

A child should never have to face abuse or uncertainty. They should live without fear. Once I found out about the Merciless Few's connection to B.A.C.A: Bikers Against Child Abuse, it reminded me of Franklin and there was no doubt my place was with them. I smile, thinking how wonderful Franklin's life turned out to be after leaving his abusive home. Or at least I hoped.

I wanted to be a two-sided coin: a champion for the silenced and also live the wild, carefree biker life full of booze, bikes, and bunnies. My bed would never be cold.

Before anything else, I had to go through the unavoidable conversation about my future since I didn't go to school or enlist right away. I was slower in taking a course of action, and my mom was concerned that my dad would push me away, so she tried to intervene as much as she could. She'd change the subject or ask dad a question and give me a wink.

I ended up with a job at the biker shop to appease them and also work towards my goal. I learned everything about motorcycles and even got to test drive a few.

I fell in love with Ducati but obviously even with my savings I couldn't afford one, but I found a bike that fit my personality just as well. She was a sleek 2019 BMW S 1000 XR Black with the color storm metallic. It was a midnight blue with greyish black swirls that shimmered in the angles of any turn. I was proud she was mine, and I kept the name Stormy.

I ended up with a small apartment near work, proudly living the bachelor's life. And after work, I'd regularly go out with my coworkers to our favorite bar, Sacred Cross.

"So, Ash, when are you blowing this town?" Trent asked me while knocking back his beer. I stared at my Dr. Pepper counting down the days until my 21st birthday, when I could legally take down every drink they ordered and then some.

"Two months, right when I hit 21, so I can celebrate getting into the Merciless Few. It's gonna be a dream come true, plus a new wave of hot chicks to bang."

He signaled the waitress, holding up two. She comes back, and he slides one over to me. "Stop acting like a boy scout, like you've never had alcohol before. I know that pretty boy smile has convinced Sophie at the liquor store to look the other way."

Well, he's not wrong.

I sip it. "Yeah, but when I become a brother, I want to celebrate openly, plus they don't want any snot-nosed kid as a member."

Just as I finished my beer, feisty little Dawn hopped in my lap. She was my guaranteed good time and, even better, she left immediately after. Her cling factor was absolute zero. If we had a local motorcycle club, she'd definitely be a bunny, head bunny if it were up to her. She sat down, pressing her tight, petite body against mine, her movements suggestive and enticing. I could feel the warmth of her ass against my lap, a subtle invitation that ignited my senses. I could feel a surge of desire building within me, a mix of excitement and control.

"Come on, let's get out of here." She licked her lips.

"Dawn…" She immediately started rocking back and forth with the beat of the song, staring back until she got the reaction she wanted when I gripped her waist to stop her torturing.

"Come on Asher, you know you're my #1."

"Right back at ya." I knew if I said anything other than agreeing, I could lose my chance and since I didn't know how quickly I'd be able to score once I settled in, I'd better be on my best behavior. She smiled as she pulled me from the table and I took her back to my place.

Her hoots and hollers while hanging on to me were exhilarating. I sped up down a straightaway and she clung onto me tighter before her hands landed in my lap. She rubbed against my erection, causing me to groan. She was asking for a licking. She's lucky I didn't pull over, turn around and slide her forward. Taking advantage of her wearing a skirt and, undoubtedly, no underwear.

But another girl would get to fulfill that fantasy.

Later, as I admired the curvature of her smooth ebony back, I really paid attention as she slid her bra back on. I didn't know how she clasped it back on behind her. She glanced over her shoulder, then sighed loudly. "When were you going to tell me you were leaving?" So much for the zero cling factor. I instantly felt annoyed.

She's breaking protocol. What did it matter? We weren't exclusive.

Especially her, she's known to play leapfrog. I luck out

being victim #1, reducing the chances of catching something being her sloppy seconds and beyond.

"We're not together, Dawn, so what does it matter to you?" I put my hands behind my head, watching the ceiling fan.

"That's true, but who's going to replace you as my #1 in making me feel so good? You're the only one I get multiple orgasms from."

Well, that's a stroke to my ego. Damn I'm good...

She bends over, ass facing me and smirking. I lean over and yank her back to bed for round four and orgasm number four, five, and six.

That was the first and last time she stayed all night. Guess I broke my own rule.

We'll call it the last hurrah before I begin my new bad boy biker life.

Chapter Two

Asher aka Wicked

PROTECTED
THE MERCILESS FEW MC: DEVIL'S IGNITED
Williamstown, Mass.

Two months later

I spent the rest of my time in Williamstown, working extra hours to afford a place to stay and figure out how to join.

The talk with the parentals was a lot…quieter than expected. I think because I was the last bird out of the nest, they were more open to whatever decision I made. Perhaps my resemblance to my beautiful Venezuelan mother, with her warm toffee skin, spoiled me; she may have defended me more because I was her legacy. My brothers took the smooth, rich bronze sandalwood tone and features of my father.

I saw my mom patting my father's hand as I explained my goal. I could tell he was not pleased.

"I want to stand for something and they do so much for this charity. Remember Franklin? When I researched B.A.C.A.

I remembered how much he suffered in silence. No child should ever fear for their life."

My mom sighed. "Oh, I do remember that sweet boy. I surely hope he's doing well. You stood up for your friend while witnessing something so traumatic. I was always so proud of you for what you did. Although this is nothing like what we imagined for you, you are a man now, Asher Thomas," I groan hearing my full government name, "all WE want for you is to be successful and happy. No matter what, you always have a home here and we love you. Isn't that right, Tobias?"

I see him straining, his military background wanting to scream me into attention and submission, but then he sighed. "Asher whatever you do, if it makes you happy then I'll be one proud father."

"Thank you, dad."

And just like that, the final baby bird was out of the house. I don't know what they'll do without us.

The morning I arrived in Briarswood, I found a decently priced extended stay hotel and paid for the first week. I chatted with the manager to see if he had any information about the group.

"The Merciless Few? Oh yeah, they're a big deal in town, but they don't monopolize on it. They're a good bunch, not like what you hear and see on TV." He eyed me for a second. "You're awfully young. You sure that's what you wanna do?" He asked while filing the paperwork that I signed.

I knew that's what everybody would be thinking. I'd always be the baby, in the family, even of all my cousins I am the youngest and more than likely I'll be the baby of the club, too. That only made me want to try harder to prove myself.

"Yeah, I'm sure." I left it at that, picked up my bags, and headed to my room for a nap.

What a dump! But it would only be temporary. I look up at the ceiling. Is that mold?! I refrained from turning on the overhead light and revealing any other discrepancies or infestations.

The clerk told me the group hangs out at this bar called Throttle. What a perfect spot to observe them in their habitat and see what type of girls they have here in Briarswood.

I laid down at half-past two. I remember because mid-afternoon trash TV was playing and when I woke up; it was pitch black outside and prime TV was showing. I check my watch, 8 pm. Perfect. I can grab a bite to eat there while scouting. I threw on some black jeans and t-shirt with my black leather lace-up boots. I finish with my letterman jacket from school. I had lettered in basketball and track. I personalized it, having *Wicked* sewn on the left side because of my inhuman speed. They'd say, "Damn, you're wicked fast!" Especially after setting the school record for the 100, 200, and 4x400 meter dash. On the flip side, the ladies would say I was wicked in the sheets. Hey, can't argue with satisfied customers.

I pull up and park my beauty next to a sick row of bikes, varying from the classics to the tricked out choppers, all individually bad ass, especially this one electric cherry or candy apple red Harley. I know that a paint job like this costs an arm and a leg, but it was sweet! A guaranteed panty dropper.

My girl Stormy was her own unique beauty. I tapped my seat, my way of letting her know she was my only girl, and I was proud to ride her.

I could hear the rowdiness from outside. It sounded like a good time to be had. I stroll in, looking around. I see girls on the dance floor whooping and having a good time. Some nice-looking specimens, too.

I saddle up to the bar and order a beer and a burger, medium well with fries. The bartender turned to pour my drink. I'm surprised he didn't card me. Judging by the sizable crowd, he either didn't care or was too busy to bother. A few minutes later, my food came out.

After finishing my meal, it wasn't half bad. I turned around and scanned the place. It's hard to miss the bearded guy with the huge club patch on his leather vest. He had a leggy woman in his lap fawning over him, probably his ol' lady or perhaps a ready and willing bunny, but bunnies were for easy access, not relationships or trotting around, so I'll assume she's his wife or something serious.

At this moment, I kicked myself for not having a plan of action other than flat out asking to be in the group, but that seemed stupid, too. I gulp half the beer to quench my anxiety before I push off the bar and head toward the small table consisting of the two guys and the babe in his lap.

It was now or never.

The big guy didn't notice me because he was busy trailing his fingers up and down her leg, but his buddy did. He eyed me as he slammed down one of the three shots in front of him. He was as solid as a boulder and had muscles upon muscles. He chuckled as I stopped in front of them. "Lookie here, Boss Man, a frat boy in his little letterman jacket. He's got to be lost. Are you lost? Looking for where the boy scouts hang out? Sorry, kid, this bar is for adults. Come back when you hit puberty." He laughs and shoots the second shot.

The big guy doesn't even move or acknowledge my presence. Both postures piss me off. "I'm old enough to kick your ass! I'm looking for the leader of the Merciless Few and obviously it isn't someone uncultured like you. You act like a… prospect." I snapped. I knew it would piss him off. He sneered in disgust and only then did the guy turn around with her still in his lap.

"I'm Lucifer, President of the Merciless Few Massachusetts Chapter: The Devil's Ignited." The name even sounds bad ass!

He holds his bear sized hand out for me to shake and I do. "What can I do for you, son?"

14

I felt a bit stung when he called me son, but I persevered.

With all the adrenaline of realizing my dream might come true in this moment, I felt all these emotions rush forward, and blurted out, "I really want to join the group! I've read up on you guys and I love what you stand for. I helped a friend of mine in an abusive situation, plus I love motorcycles. I just bought mine. It's outside, you should really see her! She's not as pretty as that red one out there, but she's mine. I named her Stormy!"

Perpetual word vomit spewed from me and I sounded like an obsessed fangirl. I was mentally kicking myself. I was supposed to play it cool, instead I took the role of a prepubescent girl.

I stop, breathing heavily while staring at them.

"How cute... a fan, boss." Another smart ass remark. He doesn't have too many more, and I made sure my face said so.

The woman chuckled at my display then held her hand out, "Name's Sam, nice to me you?" She left it open-ended for me to answer.

I shake gently, "Asher, but my friends call me Wicked."

"Nice. Well, you met Lucifer, and that's Demon. Don't pay him no mind, he's always been...difficult. So you want to be in a biker gang, aren't you a little young? Don't you have bigger dreams?"

At least she wasn't condescending.

"No ma'am, this IS my dream. I can be an asset to the club and I will do whatever you want to prove it...except you." I pointed to Demon because I knew he would make me spit polish his boots or something outrageous. He doesn't answer because he knows it's true.

Lucifer taps Sam, she stands up, and so does he. He's literally built solid, like a fridge. His eyes, cold and sharp as ice, scan over me, leaving me frozen in place. It was a long, awkward pause.

15

He thinks I'm just some kid.

He is in search of tough, relentless, and hardcore. I barely have facial hair.

This was a dumb idea.

I turned around to leave before he could reject me and his buddy to laugh in my face. It was time for me to carve an alternative path. Too bad I have no clue what that is. This is all I ever wanted.

"Hey kid."

I didn't turn around. "It's fine. I know when I ain't wanted. You won't see me again."

I heard him chuckle. Another hit to my ego. "Don't give up so easily, kid." I turn around to see what seems to be a smile from him. "As long as you're sure this is what you want, I have no problem letting you in, but there are some stipulations."

I couldn't believe it!

Me!

A Merciless Few!

I didn't squeal or anything, but my wide smile gave away my excitement. He watched me and gave me time to compose myself after I heard the words I'd been waiting for.

"How old are you, Asher?"

"Today is my birthday, actually. I'm 21."

"Well, you look much younger. That's why I was hesitant. A lot of these neighborhood kids try to hide their real age to get in when I know every family in this town and can just ask their parents. You're definitely not from here. Where are you from?"

"Oh, umm, Williamstown, close to here."

"Yeah, about an hour or so. I've fished the Grotto Lakes, and caught some excellent fish there."

I nodded. I can't believe I'm having a conversation with the President of the Massachusetts Chapter of the Merciless Few.

"Anyway, it sounds like you check out. It's pretty simple. You will be required to move into the clubhouse. It's a few minutes' drive from here. You will help around the house, anything Sam wants, and we'll start taking you on jobs to learn the ropes before you break off into teams for multiple runs. The more you do, the more responsibility you get. Don't be stupid, plain and simple. We'll go over more rules as they come. Alright?"

"Yes, sir."

"No need for formality. Lucifer is fine around the others and Rocco, if you need to really talk, got it?"

I nodded.

"Welcome to the Merciless Few...Wicked. That's a pretty nice varsity jacket. We didn't have those back in my day."

"Yeah, you also had dirt tracks to run on, old man! Did they still use the abacus?" Demon laughed before he whistled for the waitress. She quickly came with another beer. He handed her a bill and smacked her ass hard. She squeaked, but really didn't seem to mind when she leaned down for a kiss. She sauntered away while he adjusted himself.

"See, he rags on all of us. Don't take it personally, he ain't got the sense God gave him. But he will complete a thorough 21-point inspection on your bike to make sure it's up to specs for possible long runs. Let's go see your girl. I bet she's a real beauty." I smirk at a fuming Demon. He better not mess her up. Might have to check my brakes and definitely wash his dirty paw prints off of her.

Lucifer shakes my hand and we go outside so I can introduce them to Stormy. Turns out that exquisite red masterpiece belonged to him! I should have known.

He gives me his number, the clubhouse number, and the address. He said he knew I probably got a room for the night and that I shouldn't waste money. I didn't tell him I reserved it for the week, but I could probably negotiate a refund for the rest of the time. A simple complaint about the cleanliness should do. I wanted to pack up and move in now, but didn't want to seem too eager or kid-like.

I was really tired of being called a kid.

I was a man.

A Merciless Few man now.

Chapter Three

Asher aka Wicked

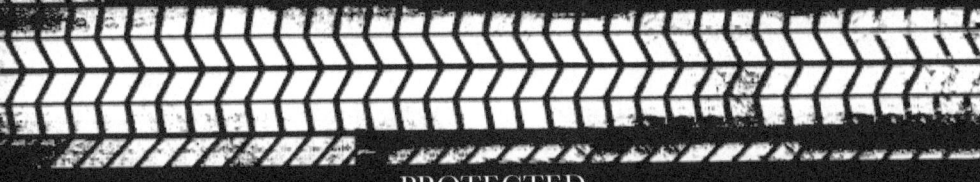

PROTECTED
THE MERCILESS FEW MC: DEVIL'S IGNITED
Briarswood, Mass.

Two years later

I was living the life! Hanging with my brothers, drinking and partying whenever we felt like it, watching the bunnies lose more and more clothing throughout the night, and making good money doing runs on both sides of the moral compass.

We ain't choir boys, but we aren't the 1% either, not until we have to be. Little did I know what that term really meant.

"Aye Wicked!" Demon calls me. We've gotten past that rough introduction and I see him as someone to look up to as he reminds me of my brothers. Demon was the type to pick up girls and have his way in his dungeon, and judging by the smiles when they left, he did not disappoint.

My room was on the other side of his, and I was often

privy to the night's activities. It usually left me with a problem I had to take care of myself.

Until my luck changed.

"Yeah?!" I answered him.

"Let's go to Throttle. I'd like something not on the usual menu." He had already gone through the roster twice this week. Wonder what his deal was?

"Yeah, ok." Our walls were so thin that this is how we held most conversations. But tonight, the music was blasting, so we had to yell. I changed my white tee to a black one, threw on my boots, and grabbed my cut. Don't get me wrong, the bunnies we have were amazing at what they did, but I also wanted more options or something different. You wouldn't eat the same dessert over and over for eternity, would you?

It would get stale.

Nothing worse than stale pussy.

Going to Throttle wearing my coveted vest would almost guarantee I could have any girl I wanted. We hopped on our bikes and headed out, revving them loudly as we parked. It was way more crowded than normal; must've been the University graduation.

I realize I would have graduated last year had I'd gone straight to college from high school. But I'm not mad I didn't attend. I can get my experience second hand.

"Sweet ass on a Saturday! Fresh pickings. Demon's going hunting. Good luck, brother." He didn't even turn his head, but I watched him approach a group of what I would call prissy rich girls who love pissing off Daddy, but also spend his money like water because he can't say no to his princess.

Demon is the type of guy dads fear his daughter would bring home.

I'm the second closest fear. I'm melanated enough to cause concern. It makes me chuckle.

I spot a few girls looking my way and rate my choices and my chances. Demon's dealing with a table full of sevens, but, from what I said earlier, that makes them solid fives, hit or miss. He just wants to hit.

The girl that actually caught my attention wasn't even looking my way. She was pouring beers faster than her male counterpart, while the group of rowdy guys in front of her cheered her on. I catch glimpses of her face through the movement of the wisps of hair framing her face.

"Yeah! Wooo! Go! Go! Go! Go!" They were chanting like they were at a college football game. She had a slight cocky smirk as she poured, slid the glasses forward, then lined up shot glasses pouring that cheap ass Smirnoff.

Goddamn rookies. Might as well pay for water.

Anyway, not thinking anything of it, I walked past her to get a drink from her not so busy coworker. I noticed her glance up. "Hey! You don't want to visit Silas the sloth." She chuckled at her playful remark.

I raised my brow. "I don't?"

"Nah, you want service from me."

In more ways than one. I only raised my brow.

Her beauty captivated me as I looked closer. Her almond skin, with its warm and sun-kissed glow, perfectly complemented her hazel eyes. In this small town, she was a truly unique beauty. I felt an undeniable urge to get to know her better.

And to see her naked.

She motions for me to squeeze in between the frat boys and a group of girls. "Make room!" She bellows and they do as they're told. I step up. She sets a bar coaster in front of me. "What'll you have?"

She leans forward, and I immediately focus on her tits in a tight black tank. "Hey sunshine, my eyes are up here. Now are you ordering or gawking cause I got customers. I did you a favor getting you VIP seating."

I scoff, "Oh really? Guess I owe you." Her smirk was a mutual understanding. "Gimme a whiskey sour, please." She leaned back, clearly taken aback by my choice. It seemed she expected me to be like the others, indulging in cheap swill.

But I was different.

I was a Merciless Few.

She placed the ingredients on the sub shelf of the bar. "So, what's your name, handsome?" She whipped the egg white, setting it aside, before pouring everything else into a chilled shaker.

"The name's Wicked." I pointed to my name on my vest. "And you? Where are you from?" She added ice, popped the top, and shook. "That's two questions. Kinda greedy, don't you think? My name is Priya and I am from Bangladesh."

That completely made sense to me. I honestly could never accurately put into words the sheer beauty she possessed. She was a kind of vision that was rare, to be put proudly on display.

It was as if time froze and I became aware that I couldn't take my eyes off her.

She must think I'm a creep!

She flipped the glass right side up, wiped it, poured my drink, then the egg white rounding out the perfect presentation. She slid it forward before she took the orders of the girls next to me. Thoughtfully ignoring me, but also curious about my reaction.

I noticed everyone ordered long island iced teas. I caught a glimpse of Priya laughing to herself. I can imagine the stories she must have from working at this bar. Of course, college students will choose the easiest and cheapest route to getting shit faced.

A tall brunette in what they considered a skirt held her glass up. "To the graduating class of Mu Gamma Alpha, cheers bitches! Mu Gamma Alpha! MGA!" They all chant and cheer, a few looking my way. I nod and tip my drink, turning my focus back on Priya. Giving them no hint of interest.

"Well?"

I finish the rest and slam the glass down. "That's one hell of a drink. How much do I owe you, gorgeous?"

"On the house."

"On the house? What's the catch?"

As she leans over the counter, I gather enough courage to imitate her. Now, her lips, tinted with a deep crimson hue, are dangerously near. "Well...Wicked...guess you'll have to find out." She holds up a folded napkin. I take it.

"Ayo, Wicked, we got a run to do! Let's go. We gotta meet up with Frankie, the fat ass."

Hearing that name makes me growl. I hate that sloppy fucker. He blew into town and thought he was hot shit. He was just some slob from South America whose boss died suspiciously, at least that was the rumor. The fact was, he killed him and took over.

"Sorry, beautiful, gotta go."

She gestured to the paper in my hand. "Understood. You got what you need. Hope you know what to do with it."

I smirk and follow behind my brothers. Hopefully, sleazing behind Frankie doesn't last for much longer. He's going to cause trouble for us, I know it.

It was a solid week of running hauls for Frankie, and a few local businesses who needed their supplies from the port, before I remembered Priya had given me that paper.

I ended up tossing it on my dresser before getting a blow job from Reba.

You know when you can tell someone's eventually going to cause trouble? That was Reba. She had been a bunny before in Georgia, but she was no peach.

She claimed the other girls were jealous she was the only one to get railed by the President. It was her badge of honor and she was attempting to repeat it here, but she was severely delusional if she thought Lucifer would leave Sam for her. The only reason she even got in was because she convinced

Lila to vouch for her and promised to be on her best behavior.

Lasted two fucking weeks before she set her sights on Boss Man.

The conversations that take place while sitting at our club bar are absolutely wild. I couldn't resist discreetly eavesdropping while taking a shot.

Sam pointed at Lila, who was trying to keep her own spot here. She knew Reba was her responsibility. "I gave her the benefit of the doubt, Lil, but I'll snatch out those cheap fucking plastic extensions if I see her trying again! She better have damn good dental insurance or she'll be gumming dicks!"

Lil is trying to calm her down. "I know! I regret putting my ass on the line for her. I'm sorry, Sam. She's crazy if she thinks he'll even consider looking her way when he has you." They both laugh to make light of the situation.

I figure my request would keep Reba out of trouble or getting her ass handed to her. Later, I figured out how wrong I was.

As I said, I took Reba up for that celebratory blowjob after we had completed a $50K run for Frankie, which only earned us a measly five grand. I don't know why we continued to let him nickel and dime us.

We weren't celebrating the money—it was the bare minimum—but the fact that we'd survived another reckless, near-death run, the taste of fear still lingering. We seldom venture into this part of Connecticut because it was under the control of the notorious Vice Lords.

Frankie reveled in the thrill of the forbidden, or the high risk, laughing at the not so whispered warnings as he struck deals that made his fortune grow. It wasn't him in the line of fire; it was us! The issue is, he'd either rip them off or give them an inferior product. That could get us all killed if they checked the inventory and our chapter only had three members. That's why we always stayed strapped. I heard we had a recruit coming from the west soon. Another brother would be great; there's safety in numbers.

A shudder jolted me back to reality; my attention was fixated on the embodiment of evil attempting to devour my very soul. Her throat worked me, constricting her muscles and triggering all my senses. The cool porcelain of the bathroom sink pressed against my lower back after she ambushed me, and ripped my pants further down from when I was taking a piss.

I grabbed her head and held her as I spilled my seed. "Fuck yeah, Reba! You dirty fucking slut! I think I'm in love." I joked. She was old enough to be mistaken for my mother. Or worse, now that I think about it.

She stood up, licking the corner of her lips while tucking me in and zipping me up.

"I've been sucking dick longer than you've been alive, kid."

I didn't need to know that and her calling me kid makes this even more awkward.

I laughed to end this uncomfortable interaction, then I got ready to head back to Throttle.

It was time to make my move.

Chapter Four

Asher aka Wicked

PROTECTED
THE MERCILESS FEW MC: DEVIL'S IGNITED
Briarswood, Mass.

It was a Saturday night, and the building was slightly less jam-packed. I assumed that the crowd from yesterday was still recovering from the bender of cheap booze.

Priya was at the center bar this time, the polished wood gleaming under the dim lights, the clinking of glasses a familiar soundtrack to her presence as the main attraction. This time, she was preparing Irish slammers. She began arranging them, allowing the small crowd ample time to set up their cameras for posting on social media.

She whips her hair into a high ponytail. Even that small movement was incredibly sexy. "Are you ready?!"

"Yeah!"

"In 3, 2, 1…" She tips the first shot glass that starts the chain reaction. Shot glasses of whiskey and Irish cream fall into the dark muddiness of the stout beer. Once it does, the guys instantly slam down the whole drink. The last one finishes and it breaks out into chaos as they high five her and each other while tipping her generously. She takes their tips and sticks it between her ample breasts in a crop top baseball shirt with the sides laced up.

I walked up after the boys; their rowdy departure made me more confident I'd have her undivided attention. She sets down the coaster, "What'll you have?" She polishes a glass while waiting. I wait until she makes eye contact. "I'll have the usual." Her face turned sour almost instantly. "And how the hell would I know what that is? You just waltzed up here and plopped down! You think I can read minds?"

"You're joking, right?" I fire back. Maybe she's punishing me for taking so long to connect.

She set down the glass with a clink, her body language seemed agitated as she shifted her weight from one foot to the other. The faint scent of her perfume lingered in the air, mingling with the stale smell of alcohol. The room felt tense. "Look buddy, either order something or get out of my face! I've got a job to do, and it's not playing guessing games with you. Alright?"

Perhaps I missed my chance, and now she has committed to treating me like a complete stranger, insignificant and unimportant. "Can I get a whiskey sour?" She rolled her eyes. "Of course, you pick the most complicated drink during a rush? You better tip big, buddy." She said as she turned her back, facing away. It was a contrast to last night when we had suggestive conversation mixed with flirting.

I didn't know what to do or say, so I sat and waited for my drink. She turned around and almost dropped the glass on the coaster. "That'll be $20 for my trouble."

"Twenty bucks?! For a whiskey sour?! Unless you're using top shelf, and I didn't see you reach up for anything, I call bullshit!" I don't know what her deal was, but it was like night and day.

"Either pay up or get out! I don't take kindly to cheap bastards who skip out on their bill!" It was only when she stepped forward and forcefully slammed her hands down that I finally realized I was standing.

Just when I was about to ask her what her damn problem was, movement broke my eye contact.

What the hell?!

It was Priya, but... I was screaming at Priya. I think? I shook my head and closed my eyes. I must be hallucinating. I haven't even had a drink yet.

"Wicked! It's good to finally see you. I thought you forgot about..." She tapered off as I pointed to her, "Priya?"

"Yeah? What's wrong?" Then I pointed to her look-alike. She still had her face scrunched up in disgust.

"Oh, don't mind her. That's my twin sister, Tamla. She's a troublemaker." She smiles and Tamla breaks her mean girl persona with a hysterical laugh. "I'm sorry, it was too easy! Hi, nice to meet you. I've heard so many things about you." She holds out her hand and I slowly approach. Shaking softer than usual but she squeezes firmly. "You're right, *bōna* (sister), he is fucking hot."

"I told you, but he's a bit slow on the draw. Had to keep me waiting a whole week, huh?"

I recoiled at first, but then I extended my hands in a gesture of peace to both of them. "I'm so sorry," I said, kissing her hand. "the club's been incredibly busy. I should have called and I apologize." Kissing it again before smiling.

"Tuh, talk about smooth." Tamla responds as she lets go to take an order beside me. Seeing Priya smile at the sight of me makes all that uncertainty go away. "Will you forgive me at least?"

She places her other hand over mine, leaning in super close. "How could I say no?"

"Good, how about I take you to dinner? When are you off?"

I knew she would say yes.

"Wicked, we need to talk." Yikes, already with the 'need to talk' chat. "I have to be upfront. If you want to take me out, you have to take Tamla, too. We're sort of a package deal. We've never done anything apart."

Hmm…anything?

"I saw that. Yes, even that, not with each other, though. My sister and I are close, inseparable. We share everything and that includes men. If you're not okay with that, then we can't go any further. I understand if this is too much to ask of you."

Are you kidding me?! Walking in with not one but two bad bitches on my arm? My brothers could never achieve this level! I'd be a god to them!

And at the thought of all the possibilities, I could feel myself stiffen at the very thought.

I look to see a sadness on her face, like she had made this deal before and they turned it down.

She was actively bracing for rejection.

"I think I can handle that. So, how about I take you both to dinner?"

"Oh brother, *bōna*, he doesn't know what he's in for!" Tamla chimes in while bumping playfully into her.

I don't, but I'm excited to find out.

"We're off tomorrow. How about then?"

I was about to agree, then I realized, "Oh shit, I only have a motorcycle. I can ask my President for the truck…" They whisper to each other, "Don't worry, we'll pick you up this time. Give us the address." I scribble it down. Priya slips it between her breasts with a wink.

"Ooh, can we see your bike? Darry, we're going on break!" They shuffle from behind the bar, each taking my arm. I couldn't wait to brag about this or, better yet, keep quiet until they come to the clubhouse. Demon will lose his shit!

The girls ooh and ahh once they set their sights on my

Stormy. Touching her, caressing her curves. This is somehow very erotic.

I am going to need bunny care to drain me so I can give them both a night to remember tomorrow.

"She's pretty badass. Perhaps one day we can each get a ride. I call dibs!" Tamla screams, causing Priya to groan. "That's fine, but I get first dibs on riding..." She covers her mouth while whispering in her sister's ear. Their expressions changed from one of innocence to lustful, their gaze lowered. Priya licked her lips while eyeing me up and down.

"That's an interesting proposal, sis. I like the way you think. Alright, you get first on that...this time." They shake hands like they closed a big business deal. They giggled as they hopped on my girl together. Leaning forward to reach the handlebars, I noticed Priya's tits against Tamla's, whose tits were on Stormy.

"Could you imagine?" Priya said to no one in particular.

Could I? My mind filled with tawdry, lewd, and lascivious fantasies of how I would fuck them both on my bike. I could stack them like building blocks, hitting the spot of one and devouring the other or making one cum all on my fingers. Or have them lying opposite ways on my bike, doing the same, fucking, fingering, and feasting. Having them cum all over Stormy and me, leaving their scent, marking their territory.

Fuck!

I step forward, leaning against the handlebars. "As much as I love to sit here and fantasize, ladies. I need to go take care of some business."

The business was taking care of this hard on.

They slide off as I hop on. I turn the key and rev the engine. I tap my cheek and get a kiss from each, Priya lingering much longer than her sister.

This ride is going to be super uncomfortable.

Chapter Five

Asher aka Wicked

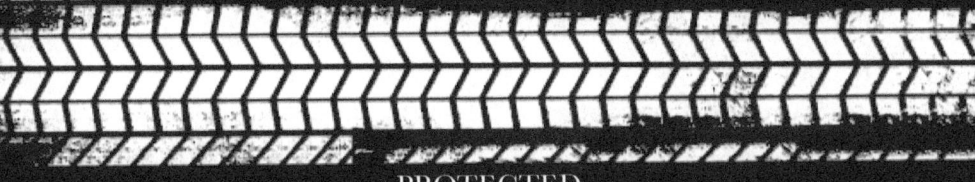

PROTECTED
THE MERCILESS FEW MC: DEVIL'S IGNITED
Briarswood, Mass.

I finally parked and headed straight inside. All the usual suspects were there, waiting for their turn. I whistled and motioned, "I need a Penny for my thoughts!" She hopped down off the bar stool and bid the other bunnies farewell. "Another needy customer. Guess I'll see you chicas later."

I throw her over my shoulder, smacking and squeezing her ass. "No, she won't. This is an all-nighter."

Once inside, I slam my door shut and pin her against it. She dropped to her knees so fast, she already had me feeling the familiar tingle of an impending orgasm.

The twins really did a number riling me up.

I was going to strip down, but I would've finished before putting my cut away. I needed to regain control. I step back, grab her by her crop top, rip it off, then toss her half naked ass on my bed. When she climbs out from being swallowed by my comforter she licks her lips while flashing me repeatedly.

Surprise, she's not wearing underwear.

I come face to face with her all too familiar piercing. Initially, Penny got her clit pierced vertically for ultimate stimulation and she claimed it made her extremely sensitive. I can attest to that, but after some careful research and consultation with her piercer, she got the horizontal piercing as well. The old and the new piercing were thinner and smaller to…fit without causing damage. She was so excited to share that she flashed us all without hesitation.

Ironically, it was Tuesday.

What a delicious site it was, too. It was a beacon, X marks her spot. Knowing what I know, I rip everything off before crawling on the bed. My body was here, but my brain was in an endless fantasy with two beautiful Indian girls. I could only imagine until it actually happened. I flick her piercing to hear her hiss.

"Are you ready?" I know why she got both, and I was going to fuck her to exhaustion tonight. Until she begged not to cum.

She started working herself up. Nothing is more exciting than watching someone get wet over the thoughts of what you're going to do to them.

"Wicked." She whispered while moaning, begging me for what she wanted. I shouldn't give in so easily. Demon says she should be in tears at how badly she wants you, but this throbbing was only getting worse.

I licked my thumb and brushed the top of her piercing while I devoured her so deliciously. She began panting, demonstrating all the telltale signs.

"Wait! I…oh god…there…right there! Fuck!" Her legs shook, and I knew she was close to…

"Yes, yes, yes, yes!!! Ahhhhh!" I welcomed the shower of

her essence. Why? Because it made the sex with her even better. Well worth the extra load of laundry.

Demon gave me the tip to have multiple sheet sets, especially if you service them right. I didn't even allow her a breather before I slid in. She instinctively clenched me so tight while gasping to my size. I guess they never get used to it.

"Jeez, Penny, loosen up or I'm going to bust. Holy fuck!" She laughed at my struggle, but I was going to teach her smart ass a lesson. I put her on her side and slammed into her. Her laugh quickly turned into screams of pleasure. In and out, her sensitivity was at an all-time high, making it easier for her to cum over and over, but only if you, "Keep going! Going to cum again! Ahhh!" She pants, gripping the sheets hard. I smack her ass and put her on all fours. "Ahhh! Oh god no more, I'm so sensitive." She says, barely above a whisper.

"Not yet, sweet cheeks. I'm almost...there! Oh yeah, squeeze me like...**smack** that! Grrrr!" **smack**

She looked back, a moment of disbelief, then mischief, before she started answering my strokes by bouncing back against me. Penny had an ass like a stripper the way she was grinding on me. I wouldn't be surprised if she had been one. She was from Las Vegas, I can only assume.

Anyway, watching her chase another orgasm was the right combination. "Oh god, I can't! But I'm gonna..." Her pussy was super sensitive, tingling, maybe even throbbing. I reach around and gently pinch and squeeze the piercings together.

The earth-shattering scream that left her lips reverberated through the entire house, echoing off the walls and sending shivers down my spine. In response, a cascade came down, drenching everything. She literally collapsed on her stomach.

"I fucking hate you. You...really are...wicked." I lean back, admiring my work until...

clap clap clap clap

"Atta boy! I taught you well!"

He didn't teach me anything. I didn't even realize he was

in his room. Usually he's out prowling for new pussy or sealing the deal.

Penny mustered up enough strength to gather her clothes, and that's it. She ran her fingers through her hair. "Both of you are bad for my pussy and my health. I'll never survive if I take you both on…uh uh." She shook her head and walked out naked with her clothes against her to the bathroom. I close my door and plop on the bed with a chuckle.

Guess I didn't need all night. She had done her job. Drained of all energy, yet strangely invigorated. I readied myself for the challenge of facing the twins.

Tomorrow is the day I become a king!

Chapter Six
Asher aka Wicked

PROTECTED
THE MERCILESS FEW MC: DEVIL'S IGNITED
Briarswood, Mass.

Since I wasn't riding tonight, I took Stormy out this morning before giving her a much needed wash. The dirt and dust were very noticeable on her exquisite paint job. Demon was doing a maintenance inspection on his bike.

"So, you got plans tonight? Or are you up for a trip to Throttle? They have an open mic night tonight."

I try not to smile, "Sorry, gotta pass. I have plans." He didn't press for details, but I knew they'd arrive early enough for him to witness.

I showered and got dressed, then took a seat in the living room. Lucifer and Sam snuggled together in his chair, watching an old black and white movie. He may have found a biker movie that I haven't watched. I'll have to ask the name of it later.

Sam peeked behind him to see me. "Look at my

handsome boy!" I groaned. "Sam...come on. It's bad enough that I'm the baby of the group. You're not helping."

"I meant no harm. I know you're a grown man, but I'm the club mom and I think of you as my son."

"Even Demon."

"Yes, even that psychopath that drives me crazy."

"Fine. I hope the new guy's younger than me." I huff. Lucifer pulls out a cigar and hands it to her. She preps it. "Sorry buddy, he's not."

Of course not.

Demon walks behind the bar, fixing a complex old fashion before he looks up. "Thought you had plans? Did she stand you up? Oh, that's hilarious! Don't worry, small fry, the college girls aren't too reliable. Easy, but not reliable." He chuckled to himself.

knock knock knock

I felt the smug smile form. "Oh no, right on time, you see." I went to open the door, and I had to keep my knees from buckling. Priya and Tamla were wearing skin tight leather outfits, Priya's a low cut mini dress, and Tamla a skirt and sleeveless vest combo with the zipper dangerously low. I heard a clank and I assume Demon dropped his drink in awe of such beauty.

"What do you think? Perfect for motorcycle babes, right?"

I spin them both. "Wow, you both look stunning." I stand out of the way. "Priya and Tamla, that's our President Lucifer and his ol' lady Samantha." They both waved and then I pointed to an open-mouthed Demon. "That's my brother Demon. He's...very pleased to meet you." I smile widely behind them.

"Holy shit." He finally choked out.

Priya holds up her hand while leaning against me. "Nice to meet all of you. Ready to go, stud?"

"Oh yeah, let's go ladies." I smack both their asses before looking back at Demon. "Checkmate, brother."

It was a silent competition between us or a cocky understanding. Either way, I won.

I close the door and take in their ride, a pristine new Lexus ES 300h Ultra Luxury, all white with tan leather interior. I didn't think they were broke college students, but how could they afford that with their jobs? Maybe they pool their money together. Either way, I'm impressed.

Priya tosses the keys to me. "You're driving." She winked before getting into the passenger seat. I drove us to this restaurant in the next town over called Fireside Grill, which was a hibachi type bar and grill. I was going all out for them. I pulled out their chairs before sitting between them. The dining area's layout accommodated multiple groups, and our trio drew a few looks from other diners.

They both pick up the menu, browsing for what they want.

I didn't want anything that was on the menu.

"Ugh, classic subpar drink selection. I should go back there and make our drinks myself. I know my skills would make this place rich." Tamla says confidently.

"Yeah Tam, you're the best bartender in Briarswood and the surrounding area."

"Damn right I am!"

Just then, the waiter approaches. "Hi, my name is Xion and I'll be taking your orders."

I noticed how he was shamelessly making direct eye contact with Tamla's tits.

"What will you beautiful ladies have?"

"Oh, I'll have a pineapple mango tequila sunrise with Mezcal only. If you don't have it, then Milagro will suffice."

"And I guess I'll have a cosmo with Ketel One or Platinum vodka only. I'm a bartender and I'll know if you use that cheap garbage on display out front."

He smirks while jotting down her order. "And your brother?"

What the fuck did he just say?!

I felt a hand on my thigh and saw it's Priya's. She shifted closer a bit and Tamla followed suit. She placed her other hand on my shoulder before kissing my cheek and, of course, Tamla mirrored her sister.

"Our man would like a high-quality whiskey sour. That is all." The revelation absolutely wrecked him. I wrapped my arms around their waist, pulling them closer, their chairs scraping the floor, and they squealed. He huffs before turning around to place our order.

"That was fun! How rude of him to assume."

"I know, right. If he were our brother, we wouldn't have such naughty thoughts about wearing him out."

They both smile so innocently as their fingers roam my upper legs. "You girls are dangerous."

"We thought you liked that. You are a badass biker in a hardcore motorcycle gang. Tell us all about it."

The waiter comes back with our drinks and takes our orders with absolutely no eye contact. I raise my glass. "Cheers to a fun night, ladies."

Following our toast, the girls tapped glasses, conveying a silent message. I can only imagine since they openly admitted to fantasizing about me.

"Now tell us."

"Well, first it's a motorcycle club. We don't ride the roads robbing people or terrorizing the town. Our mission, taken from Bikers Against Child Abuse, is to protect abused children and remove them from harmful situations. Every year we raise money for the cause. I think we're doing a barbecue this year. The girls will probably do a bikini car wash."

"Oh, you have girls there?" Tamla raised her brow.

"Yeah, they're bunnies. Dedicated to the club."

"Dedicated, huh? That's code for readily available ass. I bet you had some...bunny in your bed last night." Tamla looks at Priya, who didn't seem too fond of the idea. I swallowed hard, hoping they didn't notice my guilt.

"Yeah, probably." Priya whispered. There was sadness in her reply again. I lift her chin, "No need to feel that way, sweet pea, I'm all yours."

She perked up, "Really?" I nod as I lean closer and closer until we're distracted by a giant fireball made by the chef.

Let the show begin.

I found out quite a bit about the twins. Tamla was three and a half minutes older and thus, the bossy one. I was shocked to find out they were 25; they appeared far younger. They got their degrees in a three-year time span instead of four. Which made me wonder what they were doing as bartenders? They were actual geniuses. They told me it was good life experience.

"Brains and beauty in one? I hit the lottery twice!"

We eat and chat late into the night. They seemed really intrigued about the club and the day-to-day dealings, but they were really interested in the bunnies. Though there was no formal way to become one other than asking and pledging allegiance. I think, because they read a lot of biker romances, they expected us to treat them like common whores and openly share them or make them a part of our initiation. I could only laugh at their assumptions. We sound like dirty, sex crazed criminals. They perked up hearing vague details about our not so legal runs for Frankie. I didn't elaborate, but I definitely impressed them.

"Have you ever killed anybody and buried their bloodied and battered body in a deep, dark forest? Or circle someone with your bikes, then shoot them?"

"What do you think we are, the mafia? Listen, we are a group of bike loving men who hang out, drink, do some runs for anyone who needs security and raise money and awareness for a charity we care deeply about. That's us, the Merciless Few Massachusetts Chapter: The Devil's Ignited."

They both nod at each other and Tamla shrugs. "Well, I'm in if you're in." She says to her sister. "You read my mind as usual. Sounds like a... fun plan." Priya agreed, but to what?

I couldn't read their minds. I was totally in the dark. "Somebody want to fill me in?"

They both laughed. Priya ran her finger down my chest. "We want in. We want to be Merciless Few bunnies. But only your bunnies."

I know I had to be dreaming. There's no way two girls, two absolutely stunning girls I just met, want to be loyal to my club, specifically only to me. My hormones were messing with my hearing.

"You're kidding, right? Messing around to get me all riled up. Well played." I laughed until two hands, one on each leg, were dangerously close to my dick. I swallow hard.

"We never joke about our intentions. If we want it, we get it."

"No ifs, ands, or buts. We're way too clever not to get our way. So, how does it work?"

"And when do we move into your room?"

Fuck

Me

Sideways

"You-you're se-serious? Moving in?"

"Well...only if you want us to. Imagine waking up every morning to a blow job or one of us riding you." Tamla's lips barely grazed mine, not quite making proper contact for a kiss. She was teasing hard, but then a hand grabbed my face, turning it to face her. Priya completed the kiss that her sister teased me with while both hands roamed my lap.

I glance across from me to break the intensity and gravity of the situation. A guy and his buddy nod while giving me a confirming nod but refrain from grinning like jackals. A silent celebration of every man's fantasies.

"Hey." They're both looking at me. "Huh?"

"You zoned out. We're just making sure you didn't die of shock. That would be…unfortunate, not being able to play with our new toy."

"Or you're looking for a way to let us down." Priya adds. The differences in their attitudes lead me to believe Priya suffered past emotional trauma. Tamla gave no fucks. She was loudly emotionally unavailable. Which leads me to wonder whose idea it was to share. Maybe Tamla was tired of picking up the pieces of her soft-hearted sister. Or maybe Tamla was overly protective of her heart, which caused grief with her partner. She knew her sister could help with the emotional stuff. Each had her own flaw, but together they balanced each other out.

I didn't like Priya automatically thinking everything was negative. "Why do you do that, sweet pea?" I asked outright. She only shrugged. I could tell she didn't want to explain further. Tamla was busy finishing up her drink, allowing her sister to control the narrative.

"It's cool if you want to join. You'll need to talk to Sam about club rules and all that business. I guess I will need to clean up my room and make room."

They kiss my cheek, "Yay! We get to be bunnies!"

"We get to be *your* bunnies."

Chapter Seven

Asher aka Wicked

PROTECTED
THE MERCILESS FEW MC: DEVIL'S IGNITED
Briarswood, Mass.

Two years later

Our brotherhood was complete, and now we were stronger and more badass than we've ever been. Even with the recent additions of my brother Reaper and Fiend, I still managed to be the baby of the group.

However, I still had the one up by having two babes ready and willing just for me. The best part? Demon was persistent to get a go with the girls, but they shot him down every time.

Every.

Single.

Time.

And it put a smile on my face. Yes, he was my brother, but he was a cocky little shit and always arrogantly boasted he could get any girl.

Any girl…

Except mine.

He never stood a chance, especially after the last attempt. We were celebrating at the clubhouse and it got a little too wild that night. There was an altercation between Reaper's girl Daisy and my favorite bunny, Lila. But Sam intercepted Daisy, trying to attack Lil, by slamming her against a wall. One of the few times I saw Sam physically violent.

Even if she hadn't interfered, Lil could hold her own. Lil and I had a couple of instances together before the twins came. She's the type you should never underestimate. Anyway, Lila couldn't stand her and one day Daisy got so bold as to say that we should get rid of the 'club sluts' that she was all he needed.

But what about the rest of us? She didn't care, she just didn't want them around Reaper, but my brother was no cheater. She, on the other hand, got caught with her neighbor between her legs and he immediately dumped her ass.

Anyway, the girls were on my lap when Demon approached. "Come on, Wicked, your girls are the only ones I haven't had. Give me one night with them."

The girls looked at each other and nodded. Unspoken conversation, I learned quickly to sit back and watch.

"For the last time, Wicked is the only…"

"demon dick that we need. Get lost!" Tamla said sternly to drive the point home.

The fact that he could not have any girl he wanted made me feel invincible. He sulked away, defeated.

"I want dibs on bottom tonight, Tam."

"It suits you more anyway, so all yours."

Priya loved to claim me in every way. She wanted to bring me to my knees, and she's done so many times. She rode me as if it was her last time. I could coax four or five orgasms from her every time. Her moaning my name would send me over the edge every time, but she only knew by my body convulsions because her sister was proudly and aggressively riding my face. I had an inkling that Tam might swing both ways by how she preferred oral or my fingers over straight up sex. Her orgasms were ten times stronger doing either of those than dicking her down, anyway.

I happily consented to all their desires, eager to fulfill their every wish. Judging by the wet spots afterwards, they were.

One day while fishing, Lucifer didn't look at me while he cast his reel, but he sighed and that caught my attention. "Asher, out of all my boys, you seem the happiest and also the most lost."

I was confused. "What do you mean?"

"I stay out of you boys' business, but what are your intentions with those girls? You can't possibly be serious with both of them. It's been over two years. I don't know how to say this delicately, but this will not end well."

As far as I knew, everything had been going perfectly, but now, a seed of doubt. I shake my head, wanting the conversations to go back to what we love, fishing and catching enough to take home and fry up.

"I'm young and found myself in the fortunate situation of being presented with not just one, but two girls. Who could say no to such an opportunity? I'd be crazy not to! It's nothing serious. And I have no plans of making them my ol' lady. This is fun, pure fun."

He looked at me and I saw the concern but he sighed, "Alright, Asher. Just keep in mind that it's not only about you in this situation. There is a possibility that they might desire more, or worse, one of them does, and it causes a rift in their bond. Do you want to be responsible for that?."

What did that mean? No way, they don't know anything but sharing. Why ruin a good thing? I ignored Boss Man's words at that moment, but they would circle back. For now, I nodded so we could end this conversation and resume fishing peacefully. I caught six, and he caught nine. We had a hell of a fish fry with Sam's famous hushpuppies and coleslaw.

The next night, we had a run to make for Frankie. Thank God it wasn't to the Vice Lords. We signed over the load to the next group as our responsibility ended at the Connecticut state line. He can be their problem for as long as his product remains in their jurisdiction.

I get back to see Reaper struggling to find a comfortable position. He was still on the bench after the low-side wreck. Worst case of road rash I've ever seen! It's every biker's fear, wrecking their most precious possession. I honestly wouldn't know how to feel if I lost Stormy. She is my number one girl!

Speaking of girls, because I hear Lucifer's words constantly, I have to admit two truths. I always thought the biker life was inherently single. Because why tie yourself down when the girls were scrambling to get into your bed? Some days I want the single life and I think about dropping the twins, but there is such a strong bond between Priya and I. It's like we're in a relationship with Tam as a third wheel. And that's when his words really sink in.

Another problem was that even after two years, it's still a pain in the ass telling them apart. Emotionally I can figure it out, but if they're both ravenous and concentrated on getting off, I have to find ways to get behind them because Tam has a key shaped birthmark on her right butt cheek. Otherwise, I have to go by context clues and not to call them by their name until I'm inside one of them. Priya is so much more responsive to my dick.

One day I want them, the next I need to breathe. To be fair, seeing Lucifer and Sam when they think no one's watching makes me wonder if one day I'll get that type of happiness?

Another few weeks of security runs landed us some much needed dough. I know Reaper was saving every dime for the last bit of repairs for his bike.

Demon wanted more toys for his playroom. I swear his room has to be bigger than mine with the stuff that gets delivered, but Lucifer swears all the bedrooms are about the same. The only difference is Reaper snagged the only other room with an en suite bathroom.

How? I lost a game of rock paper scissors.

Anyway, I never go into Demon's dungeon, but my curiosity was piqued after the St. Andrew's cross arrived. Like, come on!

I knock on his door. "Ladies, ladies, the all-you-can-fuck buffet doesn't open until nine. Oh, hey small fry."

He goes to pat my head, but I smack it away. "Why must you belittle me?"

"Because you're my little brother. I got to rag on you. What are big brothers for?"

"I have brothers, and they weren't as annoying as you."

"Whatever. What can I do for you? Out of condoms? For their pleasure or yours? Trick question, it's always for yours." He chuckles and hands me a handful from this repurposed jewelry chest on his nightstand. Handcrafted, it boasted black leather and red stitching.

I hold up my hand to say no, but he puts them in there. I shove them in my pocket. I see the cross in the corner, putting his victim's ass in full view while playing. I would never tell him this, but his setup is pretty sweet. He set it up like a loft. He was here when they bought the place, so he had time to perfect his setup. He painted the room black, his loft bed frame was wooden, black, of course, and sturdier than those cheap metal frames. I always thought his bed was against the same wall as mine, judging by the banging and screams, but surprisingly, it was on the opposite wall. Instead of a couch under the bed, he had another bed but bigger, full size.

"Why do you have two beds?"

"One for playing, one for sleeping. Especially if I get a squirter! I make it my goal for her to soak my sheets, but I don't want to sleep in it."

"That's…actually smart."

"Alright, stop stalling. What are you really in here for?"

I sigh. "I'm having a dilemma with the girls."

"You finally letting me break them in?" A smile of hope formed.

"I don't think you'd have a chance if I wasn't in the picture. They're out of your league and sometimes I feel they're out of mine, too."

"What do you mean, Asher?" Use of my real name means he's taking it seriously.

"I'm not sure if this is what I want anymore. They are great in their own way, but…" I run my hand over my face.

"Are you turning into Reaper? Sounds like the same record spun differently. Well, except you have two. Which doesn't sound like a problem to me!"

"It does when you prefer one over the other, but keep up the charade because of their bond. It's all or none with them, Aven, and I knew that. But it was so bad ass at first! You were so jealous of my situation! I felt like the top dog. I always wanted to get the one up on you after our first interaction."

"Well, that you did. I underestimated you, small fry. I thought you were some pipsqueak the way you were fangirling that night…"

"Watch it."

He holds his hands up. "But I saw the spark in your eye to mold yourself to the club and you did. You went from #1 fan to a brother, keeping up with the big dogs. I grew to be proud of you."

Whoa. Talk about unexpected.

He continued while cleaning the toys on his dresser. Why does he have so many of those?

You know what, nevermind.

"I know I'm the least likely to settle down or to be giving relationship advice, but I will say this…listen to your heart, not your dick."

It was almost poetic until he mentioned my dick. I roll my

eyes and head out to the bar to make myself a stiff drink. The music was on, and it looked like the bunnies were getting ready to head to Throttle. Looks like today's outfit theme was leather and lace.

I assume my girls were going, too. I was curious to see their interpretation of the theme. I line up three shots and turn to find the good bourbon.

We have so many bottles on several shelves. I'm browsing, "Macallan…Macallan…where are you? Did someone polish it off? I swear to…" I felt frustration building, not because I couldn't find my favorite drink. It was everything swirling around at once.

I finally see it two shelves up in the corner. I finally get my fingertips around the bottle and in my grasp. I sigh. "Fucking finally!"

"Took you long enough." I turned to see them both sitting at the bar. The roles seem reversed. "What are you even doing? You know we make drinks way better than you. Let's not sugarcoat the truth." Their laughs were arrogant and touched an already irritated nerve.

"Sometimes I just want shots, not a damn drink! I don't need you for that. Don't start tonight!" I was still struggling with my feelings and wasn't in the mood. Tamla rolled her eyes and grabbed one of my shots, taking it back in defiance before walking away. Priya says nothing, and that says a lot. She's conflicted between me and her sister. I never stood a chance. Their bond was from birth. I slide the other glass to her, then throw mine back, pouring another into my glass.

I look over, and Sam is watching me. Ever since Reaper's string of bad luck, she's been observing us more closely. Maybe it's just me. I know she wants the best for us, but I left my mother at home.

She sighs hard, like she wanted to say something but had given up. Lucifer grabs her and her attention as she walks by him. She squeals as his hands wander, and I look away.

48

Nobody wants to see their bonus parents playing grabby hands.

I turned back to see if Priya wanted another shot, but she was in deep conversation with her sister. Occasionally they'd look my way, then I got distracted by my brothers. Change of plans, we were going to celebrate Reap getting his bike back. No better way than watching girls strip and dance to crappy music. I wouldn't mind a few new sets of tits getting my attention.

Chapter Eight
Asher aka Wicked

PROTECTED
THE MERCILESS FEW MC: DEVIL'S IGNITED
Briarswood, Mass.

Fiend whistles, "15 minutes until we head to the Dollhouse. If you're going, saddle up!" I grabbed my cut and my keys to ride my Stormy girl until I felt a tap on my shoulder. Both were staring at me with this innocence, but I knew better, especially after the tension earlier. Priya stepped into my space, placing her hand on my chest. Her lips close only because I leaned down in anticipation, but she didn't complete it.

"You know, Wicked...my sister and I have always had this fantasy of almost getting caught in public being naughty."

"And there's no better place than a dark corner of a strip club. Doesn't that sound like...fun?" It was Tam who completed the kiss aggressively. I wasn't expecting that. She leaned back, checking she didn't smear her flawless lipstick in the side mirror of the truck.

"I know sometimes we can be difficult, but it's not on purpose, Wicked... promise. We want to go with you." Priya's eyes are wide and glossy. She was pulling on my heart strings because she knew, knew I favored her over her sister. Meaning she could bend me to her will.

Reaper jingles the keys before getting in and starting the truck, since he'd be picking up his bike tomorrow.

I notice the mischief in their eyes. Someone would have to ride in my lap.

"Get in the truck!" I said firmly, and they obeyed. Riding in a vehicle and not Stormy was weird. I noticed they were overly clingy tonight, not that I'm complaining.

It was busy tonight, but we were able to find a booth next to my brothers. It was dimly lit, the shadows would mask their eagerness. How far it would go is up to them. It didn't take too long after sliding into the booth that their hands started roaming.

I release a low, feral growl. As I glance around, I see my brother's gaze fixed on the girl dancing sinfully on the main stage. The sound of catcalls and whistles fills the air, mingling with the scent of sweat and perfume. My eyes roll back, overwhelmed by the scene unfolding underneath the table, as a hand slips into the cool fabric of my jeans, feeling the heat enveloping me. I had settled into a comfortable slouch, making it easier to access what they needed.

"Damn, Priya. You dirty fucking girl." I moan with my eyes closed.

"It wasn't me!" She spat angrily. My eyes shot open, down, then following the hand to Tam's mischievous face. Was she trying to piss off her sister? What would be the point? No, she was just eager to please. I kiss Priya softly and sweetly. "I'm sorry, sweet pea." She seemed to perk up at her nickname I called her and only her. I take her hand and run it down my chest before intertwining our fingers. She leaned in, I smell the butterscotch on her breath, before our lips connect. She tasted so sweet. I feel her hand slide down my chest to meet her sister's hand that was stroking me to get me to cum under the table.

Tam forcefully spun my face to meet hers, her eyes intense. The movement was almost violent. "What, no kiss for me? You're not playing favorites, are you?" She pouted, then smirked before shoving her tongue down my throat. Now my hand cups her face.

Maybe this isn't so bad. I mean, they both wanted me and what's better than that? All couples have moments of friction. The best part is making up.

I lean back as they slowly stroke me, taking in the surroundings. Surprise, Demon reaches for this bubbly blonde in a barely there silver, slinky type dress. Not gonna lie, she'd be my choice for a turn in the champagne room. She grinds against him, but the cool air hitting my exposed dick under the table distracts me.

"Fuuuuuckkkk…baaaaby."

I let my head fall back. I try to open my eyes and see Reap talking to a girl.

Wait, isn't that the girl he keeps running into?

Apparently, from what Lil told me, he turned into a sexual beast when he was thinking about her. Now she was in front of him, but she was dancing at Frankie's club?

What kind of lowlife would allow his sister to work in a strip club? Or is he forcing her? What a low down dirty son of a…

She glanced over and we made eye contact before her eyes wandered down, got big, shot back up, then she focused back on him. I think she might have seen my dick, but I didn't care. It felt so good. I notice the signs of my climax and do my best to keep my cool.

I didn't even notice Reap had gone with her or how long he'd been gone. They're torturing me, minutes felt like hours as they edged me then backed off.

"You wanna cum so bad don't you?" Tam giggles, but I notice Priya looking down and licking her lips like she was eager to swallow every drop of my prize.

She even stuck her fingers in her mouth to taste my essence. "Tell us... you want to cum for us, don't you? You want to cum for me?" She whispered the last part, never breaking eye contact.

My dick is going to explode.

"Yes." I growled, "but not here." I panted.

No sooner had I said that, Reaper came barreling from the back room. He looked absolutely enraged.

"Let's go...now." He didn't even stop. He was out the door and the engine was running by the time I shoved myself back in and ushered them out of there.

Once I pass the threshold of the door, I bellow, "In the room now!"

They giggle, "Yes, sir."

They were going to get it, but first I needed a drink. Sam comes from her room once the noise levels increase from us returning. She held her robe closed as she leaned against the kitchen door.

"Hey, Asher."

"Hey Sam. Why are you still up?"

She shrugged, "Life of a club mom, worried about my boys."

I grab a glass of water. "I'm sure Reap will recover. He always does." I shut the fridge, leaning against the counter.

"I'm talking about you. What are you doing, Asher? Two girls and not just that, but the fact of how casual it is. For so long. Have you thought about getting serious with these girls or one of them?"

"It's just fun and games, Sam! Besides, I'm the baby. I can do what I want."

"I just want the best for you."

Because I was so worked up, my temper was short, and I

was easily annoyed. I should be balls deep in one of them by now. "I know you take your role seriously as club mother, but you're not MY mother." I set the glass in the sink and step around her. "Excuse me."

I scoff, the nerve! I'm allowed to have fun! I never see her disciplining anyone else! It's only because I have two girls and I'm having fun.

Anyway, I shake off my feelings before opening my door.

"Oh god!" I hear close by.

"Not god, but a demon in the sheets. Now bend over and take this…"

I damn near slammed my bedroom door. I still heard that last part and the subsequent spanking. I wipe my face and groan. My eyes adjust to the dim setting before laying eyes on them stark naked. That shouldn't be shocking to me. However, Sam's words still rang in my head, adding to my already looming doubt.

What was I doing?

"Wicked…" Their whispering brought me back to the task at hand.

"We're so wet." Both swipe their fingers between their legs before tasting themselves. In a flash I have a vision, me old as dirt with both of them on my arm. I was smiling, but it didn't quite meet. It was like I was going through the motions, but it wasn't what I really wanted.

What did I want?

"Don't keep us waiting…" I heard with a bit of sass. I look to see them both looking at me. I could almost bet money it was Tam's smart ass comment, but I didn't know who was who yet. Sometimes, I think they switch up their mannerisms to play with my head. If I couldn't tell, I'd punish them both until I was certain.

I approach the bed, and they don't move. I take off my cut.

"Belt." Immediately, one eagerly leans forward to take it off. She leans so far forward I don't see the birthmark.

It's Priya, so eager to please me. She'd never talk back. I point at her sister. "On your back!"

While Priya was squeezing me down her throat, I was putting her disobedient sister through torture. I knew how much she loved to cum all over my fingers. She'd scream for more as she came, squirting like an ATM that was shooting out money.

But tonight I'd edge her to the brink and back off, not allowing her to climax while she watched her sister get fucked into oblivion.

Was it cruel? Maybe.

Cause tension? Perhaps, but that's not my problem.

That's what happens when you have a smart ass mouth and I'm not in the mood.

Tam did as she was told, laying back, bending her legs at the knees. She teased herself while pinching her nipple. I slam my fingers in and see the shock, then the lust in her eyes. I was relentless to get her to the threshold.

My entire body shuddered as I shot down Priya's throat. Fuck, that felt so good! She sits up, leaning over to kiss me. Then she sits back, observing her sister's punishment. I lift her chin. "You're not done just because you got me to cum. Get me ready to fuck you all night."

"Oh… shi…gonna…" I felt Tam tighten around my fingers, so I pulled out. She was absolutely livid until I slid back in, resuming the motion, but much slower.

Meanwhile, Priya turned around, positioning herself in doggy. She was absolutely soaking wet. I slid into her, enveloping myself in her tight pussy. It'll take a miracle not to cum.

I notice Tam getting annoyed that I hadn't gotten her there yet. I switch my technique and she's somewhat satisfied again. I can concentrate on slamming deliciously into her sister.

"Fuck yeah, sweet pea! Throw it back...just like that! Such a good girl. Yeah..." I see Tam on the verge again and decide to edge her once more and then I'd let her cum. I'm not a complete monster.

I made sure this time to focus on her sweet spot until I had her panting. She looked at me like she knew what I was doing. A wave of pleasure, she sprawled out before bringing her knees together, "Please." She whimpered.

"Please what, Tamla?" I rub against her favorite spot. She moans, acknowledging her dire need.

I slow my motions, "Are you sorry for that smart ass mouth of yours?" She huffs and looks away. Meanwhile, Priya has cum twice and not slowed down. She's trying to break me!

I add another finger, and she arches her back. For someone who doesn't prefer dick, she loved being filled.

I retract the finger. "Alright, I'm sorry, now make me cum, you bastard...please!"

Huh, so be it.

I'm three fingers deep in her walls as she quivers around them. She's just about there and I pinch her clit hard and was rewarded with a scream as she squirted more than usual. She ended up in the fetal position as I took my opposite hand to reach around to tease Priya. I growl in her ear, "Just give me one more sweet pea. Can you do that for me?" I moved her sweat soaked hair aside to kiss her neck, biting firmly. I slide out, flip her and take over, holding her leg against me for leverage. She felt so damn good. "Wi-wi-wicked. Going to... oh god, right there!"

"I'm so close, sweet pea. Tighten up just a little more. Oh, yeah... that's it...that's fucking it! Ahhh!"

I roared up, then collapsed between them. I am drained. Looks like I'm the only one with enough energy to reach for the blanket. I pulled it over us and they each wrapped themselves around me. The room was filled with heavy breathing, sweat soaked skin, and satisfaction.

Another night living the dream.

Chapter Nine

Asher aka Wicked

Frankie tried to take us down with him. He even reported Avi to child protective services! But Lucifer had already worked out a deal.

We were required to serve six months in the state pen. I remember the night before our sentence started. Boss Man felt really guilty about everything, especially doing work for Frankie.

Lucifer stood. "Look, I know this isn't the answer we wanted, but it is the lesser of two evils. I have enough money saved for up to a year's worth of bills and utilities. The Merciless chapters from Rhode Island, Connecticut, and New Hampshire will take turns monitoring your safety and checking in. I'll leave all their contact information. They will do rotating two-week shifts and the Ace of Spades crew will monitor consistently since they are local. I will be looking for updates. I want to know if anything goes wrong, but I made sure all my girls are going to be safe. Jake and the Aces are coming by tomorrow to introduce themselves and solidify the game plan. I'm sorry that I couldn't get us off completely and that you'll have records."

All he saw when he looked at us were victims, and that wasn't the case. I made sure to let him know. "No apology needed, Boss. We knew the repercussions, and you saved us from doing more than they were going to sentence us to. Being together will help the time go by faster and I think Reap, Demon, and Fiend can agree; having a record only solidifies us more as a badass biker gang!"

I'll never forget the laugh that left him, a ray of sunshine in the impending dark times to come.

Six months.

Six long, hard months. The only good thing was I wasn't doing it alone, but with my family. I took that time to enhance my physique. Why fitness? None of the other programs they offered interested me. I figured why not leave here more ripped than ever before? Show the girls what they've been missing.

At one of the many dinners we usually had, everyone had left except Lucifer and me. He watched me while eating. He said nothing, just stared. I didn't know how to feel, so I brought up our favorite subject: fishing.

"Did you see that mile long lake on the drive here? Bet it's full of fish we can catch. We should make a trip up here once we're out of here."

"Yeah, we should. You know Asher, Sam tells me everything that happens to her and sometimes she tells me to leave it be, but I can't this time. Especially when you are disrespectful to your house mother and my wife!" His voice raised before he took a deep breath. "She only wants the best for you boys and even if you disagree, there is no need to be rude. She told me the night it happened and told me it was fine, but I saw the hurt in her eyes."

Guilt punched me in the gut. I didn't think about how our little interaction affected her, especially since I was so rude. The day after, she spoke to me like nothing had happened. I thought it was fine, that she understood my point, but I had broken her heart.

That's all he said before returning to his plate. I sat back in my chair. I had lost my appetite, and I knew he was waiting for an explanation from me. It gave me time to really think about why I reacted so hastily.

"I didn't mean any disrespect to Sam or you, honest. I've been having mixed emotions about the twins and when she asked me the same thing you did about my plan, I freaked out! I don't know what to do."

"Ready to let them go or...."

"I'm not sure. I'm not sure about anything anymore. Am I too young to go through a crisis?"

"Hahaha, you will know a crisis. Life likes to throw lessons at you, and perhaps this is a sort of lesson. Listen to your heart, that's how I learned, but don't discredit your club mother. Take our advice and do with it what you want. Love is a complicated thing."

He pats my back before taking his tray to clean.

With no answer, I head to my cell.

My logic said I needed to see them and gauge how I feel after so long. I will admit that I miss their touch. My hand is nothing compared to two sets of tits, ass, and pussy.

But is that all it is? Carnal pleasure?

The day we got released was a sight to see, watching Sam sprint to Lucifer with so much love. Priya and Tamla stood there, their emotions untelling. I wasn't sure they were happy to see me, but the other bunnies were. They screamed my name and hugged me enthusiastically.

Seeing the others react, they finally kissed my cheek. "We missed you." They say dryly. I'm not sure I believed it.

I didn't want to start something. "Missed you, too." I smacked their asses, and they giggled, hugging me tighter. Maybe everything was okay.

The other bunnies were very open about noticing the change in my physique. If the twins were around, you could see their jealousy. More and more, they separated themselves from the other bunnies.

One day I had just finished up a gym session, my shirt turned into my sweat towel.

"Hey Wicked." Kitty purred as she walked past me, scraping her fingernails across my bare chest. "Looking good now. Any chance you give a girl a sample?"

"You never know."

"Huh, yeah right. You think they'd share you with anyone? Not going to happen. They already told us to back off, but I do what I want."

That's interesting to know and super childish. Flashbacks of Daisy pop into my head, and now I'm angry. "It's not up to them. This dick is free use."

Then I heard a throat clear. Kitty looked behind me and chuckled, "Like I said...yeah, right." She strolls away to where the other girls were gossiping.

I felt the heat of their stare, but truth be told, they had no say. I could have any girl I wanted.

"Strap up boys, we got a run for Sébastien."

Thank the heavens, because this was going to be ugly.

Anyway, Sébastien was just a better dressed version of Frankie. He strolled in after they sent Frankie up the river. Frankie could never hurt Avi or Raven again, and Reap was an instant family man. It was exactly what he needed, but now we had to do runs for this vagrant. He was paying way better, but we knew it was a deal with another devil.

There was something not right about him, but I couldn't figure it out.

"We have to go. Sebastien has two trucks heading to the state line. Fiend, you stay here. We can go without you this time. Take some time off."

Fiend had been going through some family trauma with his mom dying and all. He didn't take the news well and took it out on Poppy, a bunny who we all knew was practically in love with him. I know he wasn't a woman beater, but he scared her something pretty awful, so much so she left.

I don't think she's coming back, and he's been a guilt-ridden mess ever since. It doesn't take a rocket scientist to know he cared for her. Now he was reeling. He insisted on coming, probably trying to take his mind off of the emotional pain.

I would deal with the twins later.

We made it to the docks in no time. One driver of the two white trucks met us when we arrived. He hands the manifesto over to Lucifer. After skimming the paperwork, he notifies us the exact location we got to go to. Lucifer assigned Fiend and me to the mountainous region of Vermont. That was my brother's old stomping ground, so he led the way.

Even though it was dark most of the way, I could appreciate the scenery, a change in the usual terrain. We even drove by an alpaca farm. I revved my engine to get a reaction as we passed by, some hummed or snorted in response. I didn't know they even made those sounds. I don't know what I expected, but it wasn't that.

Thirty miles down the road, Fiend turns into this old rundown gas station. We park next to each other as the truck backs in so the lights illuminate the space in front of us.

It looks and feels like a dystopian novel. Then the driver shuts the truck lights off. Now it feels like a horror movie. I check my piece, ensuring it's there and ready if anything pops off. I prop my bike and notice my brother on high alert, almost as if he were expecting something. Out of all of us, Fiend really disliked Sébastien, not sure why. As far as I know, it wasn't the same as the Reaper/Frankie fiasco.

I know he's dealing with so many emotions. "Ayo, Fiend." He looks at me and straightens up on his bike. "I'm sorry about your mom. I want you to know I'm here if you need to vent. I can take time away from Priya and Tamla. I've been considering letting them go anyway, man. I want to be wild and free, like you."

I'm surprised I even said that. Guess when you say it, it's real or becoming real.

He cocks his brow at me, "Huh, trust me, I am not a good example of anything. Besides, those girls trust their relationship with you enough to share you with others. Think about their feelings before you dump them. Are things getting serious? And that's why you're panicking, wanting to run. Don't do that; be open and honest. They are sweet and understanding girls. They don't deserve mistreatment."

I chuckled, "When'd you get so philosophical?"

"When I messed up a good thing by not giving it what it needed to grow." I look to see the face of a heartbroken man. Knowing what I know, I hope he and Poppy can reconcile.

"I hear what you're saying, but look at me! Since our prison stint, I've become nothing short of a Greek god! Not only have the bunnies been trying to get a go at me, but also random girls on the street. Besides, sometimes I feel like they can be condescending or stuck up. It's not as exciting as it once was. I don't see it going anywhere."

"Alright, but you know old pussy is better than no pussy. Think about it." He chuckles, but I get it.

"In ideal circumstances, I'd be with Priya. But she's too weak to break away from her overbearing sister. It's sad really."

The sounds of motorcycles break our conversation. From what I remember, they were called the Indestructibles. Once they introduced themselves, we told them who we were, and they seemed shocked.

"Wait! THE Merciless Few?!" The young blonde on the left says excitedly. Is this what they saw when I couldn't shut up?

He continues, "I heard great things about you guys. Why would you take a dirty job like this?" The other blonde with the face tattoo, who they called Moose, said.

I guess it was a dirty job because of who owned the shipment, but it was full of medical supplies.

"A job is a job. The driver has the manifesto. Once you take ownership, we can leave. Pleasure doing business with you." Fiend quickly says, wrapping up the conversation.

"And you as well. Hey, who do we talk to about wanting to become a Merciless Few chapter up here?"

I look at the lot, and they seem like decent people. Perhaps worthy of the Merciless Few name.

Another chapter means another area protected. Maybe we'll see them at our rally in a few years.

"It takes two to three years to go through the approval process, gain the charter, and officially call yourself a Merciless Few club chapter. Good luck." I add just because I'd been in slightly longer than Fiend and memorized all the bylaws.

They leave with the truck, and we watch their lights disappear. Fiend checks his phone, probably hoping for some sort of sign or message from Poppy or an update from the girls.

I decided not to check my phone. I didn't want to read another string of texts that do nothing but annoy me or piss me off. He sighs dejectedly before we prepare for the long drive back home.

When we all get back, Sam approaches Lucifer with concern in her eyes. "Hey babydoll, we're back safe and sound. No need to worry." He kisses her forehead, but the worry remains.

"I'm glad, Bubba, but this is about my sister. It's not good news." She pulls him into their room.

I hope everything is okay.

Chapter Ten
Asher aka Wicked

PROTECTED
THE MERCILESS FEW MC: DEVIL'S IGNITED
Briarswood, Mass.

I'm exhausted. I don't even pay attention to the goings on around the house. I frankly didn't care.

I go to my room to get things for a long, relaxing shower. I walk in and feel something is wrong. The lingerie that is usually spilling out of the drawers is gone. In fact, everything belonging to any woman, except for the smell of their perfume, is gone!

I stood there, stunned for a moment.

What the hell?

My head was spinning as I stepped out of my room in need of fresh air.

My ears tune into raised voices, "This club is a joke, that's not even funny! It's sad and pathetic, a failed experiment of losers and whores! Only the bottom of the barrel and truly low brow would call this a lifestyle!" I approach the ruckus and see the twins screaming at the group…my family.

Lil stepped forward obviously fired up, "So we're just a big joke to you? A show for your amusement?"

"Exactly!" Tamla spat. "A poor, in-bred version of trash TV. We wanted to see how the lower class lived and it's truly pathetic. And now we're bored with our playthings…you… and are moving on. You couldn't have thought we cared anything about you, could you?" Tamla laughed hysterically as she nudged Priya to join her. "I told you, sis, they'd never catch on. Dumb as a box of rocks!"

I heard enough!

"What the fuck is this? You don't talk to my family like that! Have you lost your goddamn mind?"

They spin around toward me, arms folded. Priya looked hurt until she looked at her sister, then she went expressionless.

"Ha! We're not apologizing to this band of miscreants or you. What's laughable is we don't owe you anything! Do you know why? Did you know you pocket dialed us during your run?"

"We-we heard everything, Wicked! How you don't even know you want to be with us? How little you think of us, how you think I'm just some pushover because of my sister! Well, I'm not!"

She looks at her sister and she stands taller. Her body language shifted to something I expected from Tam and not her.

"What's weak and pathetic is this group. A bunch of boys playing dress up and a bunch of women…"

"You better watch the next few words that come out of your mouth!" Sam stormed from her bedroom, no doubt hearing all the commotion.

Lucifer stepped in front of her. Sam was a woman of virtue and grace, but will also knock your teeth down your throat for being disrespectful.

Tam scoffed, "Oh here comes the club mom, only because she couldn't be a real mother." The gasps turned silence rocked all of us. Sam opened her mouth, but tears welled in her eyes before she hightailed it back to her room with Lucifer after her.

A shriek left Lil's lips as she lunged for them. All the bunnies were ready to tear them apart; however, the guys kept them at bay.

"Get them the fuck out of here before we turn them loose, Wicked!" Demon yelled.

"Don't worry. We're done with this sad life and you." Tam points at me while looking at Priya. "He never even told you his real name! In over two fucking years, he didn't even care to tell us that. Never catch feelings for a man who's obviously beneath you. Let's face facts...Wicked... even if I wasn't in the picture, you already screwed it up with that. I won't let you break my sister's heart! She's better off with me."

"Oh, is she? Or is she your crutch because you can't find anyone on your own, Tam? No one to deal with your bitchy, holier-than-thou attitude. You don't even prefer dick, but your sister does, and she prefers mine very much..."

"Even if I wanted to be with you, I can't be with someone who's so disrespectful toward my sister! I told you we were a package deal and if I had to choose, it will always be her, Wicked." She whispered the last part like it pained her to admit it.

Tam smugly smiled. I am enraged. "I thought you cared."

"I thought you cared until you told your brother it wasn't as exciting as it used to be, that you could get any girl you want! Let me tell you something, you'll live a sad life with that mindset. You want your freedom, you got it!" She screamed.

"Didn't matter, anyway. We were tired of this charade. We don't need you to have fun or get off! You think we were your plaything? You were ours. We can have anyone we want.

Why? Because we're rich. We just wanted a commoner to play with while we get our affairs in order."

"What are you talking about?" I was growing even more irritated thinking that I had a chance to pry Priya away from her sister's grasp, but I was stupid to think I could. Besides, I didn't even know what I wanted. Letting this go would be the smart thing…

"So you use me, my club, my brothers and the girls to play with my emotions? For your amusement?"

"What emotions? You used us as your own personal fleshlights! We stayed because you were pretty good at what you do, but it's nothing we would become exclusive to."

"Is that what you think? Priya? For once in your life, stop being her puppet!"

Tam laughed so hard she wiped her tears. "He still thinks you're the innocent twin, the one soooo in love with him. Such a fool! Tell him, Priya, whose idea this really was?"

Priya's expression changed to mirror Tam's. "I should go back to Bangladesh and become a Bollywood actress for the performance I played this whole time. Yes, it's true I did kind of like you Wicked, but how can I catch feelings when I don't even know your real name?! Not once did you feel like telling me or us. But it doesn't matter because we're leaving this go nowhere town for a better life. Finding an even richer man worthy of us…"

"So you're just going to trick another man with your innocent twin routine?"

"Baby, we're hardly innocent, just smarter than you. Anyway, are we done here? My sister and I have a private jet to catch."

Now the luxury car made sense.

"Priya…sweet pea, tell me, look me in my eyes and tell me you never cared." I know I said that I didn't know where this was heading, but a tiny sliver of me hoped for something more serious but I guess this was a fool's thought. I could never pry her away from her twin, and she didn't want to be separated.

Tam tapped her foot and rolled her eyes. "Wrap this up! I'm tired of explaining to this loser." She pulled the keys and unlocked the car with a confirming chirp.

She had no one to look at or help her. "Wicked...I..."

"Asher." I conceded, my last ditch effort. Her eyes went wide once she realized I had finally told her my name. I reached for her hand, but she stepped back. "I'm sorry, Asher, but it's over. The damage is done for the both of us." She whispered, each word heavy with grief, the silence a stark contrast to the turmoil in her heart. "A word of advice, although I'm sure you don't want to hear it from me...that macho chauvinistic shit you spout is not you. Be yourself and maybe, just maybe, the right girl will see your heart and be able to catch it." With a sad smile, she hopped in on the passenger side.

What the fuck is happening in my life?! I'm utterly confused and frustrated.

Have others picked up on my attempt to sound macho and ultra manly to see it was just a sham. Was I some stupid kid? I stayed outside, trying to avoid the impending backlash.

Lucifer's words ring loudly in my ear. "This will not end well." Boy, was he right and all those vicious and vile words... to Sam... what am I going to say to her?"

I rub my face. "Fuck!" I wasn't even mad they left, but the emotional damage left in their wake. I don't know how to fix this. I brought them in. They wanted to be bunnies, to be with me, but I was just some toy to play with until they got bored and they tossed me in the garbage.

I needed to figure out my life.

But first...

I trudge back into a sea of disappointed looks and anger. "I'm sorry. I guess I didn't really know them. You're not what they say at all. You're my family and I love you." That's all I could say.

"You really stepped in it this time. Were not the ones they hurt. What do we care what they think of us? Those bitches can shove their opinion up their ass for all I care! But Sam... what they spewed was hateful vitriol, and she didn't deserve it! You better fix it..."

We are startled as the bedroom door opens abruptly. He emerges from the room, but Sam is not with him. He lets out a sigh and absentmindedly scratches the back of his head. I know he tried his best to comfort her, but they purposefully brought up a deeply wounding topic. I discovered a while ago that Sam and Rocco could not have children, not because of lack of desire, but to circumstances beyond their control. They dedicated their early years to trying, but unfortunately, a doctor confirmed their worst fears.

He sighs and I meet him halfway. "I'm sorry, Rocco, I really am! I didn't know."

"Yeah, well, you should have heeded my words and hers, son. They targeted your club mother mercilessly and viciously, and I have to put the pieces back together."

I looked over his shoulder at the closed door, imagining her crying, and it broke my heart. "Let me talk to her, please. Tell her I'm sorry."

"You've done enough tonight. Let her be. When she's ready, she'll find you. I'm going to grab a snack and a shot before heading to bed. Everyone should disperse for the night." Everybody looked so shocked. He's never shut down the clubhouse before. The girls grab their jackets and head back to the bunny house and the guys to their room, but not before looking at me.

What have I done?

I trudge into my now empty and cold room, the silence pressing in on me like a physical weight.

Hoping tomorrow will be a better day.

Chapter Eleven
Asher aka Wicked

PROTECTED
THE MERCILESS FEW MC: DEVIL'S IGNITED
Briarswood, Mass.

Still feeling super guilty, I avoided interaction with Sam or anyone, really. I took Stormy on long rides and a couple of overnight trips, staying in a hotel with my thoughts. Realizing it was the perfect time to really figure out who I was, wanted to be, and what I wanted from the opposite sex and what I could provide to them. I had to treat them as equals and not objects.

I relied on my brother's paths, Reaper with Avi, Raven, and now their son, Onyx. Fiend taking responsibility for his role and declaring his love for Poppy and looking to get her back. And the epitome of the purest form of love, Lucifer and Sam. They were love perfected.

One day, in my continued effort at avoiding her because I was a disappointment, I washed and waxed Stormy girl. She had been getting extra attention from me since all the trips. I walked around her, "My, my, my, Stormy girl, you are a sight. You truly are my number one girl. You'd never hurt me or my family."

knock knock

I see Sam's hand lower from knocking on the barn door. "Hey, can we talk?"

It surprised me. I was supposed to get permission from her after they hurt her so maliciously. "Of course, you never need to ask. I'm sorry, Sam. You didn't deserve any of that."

She points to the bench and we sit down. "Are you ok? I know it was pretty shocking to you."

"It's nothing. The way they mistreated us...you...they were all wrong for me. There were probably signs, but I was too dumb to see it. Doesn't matter as long as I have my family?" I asked nervously. She leans over and kisses my temple. "Of course you do, knucklehead."

I couldn't help but hug her, but I still saw the effect of their words. "No matter what anyone says, you are an amazing mother. You ARE a mother, in every way imaginable. You take care of us like your own and we're fortunate to have you. We love you, Sam. I mean, mom." Her eyes welled up, but with tears of happiness. "You don't know how glad I am to hear that. I mean, I know and I shouldn't have ever doubted it, but it brought up some old wounds I guess I never really dealt with."

"Well, remember you're one kick ass grandma, too! Raven and Onyx love their Nana."

She sighs lovingly, "That they do."

"Can you forgive me for my part in all this?"

"Nothing to forgive, but I really want you to heal before you go into anything else. It's time for you to grow into your own. Just like I told Jett and Cullen, your heart is big and needs someone who can handle you, flaws and all." She stands and holds out her hand. I take it and we have lunch together as a family.

Several weeks later, we were celebrating Lucifer's birthday. Sam insisted on it even though he didn't want a party, but he'd do anything for his babygirl. "Come on now! Let's show Bubba some love!" As she started lighting the candles on the sheet cake with a motorcycle on it, but there were so many candles it almost covered the whole design. Someone chuckled and before I knew it, we were all laughing at the unspoken joke until he looked at us.

"When you get my age, every birthday will have meaning."

I couldn't help but blurt out, "Wise words from an old man!" But instantly felt the sting of the slap Sam gave me upside the head. "Oww, Sam!"

"Show respect; I raised you better."

She kisses Lucifer, "Aww, don't worry, baby girl, these boys keep an old man young."

After an embarrassing, off-key rendition of happy birthday, it was time for gifts.

The bunnies gifted him this limited edition Harley Davidson t-shirt and bandana. Fiend gave him a pretty stellar ass watch, which was right on time, pun intended. His current one was on life support. Sam helped him put it on.

I step forward with my unwrapped gift. How do you even wrap a...

"Happy birthday. It's the Penn Battle III." I knew no one else would understand our language of love, but it was one of the best fishing rods currently in production. He immediately wanted to test it out, and I suggested we go in the morning. He countered with this weekend and I agreed.

Demon gives him a gift card to Harley Davidson and Reaper gets him impeccable seats at the upcoming Guns N' Roses concert. I wanted tickets, but by the time I checked, even the lawn seats were sold out; the website showed a frustrating, flashing "sold out" message.

It seemed like life had gotten back to normal. I had stuck

to the bunnies for my needs, being cautiously optimistic of any outsider. It was okay being alone.

One night, Reaper came from his house dressed for a run. "What's going on?"

"Boss said we had some run for Sebastien, but he sounded different and said we absolutely had to be strapped this time."

Interesting. He never insisted before. We're usually allowed to gauge whether we were locked and loaded. I always was, never wanted to be caught off guard.

Demon comes out of his room with Penny almost stumbling out, her legs weak, body wrapped up in his sheets. "Sorry to cut it short, darlin'. But be ready to continue when I return. Massage her until I get back." He winked, tipping her chin.

"Yes, sir." She smiled through her panting. Dammit! I wanted Penny tonight. Now that's out of the question. I eye my choices, and it looks like Kitty was my backup. I headed toward the basement just as Fiend walked in. The vein in his forehead throbbed, a clear sign of his rage, and I'm sure it was the uncertainty of Poppy's condition that was the reason. He was not in the mood to do a run for a guy he hated.

Lucifer looks at us. "We got a job, but this time it's different."

"How so?" Reap asks.

"First, we'll be working with the Ace of Spades on this job. There will be four deliveries at once."

"Aye, but there's five of us. We can each take one, and you'll ride with one of us. We don't need no other people!" Demon declared, and we all agreed.

He held up his hand to quiet us. "He doesn't think a single man is enough to guard trucks this size, so we'll be in groups of two and one group of three."

"This is stupid! Why can't he deliver two at a time? That way, we're not sharing our bounty with some mediocre copycat." Demon was not a man who shared anything other than himself. When it came to money, it was his brotherhood and brotherhood only, but this time I was with him. Fuck that group! I heard too many awful things about them, especially when they elected a new President.

"Trust me, I suggested, but he was adamant about all four trucks getting to their destination simultaneously. He calls it 'on-the-job training,' especially if we have to do multiple runs such as this, plus... each group receives $50,000 once the job is complete."

"$50,000?!" We all shouted.

There's no way, something was fishy about this.

"Exactly. We may not be hard up on money, but that's a pretty good chunk for each of us, even after the percentage that goes toward the group pot."

We always put a percentage in the club funds, especially after our stint in prison, that used a good chunk keeping the lights on. We were looking to recoup. Definitely not looking to serve time again. There was no doubt that the sentence would be longer. I don't think I could do it again.

We started getting ready but found out the delivery happens tomorrow. Sam finished cooking for us and was immediately on the phone. She seemed worried with whoever she's on the phone with. Lucifer would glance at her as she paced the living room.

"No! I want to know her status! I'm her goddamned sister! What do you mean..." She storms to their room and Lucifer sighs loudly. We all share concerning glances.

The next night, we were on our bikes about to head to the location where we would meet Sebastien and the Ace of Spades. Lucifer declared this would be our last run for him. He and Sam had a spat about the circumstances. She didn't care about the money but our safety. She couldn't do another jail sentence without us. He understood and swore to find us more honest work to replace the after dark dealings.

When we parked side by side across from the Aces, it

looked like a standoff, with their President standing up. Four delivery trucks sat parked behind them. Lucifer dismounted and went to talk to their leader. He decided to not shake our President's hand, but Lucifer introduced us anyway like a respectable man. I would have knocked his teeth down his throat until he choked on them.

Their so-called leader, King, introduced his little group, but no one gave a damn about them. My brother Fiend grabbed my attention by growling. I understood and leaned over. "I don't like this douchebag."

"If you only knew." He said. I noticed the tight grip on his handlebars as he watched the exchange. King slammed a piece of paper against Lucifer's chest.

What the fuck! Oh, hell no!

We all shoot up. Fiend accidently revs his bike. It punctuates all our anger and the fucking audacity of this cheap knock off. Lucifer signals us to stand down. He handed Fiend the inventory list to check the trucks. I monitor this scumbag and his gang because I don't trust them to not be dirty. Fiend confirms the shipment and we get the group lineup. I end up with the one they called Jack. Stringy bleach blonde hair held back by a dirty bandana. He had a few inches on me, but I was definitely a lot stronger than him.

He led the truck, and I trailed, heading west. As we trekked, I realized how slow we were going. If we had to go far, it would take forever. I already felt irritated by tonight's events. This was the icing on the cake. I revved my engine, then sped up to the front to catch up with him. I signaled to pull over, and he did. The truck already stopped a few yards back.

"Dude, what the fuck? Speed up! The less time I spend on this bullshit run, the better."

"I'm following my President's orders. You follow us and our rules! Because before the night is over, the Merciless Few will be no more!"

Before I could even ask, I saw rapid movement from him before I felt this searing pain across my face. I jump off my bike, covering my face, and then seeing blood. I see the utility knife in his hand. I followed his movement, realizing he was trying to kill me!

Fuck that! I pull my gun and fire two shots. He recoils before he and his bike hit the ground. Enraged, I started stomping and kicking. "You motherfucker!" I realized what he said, that we would be no more. I had to get back! Who knows what was happening to my brothers! The truck sped past me, but I didn't care unless they wanted to die, too. I needed to get back, and I wasn't too far away. Maybe it was a blessing in disguise.

I parked back from the meeting point, working through the woods until I saw Fiend on his knees. It looked like he had been crying profusely, but why? Next to him was another body, softer, more feminine. It's Poppy! What did they do to her?! King and his cronies stood triumphantly, but they didn't know I was lurking.

Suddenly, Fiend pushed upward against the gun pressed to his chest. The movement pushed King back. "Do it, motherfucker! Pull the goddamn trigger! Put me out of my misery! I lied to my brothers, betrayed them by signing off on dirty shipments, took drugs to numb my pain, lost my girl, and YOU killed my baby! I have nothing left to live for, so fucking do it! Because if you don't, I promise I'll dismember your body while you're still conscious, then light you on fire. Preparing you for the Hell you put her through!"

In what he thought were his last moments, he cleansed his soul by admitting his mistakes with a gun pointed at him. It completely shattered him.

I didn't know.

What he confessed broke my heart and what's worse is that he couldn't tell us or ask for help. He did do one thing; he professed his love for Poppy. The sight of her made my blood boil. She had endured torturous abuse.

Then chaos erupted! A string of gunshots and I see one guy collapse. Then out of the bushes comes Reaper, who fires another round into a body.

Not paying attention to my surroundings and the sounds of scuffling footsteps, grunts of exertion, and the sickening thud of fists meeting flesh, one of his guys sees me and lunges at me. He sucker-punched me, hitting the already-sliced side of my face. It sends me into a rage. My sight becomes a blur of frantic movements and flashes of violence. Adrenaline fills the air and courses through my veins, heightening my senses and fueling the raw strength surging within me as I punch him in his head, the blood splattering everywhere. Soon he's not even covering up.

They wanted us dead, planning this ambush. They were dying tonight!

I feel hands that pull me up and off him. I almost swing on them. "It's Reap, stop, he's done. He's done!" I stare for a minute until I see his chest barely rise. I pull my gun and put one in each knee. He was alive then, screaming in excruciating pain, but it still wasn't enough! My steel-toed boots stomped down on his wounds. His existence pissed me off! "You motherfucker!" Reap again, pulling me off him.

"It's over! It's over." I catch my breath but notice he was wounded, shot! "You're shot!"

"It's fine. You got a pretty big gash yourself! Let's go make sure everyone else is okay."

bang bang

Poppy screamed as Fiend went down. He cushioned her fall with his bullet ridden body. I pull my piece, but Lucifer gets to King before me, putting a bullet in his head.

We surrounded my brother, reassuring him he would be okay, but all he could do was apologize.

After the ambulance rushed Fiend away, Lucifer made

certain that Sam would meet Poppy at the hospital; she was also in desperate need of medical attention. The wail of the siren still echoed in the distance.

Of course, the cops came and Lucifer laid it all out for them. He told them he had substantial evidence against the Aces and Sebastien he would turnover, but needed to get us medical care. He's right, they shot Reaper!

I look over, and he sighs. I think he sees my worry. "I'm fine, kiddo."

"Yeah, tell that to Avi."

"Shit! She's gonna blow a gasket." No sooner, his phone rings. I assume because Sam knew about Poppy, she told the girls and someone called Avi.

Before I knew it, a string of loud Portuguese rang from the phone. I could pick up on bits and pieces, and she was not happy.

"Avi, baby, I'm fine. It's just a little…gunshot wound."

"Just a little gunshot wound? *você perdeu a cabeça?*..." (have you lost your mind?)

She got much louder, and he walked toward the approaching ambulance. I could still hear her giving him a piece of her mind. That was love.

I check my wound and head toward the other ambulance. Only surrounded by my thoughts and regrets.

The whirlwind that happened after that turned the club upside down, but in the end brought us closer together.

Fiend entered a recovery type hospital facility for healing and detox, learning to grieve the loss of his daughter. Once he was home, he and Poppy held a memorial for her. It was heartbreaking to know I'd never meet my niece, but the memorial near the house was beautiful. I go out there sometimes to change out the flowers. It taught me how precious life was.

She didn't even get a chance to experience life.

I vowed to dedicate a small part of my life to living for her.

Chapter Twelve
Asher aka Wicked

PROTECTED
THE MERCILESS FEW MC: DEVIL'S IGNITED
Briarswood, Mass.

One day, I stood in front of the mirror, tracing the scar across my face. Luckily, he didn't cut me deep. It was healing nicely, barely there. They said there could be minimal to no scarring if I follow instructions and I did. I thought it would affect my self-esteem, but it was a war wound, fighting for my brotherhood, my family, and I was proud to have it.

I hear the bathroom door open and close. I look behind me to see Kitty. Kitty reminded me of the shy and quiet bookworm who kept to herself. How did she even get talked into becoming a bunny? After spending a few months with the girls, she has become more confident. This is clear from her experiences with Fiend and Demon, although she seemed to prefer Demon more. Why she was in here puzzled me.

"Hey, Kit, what's up? Need the bathroom?" I turn to leave,

but she blocks the door and licks her lips. I'm getting Reba flashbacks. I'm not sure where this is going.

No, I finally wanted to have my turn with you at last, now that those stuck up bitches are gone!"

I felt all the emotions again, irritation, guilt, stupidity, and foolishness. I needed to forget the damage they had done to me and my family.

"What about my new scar?" I touch it gently.

She brushes it. "What about it? It doesn't make you any less sexy. It builds character." She grabs my cut, pulling me closer to her level, slamming her lips against me.

Why the fuck not?

I grabbed under her thighs, hiking her up to my waist as she grinded her body against me. She unbuckles and unzips me with her hands behind her back. I was impressed. My pants barely hit the floor before I was balls deep. "Oh shit, Wicked! Fuck me!"

As you wish, Princess.

She peeled off her top to reveal some pretty nice tits. I latch on immediately while bouncing her against me. Fuck, she was tight! I felt my wavering and her walls quivering. She moaned my name and locked her legs when she came. I pulled her off me and ordered her on her knees. "Open." I commanded, and she held out her tongue, awaiting the taste of me.

"Oh yeah, hold that pretty little tongue out for me to bust! Ye-yeah...oh...ohhhh."

knock knock

"Is anyone...oh my god! I thought you were in your room!" She screamed out. Sam witnessed me cumming all over Kitty's tongue before hightailing it out. I grunt and tap my dick on her tongue.

No point in stopping.

She wraps her lips around me, cleaning me up. She stood up. "Thanks for the good time." She shimmies her shorts back up, opens the door, swaying her hips as she heads to the dining room.

Sam is leaning against the kitchen door. She crossed her arms and shook her head. "Do you think you should be so casual after the twin fiasco?"

"What's that supposed to mean?"

"I mean, shouldn't you be trying to figure yourself out before jumping into another situationship? I thought we talked about this!"

"It's not a situationship or relationship, it's just casual fun. Besides, what are bunnies for?! No, it's all YOU talk about. Get off my back! It's been months. I need someone to get me off, besides she came to me."

She tuts, rolling her eyes before going back into the kitchen.

What was her deal? No one else is getting lectured!

I went to my room and stayed there until the morning.

The next day I woke up but laid in bed, still irritated by Sam's third degree. Ever since Reap, and now Fiend, have moved out, she's been extra attentive. And that would be fine if she were harping on both me and Demon, but it was just me.

I needed some space. I shower and dress before skipping breakfast and heading out. I'd grab something somewhere.

"Wicked, where are you going?" I heard Sam but walked faster. "Out!"

Chapter Thirteen
Samantha

PROTECTED
THE MERCILESS FEW MC: DEVIL'S IGNITED
Briarswood, Mass.

"Wicked, where are you going?" I asked after hearing commotion from the hall. I knew it was him because Demon was in the kitchen devouring pancakes like I never fed him.

He didn't even look my way before he stormed out.

What am I going to do with him?

"Leave the boy be, Sam." I hear the rough gravelly voice of my husband, my President of this amazing club. "I can fix him, Bubba! I know I can! Look at Cullen and Jett, living their lives in love."

He pours his coffee, and I pour the perfect amount of creamer. "He's not broken Samantha. Quit trying to fix what ain't broke. When the right one comes along, he'll fall into place. In the meantime, don't run him off." I groan as I see the girls cleaning up the kitchen. My phone buzzes and my anxiety skyrockets. It's a daily ritual, but it wasn't the person I expected.

"Hello? Yes, this is her sister. You said you're calling from where? Pasadena Villa Outpatient Treatment Center. Ok, is she hospitalized? Is she hurt? Well, where the hell is her husband?!"

Later, I'm zoned out on the porch swing outside. Of course, Bubba finds me. "Hey, babygirl, what's wrong?"

The information received was so jarring and unexpected that it felt as if my world had been completely flipped upside down, leaving me in a state of shock.

My hands were shaking. "Mike had Chelsea committed to a mental facility. A mental facility! She may have needed therapy or medication, but she wasn't crazy! I told her not to marry him! He only wanted to mooch off her disability. And do you know what the facility told me? That I had no visitation right per his orders, it's restricted to only him. Not even her own daughter! I am going to castrate him with a burning hot shard of glass, you hear me!"

He was a classic gold digger. He pretended to be someone else to get close, but eventually revealed his true nature. And now, my sister is suffering in a mental institution.

"And what's worse, I realized I haven't heard from Kynlee in a while! She texts me occasionally if I don't call her to check in. Something doesn't feel right. I'm going to find out what my rights are as her blood sister. That bastard probably changed all her important documents to reflect him as her beneficiary, including her will! And if I find out he did, that motherfucker's mine!" I was not kidding.

I pull out my phone to call my old friend Phil from back home in Tulsa. He did a lot of corporate work and eventually got into local city work. He knew the ins and outs of laws, charters, and precedences needed to support complicated cases. I needed him to figure out my rights. I also asked him to stop by the house to lay eyes on my niece. I need to know how worried I should be.

He called me back the next day saying he needed more time to research because there was a new updated insurance policy being processed and no surprise, that bastard's name was on it, a $3 million dollar policy. He needed time to prove Mike had forged her signature.

"She's in a facility! No way she signed that willingly. She wouldn't have the mental faculty to! It's common fucking sense!"

I pinch my news and sigh. "Well, did you see Kynlee?"

"I didn't and her job said she hadn't been into work for at least a week. I'll keep asking around. Maybe she's staying with a friend. Don't worry just yet."

"Easier said than done, Phil. Please keep me updated. I can be on a plane and home in less than 24 hours."

He chuckles, "That's one thing I do know, Sam."

I end the call and run my fingers through my hair. I knew he was bad news. My soul burned when he was around, but my sister assured me they were in love and her mental health was better for it. He played the role of the loving mate and caregiver, making sure she took her meds and went to her sessions.

For the first year.

Then, we tragically lost our parents within three days of each other, both from heart attacks. We were both devastated, especially when we had to sell everything to cover the double funeral and tombstones. It sent my sister spiraling mentally. Suddenly, the meds were not as effective and she was skipping out on therapy because Mike said they were wasting money they didn't have sending her to talk it out when he was there to listen. Then, he said they couldn't afford both her therapist and medication. He would keep her on track, he vowed. Apparently, that meant to lock her away and have others care for her. But I thought they were struggling financially?

Nothing he did made sense. It was a crock of shit.

My thought process is if she has to be institutionalized, she should be closer to me. I'm getting my sister away from that monster! Phil assured me that even if he forced her there, they had to take care of her properly.

"Find out how they're being paid. I have a feeling he isn't and they might toss her on the street!"

I hear Phil typing, no doubt at his office. "Hmm, looks like they've been attempting to collect payment for...three months. They sent a final reminder last week, threatening to transfer her to a state-run institution at the end of the month if they didn't receive payment."

What?! My heart shot up to my throat. That's in three days!

"How much?"

"He owes $10,500. It's $3500 a month."

Hot tears sting my eyes, my anger through the roof.

"I can pay! I'm on my way. He won't get away with this!" I slam my phone onto the dresser. I forgot Rocco had walked in earlier and disappeared into our walk-in closet. He heard the entire conversation and came out with a suitcase.

"I know you don't think I'm letting you go alone, do you? I am keeping your sweet ass out of jail." He smiles to break the tension. I laugh, but it masks the pain, the unknown. He catches on and pulls me in and I sob. "We'll pull from the club fund, okay?"

He is my sanity in this storm. My hero.

I needed answers.

What happened to my sister?

And where is my niece?

Chapter Fourteen

Kynlee

PROTECTED
THE MERCILESS FEW MC: DEVIL'S IGNITED
Location Unknown

Despite picking up some really shady characters at the St. Louis stop, I feel a hundred times safer on this old Greyhound bus than I do in my own home.

To avoid any trouble, I made a point not to make eye contact and turned up my music to show that I wasn't interested. I gripped my duffel bag tightly against my chest and occasionally dozed off, but not for long.

The nightmares kept haunting me, even as I sat upright, putting miles away from my misery. I still dream of lying in my bed, with the covers pulled over my head but my eyes wide open. It was because I knew I had to be prepared in case he went too far that night.

As the door creaked open, I was instantly aware of his presence by the thick stench of cheap beer and cigarettes wafting into my room. Before he entered, he always hesitated, standing there... just standing there, fixated on my sleeping body. I try not to imagine what thoughts are running through his sick, twisted head.

After a while, I would hear the thumping sound of his approaching footsteps, and it would leave me frozen in fear! I could feel my bed sinking as he sat down, accompanied by his heavy breathing. This was the furthest he had gone. Probably because of earlier.

It was dinnertime, and if I didn't cook, he would starve. I made spaghetti and meatballs, quick and easy after working a full shift. I was exhausted and somehow he complained about being tired after doing nothing except drinking and gambling what money he had down the drain. He plopped down at the table, beer in hand. I set a plate in front of him. "What the hell is this?"

My senses are still sharp as I avoided his hand that was trying to grab me and possibly pull me into his lap. "What does it look like? It's food, eat it." I sat opposite him.

He looked at it, grunted, mumbled something incoherent, and started eating.

I ate fast because I hated being in his presence. Especially since he had my mom committed. He said he was her husband and knew what was best for her. That was a load of bullshit! He wanted her out of the way, but close enough to still collect her disability paycheck.

He never cared about her, but my sweet, naïve mother was completely shattered when my dad died. The stress of having his body transported back overseas really took a toll on her. She fought with his family over his burial arrangements, the ceremony, and his estate.

His death likely took what sanity she had left. And then my grandparents died.

"You know..." Mike startled me out of my thoughts. "Since you're doing all the things my wife used to do, you might as well do everything else."

"What are you talking about?" I already did all the cooking, cleaning, and laundry. What more did he want?"

He leaned back, a slow smile spreading across his face as his hand slid down his chest, and then he looked up and winked. "I think it's time for you to perform those wifely duties your mom used to.

Is he suggesting? I kept myself from gagging violently.

He got up, "You have to eventually, especially if you want to live in this house. We can start with a nice, relaxing blow job." Then his phone buzzed. "Hold that thought. Keep those lips warm for me."

He stepped away, so I took my plate to my room and quickly shut the door. I hear his voice raise before he scrambled out of the house, my mom's car screeching out the driveway. I booked the next ticket I could afford to Massachusetts, but it wasn't until early tomorrow morning. I had to endure one more night of hell.

If he so much as tried to stick that thing near me, I'd bite it off!

I threw only the most important stuff in my bag and hid it in my closet. I wore my traveling outfit to bed just in case.

Now he was on my bed, breathing heavily. You know, the type of panting you hear when men touch themselves.

He just recently started touching himself and finishing before he slunk back out of my room, satisfied. I was hoping for one more incident before he wanted to enact his carnal fantasies about me. You'd think the drugged up hookers from down the street would be enough. I couldn't risk it.

I knew Aunt Sam would be my refuge.

Chapter Fifteen

Asher aka Wicked

PROTECTED

THE MERCILESS FEW MC: DEVIL'S IGNITED

Briarswood, Mass.

Lucifer and Sam let us know they had to leave immediately for an urgent family matter.

I hope everything is okay. I was relieved to not be the center of her attention for a little while.

With Reaper and Fiend thriving with their significant others, it was just Demon and I. The day after their departure, Demon decides we need to throw a wild party. No inhibitions!

As if he had any.

The music was loud, the drinks flowing, and Demon had paid some Dollhouse girls to come over. Something we would never do! He was pushing the boundaries, but promised he had picked three of the most beautiful girls. No doubt he'd be trying to bang them all.

They stroll in wearing the very least under their trench coats. Demon rubs his beard as he scans all his options. He closes the door, then sits on the couch, pulling out a stack of cash.

"Oh yeah, ladies! Show me what you're working with!" He throws a handful at the girls who squeal while stripping out their coats.

Whoa! That redhead is smoking hot. We exchange looks and I'm determined to get to her before my brother does!

I reached for my wallet and forgot it was on my dresser. Wonder how much a private... dance is?

boom boom boom boom boom

It sounded almost like a police knock, but not quite. I couldn't explain it. Demon didn't even look at the door. He was face first in a pair of tits, slipping bills into a g-string.

"Don't worry, I'll get it." Probably another girl who ran late. The more the merrier, I suppose.

I open the door and immediately hear panting. I look down to see a girl sitting on the ground. It appears she had been running, as she desperately tried to catch her breath.

"I need...I..." She was drenched in sweat and covered in dirt. Her bag was halfway off her back, it looks like she had collapsed right after she knocked, the motion draining the very last of her energy.

I tried to pull her up, but she was too weak and just slumped against me.

"Sa-sa-samantha." She sputtered, then exhaled before she passed out.

Oh shit!

I carefully scooped her up in my arms, feeling the weight of her frail body against my chest, shut the door with my foot and carried her to my room. I removed the bag and her very worn sneakers and realized she wasn't wearing socks. Her bare feet were swollen and reddened. How long had she been walking? She must be in so much pain!

As soon as she hit the bed, she sighed. I fetched a warm towel, preparing a basin with a splash of soap and water.

I came in and her chest movements were slightly faster. Hopefully, this meant her body was finally finding the rest it had been so desperate to get. Who knows how long she had been out there!

I take the hand towel, wring it, and gently wipe her sweat and dirt covered face. She winced as if in pain, then settled into her slumber. Her cream-colored skin showed from underneath the filth. I was close enough to notice her long eyelashes and manicured brows. I didn't really see her eyes before she fainted, now I was curious.

I dip the towel back and sit at her feet, placing the towel against her foot to ease the pain and soreness, then gently wiping them clean. Again she winced, but this time in pain.

"I'm sorry, I have to do the other one, too." Once done, I went into Sam's room. I knew she had those fuzzy spa socks she uses during the winter. I thought they would help better than my regular crew socks.

I got the socks on, then covered her with the blankets. I went to clean out the basin, and then got some towels together and placed them on my dresser. I opened her bag and saw all her clothes were just as dirty as the ones she had on. I put them in the wash, ignoring the ruckus going in the living room.

Who was she? Who was she to Sam? And how had she gotten to these circumstances. It was exhausting to even think about. I sat in my chair, turned off the lamp, and nodded off.

I woke up to a gasp and frantic movement. I turned on the light, rubbing my eyes. She was standing, holding her empty bag, glaring at me. She asked, "Who are you? Where is my stuff? Where am I?" She looked absolutely petrified and angry at the same time.

I hold my hands up. "You're at our clubhouse. You knocked at our door. You asked for Sam, then you fainted. I brought you in and put you in my bed.

"Where are the rest of my clothes?"

"I washed them. They're in the dryer. I'll get them." I came back with the basket and set it on the bed next to her before standing by my dresser.

She touched it, rubbing her fingers against it, smelling it, then smiling. "Thank you." She whispered.

"And I have some towels here and the bathroom is next door. Hope the body wash is okay. There's an extra toothbrush in the cabinet, shampoo and conditioner!" I blurted out.

She chuckled, "Thank you." Grabbing some clothes and towels, she glanced down at the fuzzy socks on her feet, then looked at me. I shrugged my shoulders. Her smile was even bigger in appreciation. She tiptoed towards the bathroom, carefully closing the door behind her. As soon as the water started running, I let out a loud exhale. I lay out my clothes on the chair.

I trot off to the kitchen to start the coffee pot. I glance in the living room. It's a wreck! I curse Demon under my breath as I sweep up the aftermath, putting the bottles in a trash bag, taking them outside, and wiping down everything. God knows what they touched and rubbed on, besides my brother.

Afterward, I set out the stuff for breakfast. I'm so used to Sam doing it, but I watched her enough to provide sustenance to everyone. I check and see the bathroom door open. She must be done. I knock before walking in my room. I see her hands full of my sheets, my bed stripped, and my comforter in a pile on the floor.

"What are you doing?"

She jumped and screamed, "Ahhhh! Don't do that! I wanted to throw your bedding into the washer. I soiled them with my dirty street clothes last night. It's the least I could do." I knew by her tone to let her do what she wanted to do. She had the same look as Sam. She definitely was her kin somehow.

I grab my clothes to shower as she drags my sheets to the laundry room. I laugh, watching her struggle a bit.

After a long, hot shower, I come out to the smell of bacon. I throw my dirty clothes in my hamper and head to the kitchen.

There she was, cooking breakfast. She looked back, "You hungry? I got bacon, eggs, toast, and found some cinnamon rolls in the fridge. Orange juice with the coffee you made is over there. She put another layer of bacon on a paper towel to soak the grease.

Wow, I was impressed.

"Grab a plate!" I did as I was told, but set up shop in the kitchen instead of the dining room.

"I never got your name."

"Kynlee. Yours?"

"Everyone calls me Wicked."

"Right, biker code. Club names only." She gave me a thumbs up.

I wonder how much she knew about motorcycle clubs.

"You said you were looking for Sam?"

She pops a piece of bacon in her mouth. She offers me a slice and I take it. "Yeah, she's my aunt. I had to get away, things got too… it's all bad and I need her help. Where is she?"

"She said she had to go home to handle some business. They left yesterday. I didn't ask where…"

"Tulsa, Oklahoma. She's going to go nuclear when she finds out what he did! I hope she separates his balls from his body!" She screeched before regaining composure and fixing a plate for herself.

We ate in silence, her fork noticeably scraping the plate hard as she pierced the eggs.

I hear a door open and giggling as Demon emerges with all three dancers.

I must admit, even I am impressed. I can't believe I was so worn out that I didn't hear any of his sexual escapades.

THE MERCILESS FEW MC ANTHOLOGY: PROTECTED

He yawned and stretched, bare chested but in his jeans and barefoot, "Morning, bro. Who's the broad?"

I saw her brow arch.

"This is Kynlee. She's Sam's niece."

"Huh, bad timing, sunflower. They left yesterday."

"Don't call me that. You don't know me. I'm well aware, Captain Obvious. I'll wait here until she gets back. How about stop asking questions and shutting your pie hole with food. I'm sure your ladies of the evening are hungry. It's the least you could do after a night with you." The girls' mouths fell open in shock.

I couldn't help but laugh. She was quick witted and held her own.

He didn't respond, only grabbed a plate to dig in. The girls follow behind.

I finish up and start washing dishes.

"What are you doing?"

"It's the least I could do and since the bunnies aren't here, I'm the default clean-up crew." She laughed. "Aunt Sam taught you well." She smiled before joining me in cleaning up.

Afterwards, she puts my sheets in the dryer before stuffing my comforter in the washing machine. She adds a ton of dryer sheets to the sheets, something I don't do, and hits start.

"Can I borrow your charger? My phone has been dead for two days."

I show her and she plugs in. The familiar low battery icon glows before fading back to black.

"Well, that'll take a while. So, what do you do for fun around here? Wait! Can I see your bike?"

I led her to the barn where Stormy was resting. "Stormy girl, this is Kynlee. Kynlee, my Stormy."

"Thanks for the introduction?"

"If a biker really loves his bike, he introduces any new person who might ride her, especially female. It lets them know they're still their number one, and no one comes before them. Can't have my feisty girl jealous."

"I see. She is a stunner, though. Beautiful paint job." Her fingers slide across Stormy until she holds the handlebar. A mischievous smile forms, "Can we go for a ride?"

"Do you always ride with strangers?"

"If you knew how I got here, you know I am not afraid. I never rode on a motorcycle before. Come on..." She nudged my shoulder.

I relent. "Let me grab my keys." I look back and see her grinning at Stormy. I changed from my graphic to a simple black tee and put on my cut. Grabbed my sunglasses and keys and was out the door.

I come back to see her sitting on Stormy. I did my damndest to not let my bike fantasies start manifesting. I just met this girl. She giggled when she saw me, leaning forward to grab the handlebars.

Fuck me.

I signal for her to sit back and hold up the extra bike helmet from the rack. She pouted. "No fucking way. Sam would kill me if anything happened to you. No helmet, no ride." Reluctantly, she put it on. I check it and put her visor up. "Pull it down when we start moving, alright?" She gave me a thumbs up.

I slip on my helmet and straddle my bike, giving her time to adjust. This is crazy! She literally showed up on our doorstep last night, and now she's riding on the back of my bike. Her arms wrap around me for safety and she leans forward. "Woo hoo!" She squealed as we hit the main road and I hit 75 mph.

It was nice.

I knew where to take her. It was at my brother's new house. He and Poppy were on a road trip with his sisters and brother in their new RV. We all had keys to the place to keep the plants alive. I didn't need to go inside this time. I turn down his excessively long driveway and park toward the back of his house.

She hopped off and almost lost her balance because of the helmet.

"Whoa!" She screamed before I caught her, pulling her against me. After a moment of looking into her eyes, I pulled the helmet off slowly. She exhales. "It's kind of claustrophobic. I'd have to get used to it, but it was super fun! Is this your house?"

I hooked her helmet on the helmet lock and pulled mine off, resting it on the seat. "My brother and his ol' lady. They moved in recently. It was her childhood home, and he bought it for her. Follow me, the real prize is out back."

"Okay." He must have mowed the yard before he left because it opened up beautifully to the lake out back.

"Wow, how beautiful! If I lived here, I'd always be outside. I pointed toward the firepit, but she shook her head as she walked toward the edge of the lake. She sat down, leaning back on her hands. She inhaled deeply, then exhaled. Her body seemed to relax.

"I wish my life were as calm and serene as this body of water."

I sat beside her, not as comfortably because my jeans were snug. I sat with my legs straight out while she crossed her legs under.

I finally take note of her features. Noticing now that her hair was straight and in a ponytail last night, but today was big and in loose curls. Or was it wavy? The sun caught her brown eyes as she watched the movement surrounding the lake. She looked at me before pointing at a flock of birds.

She was in awe of all things nature. We chatted about her favorite animal, what owls look like under their feathers, and when they run. Her ultimate goal was to visit Yosemite National Forest and touch the giant sequoias.

Then the tables turned, and I had to answer the same

questions, spilling my dream to drive from coast to coast on my bike.

"That would be a cool ride. I'd totally be down." I gaze at her, and she casually shrugs her shoulders.

We sit in silence until a sudden shiver runs through her. I quickly go into the house and fetch a cozy blanket, then light the fire pit. This brought some relief, making the chilly weather bearable for a few more hours, until eventually, I almost couldn't squeeze my hands and I needed to drive back. I carefully pack everything away, warm my hands, then ensure the fire pit is completely extinguished. And together, we make our way back to the clubhouse.

Chapter Sixteen

Sam

PROTECTED
THE MERCILESS FEW MC: DEVIL'S IGNITED
Briarswood, Mass.

"I ought to torch that house, that dirty son of a bitch!" I scream while pacing the hotel room.

"Babygirl…" He tried to calm me down.

"Don't patronize me, Bubba. I am not in the mood! All he had to do was pack up his shit and leave! I would have picked up the pieces, taken care of my sister, instead he has her committed with no way to see her unless I get his permission or get a court order? Do you know how long that's going to take? On top of that, he emptied their account and left. He wanted to cause as much chaos as he could on his way out! And now, Kynlee is nowhere to be found?! Murder, I'm going to commit murder. I know a few pig farmers! It's Tulsa, for fuck's sake!"

I vented my frustration in a scream that might scare my hotel neighbors into calling the police, but I didn't care. The cops couldn't even help me with my sister. They are goddamned useless.

"Listen, Phil said he would ask around town, see if she told anyone her plans. We filed the paperwork at the court and they will tell us what we need to provide to reverse what he's done. I need you to calm down because in the end, your sister will be safe and we will bring her closer to home."

I couldn't help but cry, "Really?"

"Oh darling, I know you didn't think you'd do this alone. Your sister has always been my family. I'm to protect her and Kynlee just as much as you. You should start researching facilities near the house."

I am absolutely amazed by the man standing before me. It's no wonder, really, considering he possesses the biggest heart one could ever imagine. I lean up, pursing my lips and he leans down to connect. "I love you, Bubba."

His hand smacks, then squeezes my ass.

Uh oh...

He had that look in his eye as he picked me up. "I love you, too, my beautiful and badass wife. I want to hear my real name tonight."

Chapter Seventeen
Asher aka Wicked

PROTECTED
THE MERCILESS FEW MC: DEVIL'S IGNITED
Briarswood, Mass.

The bunnies were playing pool with Demon when we came back. It was a tournament. Win and get a night with him, lose and try again. He could have multiple winners if he wanted.

Lila is the only pool shark here. She's dating someone from the Aces, not the ones we got rid of, but the few who didn't take part in the ambush. Lila really liked Everett, so she wouldn't cheat on him. Plus, she's the only girl who has left Demon's room unscathed. But if Lila wanted to, she could easily wipe the floor with him.

Right now, he was playing Kitty. He had three striped balls remaining, and she had five solids. I know she wanted to win desperately, being infatuated with him since day one. It was obvious to everyone.

We head into the kitchen. "Hey Wicked, who's that?" Penny said, and I heard a bit of malice behind it. Any outside female was now subject to judgment by our girls. They trusted no one, and it was my fault.

Kynlee stopped, rolled her eyes, and put her hand on her hip. If she is anything like Sam, I better nip this in the bud.

"Kynlee, our bunnies, bunnies, Kynlee, Sam's niece." I put that in there so they could retract their claws and calm the hell down, and it worked. Penny sucked her teeth and rolled her eyes before giving Kitty some encouragement.

"I'm sorry. Our girls can be a bit territorial. There are only two of us left to share among them."

"Interesting. No wonder she was so defensive. So I probably slept on your recently fucked sheets with her. Is what you're telling me?"

I stopped. "As a matter of fact, no. Last time was on the bathroom counter, if you must know. It's been months since anyone was in my bed and I washed them after."

"Uh, huh." She opened the cabinets and fridge, taking inventory. "How about pizza and pasta? There's two pizzas and all the ingredients for my pasta salad."

"Sounds like a plan. Can I help?" She pulls the onion, peppers, olives, and tomatoes from the fridge. Searching for the cutting board, "Preheat the oven to 375 and put the pizzas on a baking sheet. Thank you."

I did as I was told, taking a moment to locate the baking sheet. I helped often, but dishes and dish placement were not my responsibility. Who knew we had so many cabinets!

She's cutting the vegetables for the salad. "Put a pot of water on the stove and set it on high." I pulled a small pot, and she told me it needed to be bigger, so I grabbed a pot we use for chili. She said it was perfect for the number of people and threw the pasta in.

I stood next to her, and she put me to work, making me clean vegetables and cut them in half and she would cut them to the perfect size. After that, she tells me to chop the ham into cubes. I did my best to figure out what that meant, cutting in half, then half again, and again.

She poured the now cooked pasta in a bowl; the steam billowed out and she waved the smoke away. She poured the Italian dressing, then added black pepper, onion powder, fresh garlic, and some red pepper flakes. She stirred it to make sure the pasta didn't clump together. Then she added the veggies, the cheese and she looked my way and I held up the board.

"Oh my gosh! You don't help too often, do you? It's still a bit too big. Cut them at least two more times, then it should be good." She continues to laugh as she checks the pizzas. They looked almost done. I chop quickly and when she turns around, I present it again. "Much better, thank you." She slides the knife, and the ham falls into the bowl and she stirs vigorously. It looks mouth-watering.

I think she saw my curiosity as a spoonful was in front of me. "Be my taste tester. Tell me how it is."

I take a bite and it's the most delicious thing I ever ate. "Wow, that is amazing, yet so simple. I could eat seven bowls by myself." I saw her cheeks blush.

"We have to share with the others, but I will make it for you if you ask nicely." She winked.

Ten minutes later, I pulled the pizza from the oven and on the freshly washed cutting boards.

"Guys! Dinner is ready." I heard the pool cues being put away and their movement toward the kitchen.

"Ooh! This is amazing, Kynlee, thank you!" Lil said, grabbing a plate. Everyone thanked her. Looks like food is the key to everyone's heart. "It was nothing. My way of saying thanks for taking me in while my aunt and uncle are away." Her face fell. "I know she's trying her damndest to save my mom. She's the only person who can." Her shoulders slumped a bit. Only the shuffling of feet and clinking of utensils brought her out of her thoughts. I hand her a plate and she joins the chow line.

After dinner and a movie, the girls decide to head to Throttle for fun and invite Kynlee. Penny seemed to have warmed up to her. "Aww thanks ladies, but I'm super tired. Maybe next time?" They nod and head out. "Hey, wait up ladies!" Demon followed behind like a puppy.

"I'm going to get ready for bed. Where are the towels?"

"In the closet next to the bathroom door." She whispered a thank you. Once I heard the shower, I got the bed ready for her. I would resign myself to the couch this time. At least there I could stretch out.

Just as I peeled the comforter back, my door opened, and she stepped in wearing an oversized shirt. I'm not even sure what she was wearing underneath.

"Oh no, I couldn't take your bed again. I can sleep in the living room. I'm small. It should be okay."

"Absolutely not. You're a guest. Besides, I insist. You deserve a good night's sleep."

"I know, we can share! I don't take up much space."

She looked at me so innocently and I know she meant well.

"Kynlee, I don't think that's a good idea…"

"Already thinking about banging me?"

"What?!"

"Kidding. Look, you can sleep on top of the covers and I can sleep under them. Easy peasy." She looked at me with brows raised, then this wide smile appeared.

I roll my eyes, "Fine. I need to shower first." I grab a shirt, boxers, and some basketball shorts. The shower was magical, my muscles sore from the ride. I also had to rub one out because even though she was joking, she was right. I was thinking naughty thoughts about her. After blowing my load, I felt a hundred times better and could sleep in peace.

The house was dark and quiet. I walked in and found her peacefully asleep, softly snoring, still exhausted from her long journey. She had to be if she came all the way from Tulsa.

From how she phrased it, something tells me she didn't just hop on a plane to get here.

A yawn catches me off guard. I casually tossed my dirty clothes in the hamper, grabbed the blanket that covered my chair, lay on the bed, and used it to cover me. It didn't take long until I was asleep.

Chapter Eighteen
Sam

PROTECTED
THE MERCILESS FEW MC: DEVIL'S IGNITED
Briarswood, Mass.

I was so glad to be on the familiar road back to the clubhouse. It was a two-hour drive from the closest airport. Bubba kept tapping his fingers and humming to the radio station, probably to keep himself awake. I know he was just as tired as me. I stayed awake to keep him company, singing along to our favorite bands.

When he parked beside the house, I sighed loudly, "Home sweet home! But why is it so dark?" He shrugged while yawning, hopping out of the truck with our bags. I grab my bag and his hand. It was indeed pitch black inside, not a peep.

"They must've gone out. Fine with me. Maybe I can get some sleep with the kids out of the house. Come on."

"Let me check the place. I don't put it past them to have had a wild sex party. There's probably used condoms in between the coach cushions." I shudder, thinking about the chances of that actually being true. I mean, we left Demon here. "I'll be right there." He made his way to our room while I looked around. I was amazed by how nice the place looked. No random underwear or bras, no used condoms, and no liquor bottles everywhere. In fact, the kitchen was freshly clean, with the dishes piled on top of a dish towel to dry. I have a dishwasher, but at least they cleaned them. I open the fridge to see leftover pizza and pasta salad put away.

"Who made pasta salad?" I wondered, because none of my guys or girls have made this before. I was intrigued, but exhausted at the same time. I look over and see a cut hanging off the chair. His name patch solving the mystery.

"Wicked." I pick it up and head to his room. It's pitch dark and I don't have his layout memorized enough to risk it. I open the door and turn on the light. I see two bodies in his bed. Asher sits up.

"Sorry. I was just putting your cut away…"

Then the other body sat up, rubbing their eyes, yawning and stretching.

"Kynlee?!"

"Auntie Sam!" She jumped out of bed and I noticed she was in only a sleep shirt before she hugged me hard, but I glared at Asher.

"Nothing happened Sam, we weren't even under the same covers, see?" He lifted the blanket to show he was on top of his comforter and she had folded back several layers, showing she was underneath. "She insisted."

"Yeah. After he helped me last night and hung out with me all day, I couldn't kick him out of his own bed. There was enough room to share."

Lucifer peeked his head in. "Everything okay? Oh, hello."

"Rocco, you remember my niece, Kynlee."

"Wait, the one that went missing?"

"Yeah, apparently she made her way here while we were in Tulsa. How did you get here?"

"I took the bus."

"The bus station is like...12 miles from here!"

"I know, I walked. My phone was dead, so I fought the elements and fatigue to get here, but the pain was finally too much and I passed out in Wicked's arms. He took care of me."

I didn't like how that sounded, but I kept my cool.

"Well, we'll talk more in the morning. We just got back. Come on, I'll put you in Reaper's old room. The bed's all made up."

I could see she wanted to ask me why, but she grabbed her bag and followed me out.

No way was I leaving her alone with him.

Chapter Nineteen
Asher aka Wicked

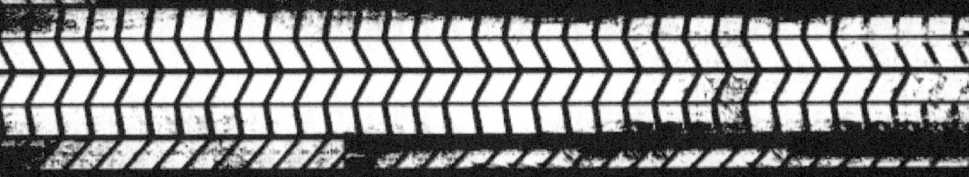

PROTECTED
THE MERCILESS FEW MC: DEVIL'S IGNITED
Briarswood, Mass.

Sam's expression was one of pure, unadulterated disgust; her lips curled into a sneer, her eyes burning with hatred, at the sight of me in bed with her niece. Not the fact that all I did was help and care for her while she was gone.

I felt too exhausted to deal with it, so I crawled back into bed, where the cool sheets provided a welcome relief.

Chapter Twenty

Sam

PROTECTED
THE MERCILESS FEW MC: DEVIL'S IGNITED
Briarswood, Mass.

I stepped into Cullen's old room. I had washed all his bedding when he left in case one of the bunnies needed to stay over. This was a safer space for her.

She steps in and puts her bag on the dresser. "What is your deal?" She crossed her arms and popped her hip.

"What are you talking about?"

"Don't play dumb, auntie. You were rude to him!"

"It doesn't matter. Why didn't you let me know you were coming? I would have paid for a plane ticket."

"I know you would have, but I had to leave abruptly and super early in the morning. Mike said that because mom was unable to, it was my duty to fulfill her wifely duties.

A flash of anger made me blink really hard. Is she saying what I think is?

"Did he try to…"

"I left after he said that. I wouldn't risk it. The only person I knew who could help me was you. I'm so happy to see you!" She hugged me so tight while I had murderous thoughts of ripping Mike apart, slicing his dick in half, and setting his pants on fire from the bottom and watching him burn alive.

I separate us. She looks so much like her mother. It brings me a little pain, knowing my beloved sister's current situation, but I would fix it. For now, my niece was safe, and that's all I could ask for.

"I'm exhausted. We'll talk more in the morning, okay? Night, sweetie."

"Night, auntie." She slides underneath the sheets, hugging another pillow against her. I shut the light off and close the door.

Rocco is already in bed asleep, or so I thought.

"What was that, Samantha Ann?" He did that when he was angry with me.

"I don't know what you're talking about." I looked over and his eyes were still closed. "You were nasty to Asher."

"She's my niece!" That's all I was going to say about that.

"And he's practically your son."

"Almost, but she's my actual family. She's been through god knows what and I find her in his bed?! Absolutely not, Rocco."

"Fully clothed after he took care of her while we were away. Don't punish him for something that didn't happen. I believe we raised him right."

"Did we?! Because according to his little girlfriends, I can't cut it as anyone's mother!"

There's that sting, like running my heart into a brick wall.

Now Rocco was up and holding me so lovingly. "Hey, we all know you are a wonderful wife and mother. Dedicating your life to me, these boys, and this club. I will not let you beat yourself up over words from people who don't know you or matter. Do you understand?"

I nod and bury myself in his big, warm, burly arms. He smells like warm tobacco and, oddly enough, honey. I sigh, basking in the love of my man, but the family drama makes me queasy.

I look up, brushing my forehead against his beard. He squeezes harder and kisses my temple. "It's been a long day. Let's go to bed."

Chapter Twenty-One
Kynlee

PROTECTED
THE MERCILESS FEW MC: DEVIL'S IGNITED
Briarswood, Mass.

Aunt Sam is overreacting. Wicked was just taking care of me. What's the big deal, anyway?

There's more than what she is letting on.

Another time for that. I search in my bag for my charger to plug in my phone.

I should leave it dead. I should have left it behind, but I brought it in case I ran into trouble on my way here.

It buzzed with that familiar tone of powering on, followed by the repetitive buzzing of new text messages and missed phone calls. Reluctantly, I checked.

Where are you?!

You better answer me or you'll regret it!

Now you owe me more than that blow job and I WILL get it, do you hear me?

ANSWER ME!

I will find you. You'll never be safe!

As the buzzing persisted, it filled the room with an incessant hum. The air felt heavy with dread, making me feel lightheaded and disoriented. Pulling the blankets back, I turned away from the source of the noise, seeking solace in the darkness. The sound seemed to vibrate in my ears, creating an unsettling sensation. My fatigue won out over my uneasiness, and I soon fell asleep.

Chapter Twenty-Two
Asher aka Wicked

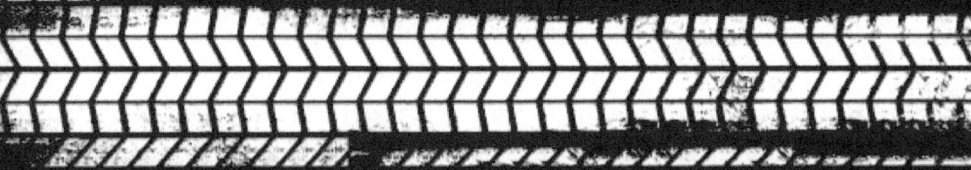

PROTECTED
THE MERCILESS FEW MC: DEVIL'S IGNITED
Briarswood, Mass.

I woke up, my eyes fixed on the textured pattern on the ceiling. I couldn't help but feel a mix of frustration and confusion. The sound of my breath seemed amplified in the quiet room, filling the air with a sense of unease. The faint scent of her lingering perfume still hung in the air, a reminder of the events that had transpired. Did she think I was some sex crazed pervert? Trying to bag her niece overnight. Another notch on my belt? It was absurd!

My room became a reflection of the tension within me, a battleground of emotions. At that moment, I made a silent promise to myself: if she didn't think I was good enough to hang out with her niece, then I wouldn't.

Stormy and I went back to the lake. I needed peace for my thoughts. I've never been so angry towards Sam ever but she didn't even blink before calling me trash.

I catch myself throwing rocks instead of skipping them. Putting all my anger into chucking them as far as possible. Until I heard an all too familiar sound. I look back to see the truck barreling down the long, dusty driveway towards me. The rumble of its engine grew louder with each passing second, filling the air with a deep, resonant hum. A cloud of fumes billowed from its exhaust pipe, permeating the atmosphere with the acrid smell of gasoline. I rolled my eyes and picked up more rocks.

"I'm not in the mood to be belittled by you right now, Sam. You made how you feel crystal clear."

"She can be a bit overprotective. I mean I am her only niece, but I'm also an adult and can make my own decisions."

I look back to see Kynlee slamming the heavy door shut. My eyes wander to her legs in short shorts, but covered by a light cardigan coat and ankle boots. They had little metal embellishments that jingled as she walked.

I scoff. "What are you doing here?"

"I followed you since you didn't come to breakfast. I knew you'd be feeling some kind of way about what Aunt Sam said."

I angrily threw two more rocks.

She bends down and grabs a rock and tosses it gingerly. I laugh at the sound it makes in comparison. She casually throws another. I step behind her, "Here." I place a nice sized one in her small hand. "Don't throw it overhand like an arch. You want the movement to explode the moment you release it. Like this." I step back over to my spot and launch it a good distance, the splash echoing against the trees.

"Whoa, nice. You're either a great thrower, or my aunt really ticked you off."

"Both." I said bluntly, throwing another. I see, out of the corner of my eye, her staring at me. I don't look over.

"So what's her deal, anyway? You seem like a nice guy."

"Not too long ago, there was some drama that was my

fault and…" I shivered at the memory of the drama I caused, the echo of vicious words haunting me like a chilling whisper in the dark. "Horrible things were said."

"By you?"

I sigh, "No. I had a set of twins who were bunnies and were only loyal to me. I thought it was the best thing ever, basically having a threesome every night…"

"I bet." She mimicked my throw, her distance improving.

"It was until I started favoring one twin over the other. To be fair, I always liked Priya over Tam. I met her first, and the sparks were immediate. But she was crystal clear. It was both of them or nothing. Back then, the idea seemed like a no-brainer. Until…"

"Uh oh…"

"I came back, and they had moved out of my room. I caught them disrespecting my family, telling them they were losers and useless. That they were better than them and this was all a joke to them. There was a lot of yelling and Sam came to see what the commotion was. They turned on her and brought up the fact that she couldn't have children. Her heart shattered, and she ran back to her room. I'll never forgive myself for allowing that to happen. They left me saying my macho bravado would get me nowhere, and they were right. I need to grow up."

There was a long silence between us. "That is a lot. They sound like horrible people, all high and mighty. I'm glad they're gone because if I had heard that, you'd be peeling me off both of them."

"Huh, I bet. But that's why she doesn't want you around me. I make poor decisions and apparently am a sex crazed lunatic. I mean, we already ended up in bed together after the first night."

She chuckled, "Right. She reacted as if she caught me riding you."

I damn near choked, and she burst out laughing. "Thanks for the visual, Kynlee."

"I'm just saying. She can be a little overprotective, but I'm an adult and a pretty good judge of character. You're a cool dude, Wicked." She punched my arm.

"It's Asher." Hearing her calling me by my biker name seemed wrong, so I bit the bullet. I didn't want a repeat.

"Asher. Suits you perfectly. What's your middle name?"

"Not a chance."

We spent the day at the lake. We laughed almost the whole time. I think she thought I wouldn't notice that she was steadily scooting closer and closer to me. I felt too many familiar feelings. I put some space between us by going in and making sandwiches. I left a twenty-dollar bill on their counter. Eventually I'd replace the food, but in case they come home early.

Afterwards, I sent her home first, putting a ten-minute buffer between us. As I turn in, I rev my engine. I see Sam and Kynlee by the truck. Judging by the wild hand movements, Sam wasn't happy she took the truck.

That wasn't my problem, but I'm sure she'll find a way to blame me.

I hop off and push Stormy into the barn. I can hear her screaming at Kynlee. "Are you kidding me, Kynlee? Someone might have kidnapped you, or who knows what else could have happened! You've got to tell me where you're going! It's common decency!"

"Trust me, I've endured things you couldn't even imagine! I wanted to explore my new surroundings, to find a place of silence so I can just think! That motherfucker has my mother locked up only because he didn't want to take care of her! He never took care of her. I did! He only cared about the check that came in the mail to support his gambling habit. And let's not talk about decency the way you've been acting toward people!"

THE MERCILESS FEW MC ANTHOLOGY: PROTECTED

Kynlee was red in the face as I walked by. I knew she was talking about me and I appreciated it. I would deal with that eventually, though I hated how emotional it made her. She angrily wiped away the tears, tears of frustration. My eyes meet Sam's before I continue into the house.

Inside, Lucifer and Demon were watching football. Looks like the much anticipated semi-final game, winner goes to the championship bowl. A lot riding on this, probably money the way Demon is pacing the floor.

The score was close, and they were in the last critical minutes of the 4th quarter.

"Are you kidding me? That was a clean block! Get your head out of your ass, ref!" Demon screams at the TV, still pacing like a new dad waiting in labor and delivery while they set up the next play.

Lucifer sits up in his recliner. "Okay, let's go. Good defense." He claps his hands. I stand by the kitchen. They snap the ball and it's clean. The quarterback is looking for his target and he spots him near the eight yard line. He launches it before he's sacked hard by two opponents. The ball spirals toward the end zone. His hard throw allowed the interception, despite the catcher's attempt to adjust his position. He takes off toward his goal line, the other team scrambling after what they thought was an easy play, but it was too late.

We didn't even have enough time to celebrate the interception before…

"Touchdown! We won! Hell yeah!" We all cheered and clapped.

Lucifer sparked a celebratory cigar. "Good game. Good game. Hey, isn't the Liberty Bowl semi-final about to start?" He picked up the remote to find out.

I was tired and to avoid any upcoming interaction; I went to take a nap. I peel out of my cut and shirt, kick off my shoes, and plop face first into my bed.

Soft hands glide across my skin with a sensual, delicate touch, the sensation of their fingertips leaving a trail of soothing warmth along my entire back. As their hands start to knead and work their magic, I can't help but let out a contented hum. The stress that had weighed me down seems to dissolve under their skilled touch, as if every knot and tension in my muscles were being untangled.

"You have the hands of an angel." I groaned.

"You know I've been told that."

My eyes shot open, and I looked back to see Kynlee seated next to me. Her hands are kneading my lower back. "Ohhhhh." I shake my head. "You can't be in here! Sam will kill me!"

"Well, if you're quiet, she won't know." She continues pressing her thumbs deep into my muscles. I sigh and admit defeat. It felt too damn good.

"Deeper on my neck and shoulders, please." Instead of just scooting up and placing her hands on my shoulders, she slides her hands, palm down, up my back to my shoulders. Then she raked her nails down my back.

"Did that feel good?" My eyes rolled to the back of my head.

"Abso-fucking-lutely." Then I jumped up. "No! You have to go. No!"

"But…" She tries to counter, but I'm insistent. I opened the door to let her out and Sam had her hand up, ready to knock.

Of course.

I step away from her with my hands up. "It's not what you think!" Spills out my mouth even though I know that's what guilty people say.

"Kynlee, out, now! You, take a seat!" Kynlee storms out and I hear her slam Reaper's door with a scream. Sam stepped in while I stepped back until I'm seated on my bed.

I found myself slightly irritated before she even opened her mouth.

She shakes her head while pacing. "Why her Asher? Huh? Why?"

"Why what, Sam? Nothing has happened other than two people hanging out. I took care of her while you were gone! You're welcome!"

"Please. You and Demon are like bookends, all you want is sex. Look at you, you're half fucking naked! You don't know emotion or feelings or genuine connection. You just want another notch in your belt!"

I'm pretty sure everyone can hear her. Gloves off!

"Do you really think so fucking little of me?"

The air crackled with tension as my words hung in the room, the anger unmistakable. "All you do is think with your dick! I told you that masculine arrogance would get you nowhere and I haven't been proven wrong yet!"

Wow.

The scent of frustration filled the air, mixing with the scent of the body oil Kynlee was using to rub me down. The hostility lingered, leaving a heavy weight on my shoulders.

"I like Kynlee because she's sweet and doesn't see me as the monster you do. Just tell me how you really feel, Samantha!"

"Fine! I don't think… no, I know you're not good enough for her! I don't want you messing up my family!"

"Wow. I thought we were family." I choked out.

"Samantha!" I look to see Lucifer shocked by his wife.

All I saw from him was pity. "We got a job to do, son. Meet me outside. Go on."

I was so mad that I was clenching my fists without even realizing it. I glare at her before storming past.

Chapter Twenty-Three
Sam

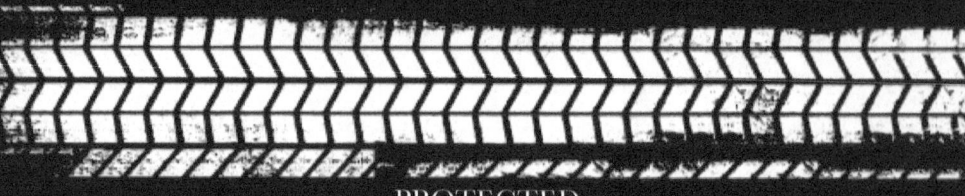

PROTECTED
THE MERCILESS FEW MC: DEVIL'S IGNITED
Briarswood, Mass.

"What the hell is wrong with you? We could hear you throughout the house! Do you even know that Kynlee took off in the truck in tears after what you did and said?"

"I'm protecting her! She doesn't know him like I do. He is no good! He needs to grow up!"

"And right now, I could say the same about you."

Then he slammed the door!

When did I become the goddamn bad guy? Just because I don't want Kynlee to be used and tossed aside for the next pair of legs that open for him! If that makes me the bad guy, so be it!

ring ring

I wasn't in the mood to be social, but I knew I was awaiting a call from Phil about a ruling on making me my sister's guardian.

"Hello?"

"It's Phil."

Chapter Twenty-Four
Kynlee

PROTECTED
THE MERCILESS FEW MC: DEVIL'S IGNITED
Briarswood, Mass.

Un-fucking-believable! I cannot deal with this! She was being so mean and disrespectful, and he hadn't laid a finger on me.

Though I want him to. I really wanted him to.

sigh

He's so handsome, sweet, and has been a perfect gentleman. Way better than the boys back home, nothing more than slightly evolved monkeys.

I ran out of there to get away from the fighting. I was so sick of drama. I wanted to run far and fast.

I grabbed the keys to the truck and didn't listen when someone called my name. It was probably Uncle Rocco. He was with me when they started screaming at each other.

I need a drink!

Chapter Twenty-Five

Asher aka Wicked

PROTECTED
THE MERCILESS FEW MC: DEVIL'S IGNITED
Briarswood, Mass.

I angrily stomp past my brothers, exerting so much force on the front door that it comes off the hinges, adrenaline surges through my veins. The world around me blurs.

"Fucking bitch!" I scream, walking to the barn. The pounding of my heart drowns out all other sounds.

"Hey, hey!" Lucifer spat out. His big hand stops me and turns me around. His words were sharp and laced with venom, face flushed with rage. "Don't talk about my wife like that! I know you're upset, but I do not tolerate disrespect!"

"What about my respect or dignity?! She didn't have a problem telling me I wasn't shit. Whatever…"

I'm so fucking over this because my intentions were pure. Sure, she was a beautiful girl, but I also enjoyed getting to know her. A breath of fresh air. I didn't have to pretend or puff out my chest. Even if I wanted to create something with her, I know I'd never be good enough in Sam's eyes.

And that hurt.

"That's it, Asher! Take a fucking knee. We'll handle this. Go cool off!"

"Are you serious?! I lose money because of your…" I stopped because I felt I was about to go too far.

"No, you're a goddamn liability. Emotionally compromised and we're working with the Vice Lords again. I can't risk it. You'll still get your cut."

I watched my brothers leave for their run. Fine, I needed a drink and out of that house. I started up and after a lot of back and forth in my mind; I headed to Throttle.

I know the twins wouldn't be there. They bragged so much about being rich and this was their little social experiment, but a tiny part of me still feared running into them.

They turned my life upside down, and I hadn't quite recovered from it.

I step into the soothing embrace of loud music, yet there is a distinct change in the atmosphere. It's live music. Tables and chairs fill the room. Everyone is watching the stage. Someone announced, "Give it up for Pepper Ann and her rendition of My Heart Will Go On by Celine Dion." Everyone clapped.

Ahh karaoke night. Maybe this is good, I could use a good laugh.

I found an empty seat in the back. Once settled, a waitress approaches, pulling her pad to take my order. "Hey, what'll you have?" Her smile is a breath of fresh air. Even with minimal lighting, I could see she had a similar skin tone to me. Her beautiful curly hair looked like a lion's mane.

"Can I get a beer? Domestic." I knew getting plastered and driving was a stupid decision.

"Coming right up. Enjoy the show!"

The announcer steps on stage. "Next up, we have Aria singing…let's see, Gwen Stefani! Come on up!"

Everyone cheered for her as she got on stage.

Aria definitely had a few drinks as she queued up Hollaback Girl. She was also hyping the crowd up to sing with her and before you know it; we were all spelling b-a-n-a-n-a-s.

I shake my head. The fact that I actually took part was hilarious.

"Alright, are we ready for our next contestant? Remember, the crowd's favorite will win $500! Next up is Kynlee! With her singing Mariah Carey."

I stopped drinking when I heard her name. It was unique. It could only be her. She was still wearing the clothes from earlier.

She cleared her throat; the sound echoing through the room, and then nodded for the music to start. Anticipation built as she closed her eyes. As she hummed with the instrumental, the sound resonated in the air, adding a melodic layer to the atmosphere.

With a sudden flicker, her eyes opened, revealing a glimmer of determination. A soft glow filled the room, illuminating her presence with the stage lights. Her arm movements were slow and graceful, each motion flowing seamlessly, mirroring the ebb and flow of the notes that she effortlessly hit.

With each word sung, her voice soared, filling the room with a captivating melody that resonated deep within the hearts of the audience.

This song was more than just a performance for her. It held a special place in her heart. The emotions hit heavily as they envelop her. They transported her back to when she first fell in love with this song. It was a love affair that had grown over time, becoming one of her favorites, and tonight, she poured her soul into every word, every note, making it a truly unforgettable moment.

During the chorus, she received a roaring applause. The second verse was elementary work as she hit those high notes.

I felt goosebumps as if she were singing to me, but that can't be. She doesn't know I'm here. She must be thinking of an old or even current boyfriend.

Wishful thinking, Asher. He's probably some NFL bound college football star with plans on taking her with him.

When the breakdown and end of the song came, she put all her emotions into it and killed it. I was in awe of such a beautiful and powerful voice. She had a standing ovation before finishing the last note.

She bowed, blushing profusely, "Oh, thank you." She said quickly before walking off the stage. The applause followed her as she headed...my way? She stopped at my table and I clapped, "Bravo, madam. You have an amazing voice."

"Thank you." She sat on the other side and I ordered her a beer.

I sip mine as we wait on hers. "You know, I didn't know you saw me."

She glanced at me, then away, her hair falling forward as if she was trying to hide. "Yeah. It was the only way I could sing with full emotion and not be nervous. You made me feel safe." She glanced away again.

"Oh." Was all I could say. I recall the words to the song that she was singing...singing to me. The waitress sets the beer down and I hand over a twenty and tell her to keep the change.

Although someone is singing another Mariah song, my attention is still on her. She turns her attention to the stage, humming in the correct key the girl should be singing. A few people notice and look back to see.

Then she sang full volume again, hitting that breakdown like a pro until the end. "*Certainly the Lord... will guide me...where I need to gooooo...*" I got goosebumps. Everyone turns around and cheers for her again. The girl on stage, not too happy.

Kynlee hides her face. "I couldn't help it. Mariah is my

favorite artist of all time. She helped me through the toughest times of my life."

I find it ironic the verse she chose to start singing. It didn't fall against deaf ears.

"Tell me about it."

She shook her head. "You don't want to hear about my sad, pathetic life."

"Stop it. Whether good or bad, it makes you who you are, and I think you're a pretty cool girl."

Her eyes grew wide. "You do? I suppose you're right. Wait, I thought you had a job to do. Why are you here?"

"Boss Man said I was compromised. Told me to cool off."

"I heard the fight. She was way out of line! I left before I said something I would probably regret."

"Don't. She's just being protective. You know what they say about bikers…nothing but street trash."

Then she takes my hand and smiles, "No, you're not."

I stared at our hands together, then sipped my beer, and she followed suit. She kept squeezing me and the silence was welcoming.

The host taps the mic. "And now it's time to announce the winner!"

"Sounds like that's my cue. I'll be right back." I clapped loudly as she made her way to the stage. I wanted everyone to know where my vote was going.

"Alright, I'll hold my hand over the contestant and the person with the loudest cheer wins!" He started from the beginning. She was second to last. I kept my clap light and steady as he passed over the others. When his hand stopped above her, I stood up, clapping loudly. "WOOO! YEAH! GO KYNLEE!" Then I put two fingers in and blew, producing a loud whistle. Everybody cheered loudest for her. Once he passed over the last contestant, a girl came up and handed him an envelope.

"The crowd doesn't lie! Give it up for Kynlee! Congratulations to tonight's winner!"

I was still standing and clapping hard when she came back.

She grabs my arm and pushes me before my arms instinctively wrap around her waist and there's silence. "Congratulations, you deserve it." I separate us, Sam's words poisoning my brain.

"Let me buy you a celebratory drink."

"Umm, okay." She returned to her seat as I signal the waitress.

She jumps, pulling her phone out. "Ugh! Why can't she leave me alone?" She slams it face down with it still buzzing.

"She's your family and loves you. And you know that because you came to her."

"How can you be so forgiving after everything she said about you?"

I finish my beer, pulling the new one back. "Because as hard as it is to say, she's right, and this isn't new. Growing up, I watched my older brothers behave like hormone-crazed, chauvinistic jerks, and I desired to be just like them. I treated girls like bingo cards, marking each one off until my card was full. And when I landed the twins, my ego exploded, and I got cocky. They put me in my place and I came crashing back to Earth and reality."

"You're young, you get to make mistakes, it's called growth."

I shrug my shoulders, not as motivated as she liked me to be. "It proves I'm not ready for anything, even if I wanted it. I look at my brother's Reaper and Fiend, what they went through, and in the end they were able to find or confess their love. I have to prove myself worthy...of anyone."

"Yeah." We both sipped our beer in comfortable silence until there was a crash and scream. There were two guys fighting at the bar and their friends trying hard to pull them apart, but when they got caught in the crossfire, they instinctively started throwing punches back. It was chaotic and spilled over into the stage area. People were rushing to get away from the melee.

I stayed calm and acted quickly. I took her hand and led her outside to safety. The cars were all trying to leave at once, causing a lot of near accidents. I knew it wouldn't be safe to leave right away. I located the truck and opened the truck bed. I held her waist and helped her up onto it. I noticed her gasp when I did. When she sat down, I saw her squeeze her thighs before biting her lip.

She's watching the chaos surrounding us as I scoot back on the bed. She shrieks and points as the guys spill out the door and are now scuffling in the dirt. Her hand landed on my thigh and I damn near choked. It was so nonchalant, but inside, my desire was raging. I found myself staring at her while she was watching this fiasco like pay-per-view. Dust was flying everywhere. There were girls screaming at them to stop.

"Oh my gosh, it's a good old-fashioned brawl! They don't do this in Tulsa! I wish I had popcorn!" She squealed excitedly, kicking her legs. Which made her breasts jiggle.

Finally, I hear the distant sounds of sirens. "Oh, time to go. I've heard that too many times in my life."

She ran her finger down my arm. "Oh, a bad boy with a record." Now her breasts press against my arm. I inhale sharply and catch her grinning.

Tease.

"Yeah, whatever. I need to get you out of here before they accidentally detain you."

"Ooh, my hero."

I help her down, close the bed, and send her on her way, watching to make sure she doesn't get stopped as the cops pass her, blocking the exit, detaining those who remain.

Including me.

Chapter Twenty-Six

Sam

PROTECTED
THE MERCILESS FEW MC: DEVIL'S IGNITED
Briarswood, Mass.

"I've written my statement, provided proof we're related multiple ways and proved his wrongdoings and neglect! And I still need to provide more? How is this fair?"

"You have to be smarter than him, Sam. He provided very convincing paperwork and lies to get her committed and to place those strict regulations. Saying any other visitors would be triggering to her mental state or cause an episode."

"Yeah, he wants her to die in there so he can collect her policy and I'll be damned if I let that happen! Can we put an injunction on her policy in the meantime? It should go to her daughter, not her worthless husband. Has anyone even seen the cowardly piece of shit?"

"If they have, they're not talking, but I don't think he has friends like that. He's constantly burned bridges."

"Probably sleazing it up with some whore in Vegas or

something. Maybe they'll find him dead from an overdose, at the very least."

I hear their bikes going into the garage. For the first time, I was not filled with happiness. It was dread and concern. Bubba and I have never left an issue on the table like this. We always talk it out, but this was different. I don't understand why he didn't see my way!

Phil was still talking, but I couldn't concentrate. "Let me call you back. I'll get the additional information somehow."

"Alright. Remember your end goal, Sam. It's not about retaliation, it's about getting Chelsea home. I know she would love to see her sister."

That got me. Tears ran down my cheek and my throat tightened. "God, I would love to see her so much."

"Focus on that and not the negativity. Talk to you later. Bye."

"Bye." I smile because I know I'll see her again. I have faith on my side. I quickly wiped the tears from my face.

My boys stroll in cautiously. I don't know how they feel about what I said about their brother. Did they hate me, too?

They made their way to the bar, a tradition to celebrate completing the job. I see them pour three shots each.

"To the Merciless Few." They clink and shoot it back.

"To our brotherhood." Another.

Then they paused, looked at the last shot before raising it high. "To our brother."

My husband walks in and our eyes meet. I felt my heart shift. I wanted to say something but couldn't. Instead, he joined his boys at the bar. Reaper turns to grab his favorite scotch. I usually pour his celebratory drink, so I'm hurt as he accepted it from Reaper. He sighed and shot it back, signaling for another. Reaper looked at me knowingly. I could tell he knew how I felt.

Then I hear the truck squeal to a stop, the door being slammed and Kynlee runs in, "Asher's in jail! They rounded him up when they broke up a fight at Throttle! He's innocent! I was there!" She sees me and runs to Bubba, "You got to help him!"

"You boys take the truck. Reaper make sure his bike wasn't left there. If it was, grab it. Kynlee, you stay here."

"No way, Uncle Rocco…"

She cut her eyes at me. "I'm coming with you."

Chapter Twenty-Seven
Asher aka Wicked

PROTECTED
THE MERCILESS FEW MC: DEVIL'S IGNITED
Briarswood, Mass.

This is great.

Third time's the charm, even though they didn't formally charge us for the Aces ordeal. It was another case of self defense, but they still drug us in. Not sure how many more times they'll let us slide.

The actual brawlers are in two cells to prevent further disruption. I'm handcuffed to an interrogation table. I hear the unmistakable sound of motorcycle engines and the truck doors slamming shut.

I look to see Lucifer, Kynlee, and Sam.

Great, incoming lecture.

My brothers trail behind. Even better, everyone witnessing my embarrassment.

Lucifer approaches the Sheriff, and they shake hands. "I was going to call you. The boy's not in trouble. We gathered everyone, ran a background check, and sorted them out according to eyewitnesses. He's free to go." The officer takes his keys and uncuffs me. I rubbed my wrist. They were a little tight, but didn't want to complain.

"Asher!" Kynlee yells and wraps her arms around me. It's good to see her, so I hug her back. "Hey, kiddo. Thanks for telling them." She holds onto me but moves to my side. "I would not let you rot in here. You did nothing except keep me safe."

I saw realization in Sam's eyes. Maybe I'm not so bad after all…

She squeaks, "Asher, I…"

"Save it, Sam!" I walked out and saw someone rode Stormy here. "I'm sorry for leaving you, beautiful. I'll make it up to you."

"Are you talking to me or the bike?" I saw Kynlee had jogged behind me. She swayed from side to side with her arms behind her back.

I felt my whole body flush in excitement.

I hand her my helmet. "Get on!"

Chapter Twenty-Eight
Sam

PROTECTED
THE MERCILESS FEW MC: DEVIL'S IGNITED
Briarswood, Mass.

"Save it, Sam!" He spat so angrily. I wanted to follow him, to fix it. He's never been a bad kid, just learning and growing. Everyone's allowed to make mistakes, and he's no different.

I look to see Kynlee follow him out. I run my fingers through my hair and follow everyone. "Kynlee, wait, please!"

"I think I'll mirror Asher's words exactly. I'm going to ride with him." She says before saying something to him. I know he wanted to tell her no, to appease me, to make me happy that he was staying away from her, but I was wrong. He has been a perfect gentleman these few days since she's been here.

He even hands her his helmet so that she would be safe during the ride. He risked injury, or worse, to protect her.

His attitude and manners differ tremendously from when he was with the twins.

"Samantha…" My husband says cautiously.

I couldn't help the tears that fell at my realization. "Bubba, I'm sorry, I was wrong. How could I be so cruel to my boy?"

"He's a man, a man you've watched grow for years. We knew he wouldn't be girl crazed forever, that he'd find his grounding soon and she may be the key. You have to let them figure it out. He's been so attentive and caring. We've never seen him like this before."

I nod, wiping the tears away.

"I love you, my beautiful, stubborn girl."

"Thank you for loving all of me." He takes my hand and we ride home in peace.

He was right about Asher and tomorrow, I'm going to make this right.

Chapter Twenty-Nine

Asher aka Wicked

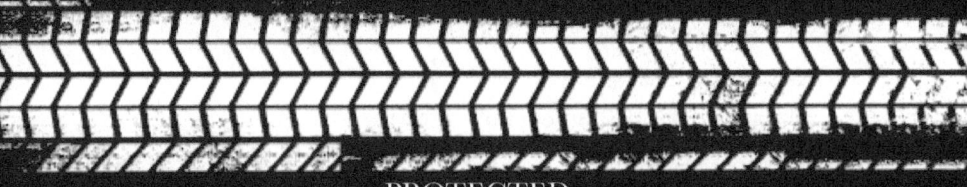

PROTECTED
THE MERCILESS FEW MC: DEVIL'S IGNITED
Briarswood, Mass.

I'm drained, physically and emotionally. She hops off, forgetting about the weight of the helmet and almost bites it again. "Dammit! Why didn't you wear this thing?" I try not to laugh. "Because you are the precious cargo. I'm supposed to keep you safe." She blushes hard before turning and going inside. I smirk and push my bike into the barn.

I can barely keep my eyes open as I peel out of everything except my boxers. I barely remember hitting the bed before I passed out.

knock knock
knock knock
knock knock

I opened my eyes, about to stretch, but I noticed something against me, rather someone. Those knocks I thought I dreamt obviously weren't.

Half her soft, sweetly smelling body lay on me in cute pink pajamas. I raised my hand to scratch her scalp, and she sighed, holding a little tighter.

She was absolutely gorgeous, like a rare gem. Her flawless complexion, with a hint of a rosy blush, made her look ethereal. A subtle shade of pink painted the soft curve of her lips. I thought I knew beauty, but her laying on me, I could really take it all in.

Then her body jolted, and her face looked pained.

"No! Get out! You're not supposed to be in my room! NO!" She sat up, panting. She was looking around as if she didn't know where she was.

"Hey, you had a bad dream. Are you okay?"

"Asher?"

"Yeah." She hugged me and laid back down. I knew she wasn't asleep because she started humming. I started scratching her scalp. "Do you want to talk about it?"

She shook her head vigorously. "No, he can't get me now. I'm safe…I'm…safe…with you." She resumed her humming until eventually I heard her snoring lightly.

I couldn't go back to sleep. All I could think about was what she had experienced in Tulsa? What had compelled or forced her to travel across the country to come here? Whatever it was, I sensed it wasn't good. Maybe Sam knew something or could help her.

The next morning, she had slept through the night without another nightmare. I cover her and she snuggles up to my pillow. I throw on a t-shirt and sweats before slipping out quietly.

I hear the familiar sounds of breakfast making. I go wash my hands before walking into the kitchen. Sam is whipping the pancake batter and greasing the griddle. I clear my throat and she looks up.

"Morning Asher."

"Morning Sam. Can I help?"

She smiled widely. "I'd love that. Can you put the bacon in the skillet? Probably the entire pack, you boys could always eat. Now that I think about it, with Kynlee here now, you better grab the other pack, too."

I nod and go to the refrigerator to grab the other pack of applewood smoked bacon. I lay out the first batch that sizzles immediately.

"Is she still asleep?" I almost dropped the fork. "I swear nothing happened! She snuck in!"

She laughs, catching me off guard. "I know that. I peeked in once I saw she wasn't in her room. It was very cute." I flipped a strip of bacon over.

She poured out one plate sized pancake and then another. "You're a good kid, Asher. I shouldn't have attacked you. You did nothing to warrant it. I guess my sudden family problems overwhelmed me and I took it out on you. My sister, Chelsea was forcefully institutionalized by her husband. I'm currently working on reversing it and getting her treatment closer to me.

"Wow, that is insane. No wonder Kynlee trekked here to find you. I have a question for you, Sam. She had a nightmare last night. It sounded like someone was coming into her room and she was telling them no. When she woke up, I told her she was safe, and she went back to sleep. Do you have any idea what that could be about?"

I look to see Sam absolutely seething, "If that motherfucker touched her…"

My fists clenched, and a knot formed in my stomach as I felt myself getting angry. "Who?"

"Kynlee's stepfather. I'm thankful that my sister had the good sense to pick an amazing man to be Kynlee's dad, unfortunately he died overseas. She raised her as best she could, but my sister always had mental issues. She was a great mother, working and providing, then she met this loser when he delivered a package to her job and it was downhill ever since. I tried to convince her she could do better, but she swore he could be her caregiver, since I wasn't home."

"I hear a but."

"And you would be correct. She started having problems at work when he quit his job and moved into her house within a matter of weeks. Giving some crap about starting a business. Guaranteeing they'd be living the good life in no time.

So she started working more to compensate, but soon she started coming in late or was constantly on her phone with him because he needed something. Eventually, he convinced her she would earn more on disability and unemployment and she believed him! She left her comfortable job and became a stay at home wife once they got married. They didn't even have a ceremony; they went to the courthouse. He said they didn't need all that fancy stuff to profess their love to each other.

Anyway, he then convinced her to stop taking her meds and then persuaded the courts she was mentally incompetent to care for herself! It's even in his stipulations to not give her the medication she needs! He knew how to play the system, but he won't win. He wants to claim beneficiary to her insurance, but I started the steps for an injunction until I can provide further evidence he's a gold digger." She sighs after telling me the story. "I need every bit of dirt on him I can conjure up to get my sister home and Kynlee as the rightful beneficiary."

I plate the first round of bacon, putting the second in the pan. Sam plates the pancakes and pours two more of the same size.

"Did you consider getting info from Kynlee? She has firsthand knowledge of what went on. She knows the good and the bad."

"Oh my god Asher, you're a genius! Her testimony will be the nail in his coffin!" She squeals happily. "I have to talk to her anyway and apologize to her for trying to keep her from knowing such a nice boy." She reaches over and pinches my cheeks. "Come on, stop! You said I was a man!"

"You are, but you're also my boy!"

"Okay, fine, I'll let that slide." She musses my hair and resumes flipping pancakes.

"Mmm, pancakes and bacon, my favorite. Morning, babygirl." Lucifer smacks her ass, and I turn away and groan.

"Good to see you both together. Oh, Wicked, we got six trucks today. Heads up since we're the relief dock for Boston harbor, we'll have more and consistent days like this. Good thing it's all legit and pays just as well. I told you I would keep you boys out of trouble."

"You did, Boss, look at us now. We only go 1% when absolutely necessary." The incident where we successfully eliminated the Ace of Spades and rescued Fiend and Poppy. That incident was a prime example of the 1% rule. Otherwise, we're the nicest guys on two wheels.

But don't cross us.

"Hey, morning." Kynlee comes in, her hair messily tossed on top of her head. Sam kisses her forehead. "Good morning, Peanut."

Kynlee looked mortified. "Not my childhood nickname, no!" She covered her face with her hands. I couldn't help but laugh. She punches my arm before stealing a piece of bacon. There was a teasing gleam in her eye.

A little later, we ate breakfast as a family. Then Lucifer brought us down into the basement to conduct church immediately to discuss the details of today's runs and routes.

"All six are for Prion Tech Industries. We can split and do the two loads to Springfield and the two to Providence, and whoever gets back first can do the last two to McKinley, about an hour away from Briarswood. Demon and Reaper take Springfield, the rest of us to Providence. Unless necessary, maintain radio silence, radio frequency Alpha Tango three, got it?"

We get our radios and all tune in to the radio frequency. There was a lightness in the air knowing we were securing legit shipments with no need to check the loads. Lucifer was very proud he finally got us out of the gutter.

"Let's go. We should be back by dinner."

Chapter Thirty

Sam

PROTECTED
THE MERCILESS FEW MC: DEVIL'S IGNITED
Briarswood, Mass.

After breakfast, I got dressed for the day. As I was brushing my hair, I looked at the stack of papers and evidence. What more do they want from me? My blood!

Well, I was going to give them everything they needed and more. But first, I need to talk to Kynlee. I look around and she doesn't seem to be inside the house. I see the bunnies were discussing the menu for the B.A.C.A charity event.

"Hey girls, remember we'll be having hundreds if not thousands of hungry bikers and babes. Make the list and we'll split up the responsibilities later.

"Alright, Sam." They yelled.

I stop at the place where the screen door was supposed to be, but it's lopsided against the wall.

That's coming out of his pocket.

I saw Kynlee standing in the yard, but she was staring at her phone and then frantically typing.

"Hey." I whispered.

She screamed bloody murder and almost dropped her phone.

"Sorry, I didn't mean to startle you." She looked panicked. "Are you okay?"

"Ye-yeah yeah, you just scared me is all." She quickly puts her cellphone in her pocket.

"Come sit with me." I say, leading her to the porch swing. Once we sat down, we pushed back lightly, enjoying the breeze.

"I've been working hard on undoing what Mike did to your mother. I've sent what the courts asked of me, but it seems like they want even more."

"I'm not surprised. I'm her child and they looked at me like I was inept! I was the one taking care of her, driving her to therapy, making sure she was taking her meds, not him! He had her committed while I was at work!"

"I believe you." She was still breathing hard. "Do you know how heartbreaking it was to watch my friends venture off to college and I couldn't because we couldn't afford it and I had to get a job to pay the bills, to keep the lights on?! I have so much...rage Aunt Sam!"

She leans against me, her hands fisted in anger.

"I know. I should have been there after our parents died, but she convinced me everything was okay, that she was living in love. That's all I wanted for Chelsea. I should have paid more attention! God knows what you endured."

She scooted away, placing her hands on the swing. "If you only knew." I want to ask, but I'm afraid to know, terrified of what I might do.

"I need something from you to help strengthen my case, a sworn written statement. I need you to tell every minute, every detail..."

"Every disgusting interaction."

My heart stopped. "What do you mean, Peanut?" I know she hated that name, but when she was a baby, she was cuteness in such a small package, like a peanut.

"Nothing, it's nothing. I'll work on that written statement…right now." She quickly disappeared into the house.

What was that about? I knew she'd clamor up if I probed for information. I'd have to let her open up when she was ready.

I had little time to turn the evidence in, so I went to see what else I could gather.

Chapter Thirty-One
Kynlee

PROTECTED
THE MERCILESS FEW MC: DEVIL'S IGNITED
Briarswood, Mass.

He was so angry!

It gets worse every time I block a number. Why won't he leave me alone?

I want to throw in the towel, let him have the money, but a part of me, the part that hears my mother's voice, wants to stand up to him. He won't get away with this! I am going to get my mom from that mental prison, bring her here, and live in peace together.

I have an idea why he wants me to come back. You see, Mike not only had a drug habit, but he gambled like it was his job. He'd come back wasted and even more broke. He started pawning things and even took money I put in for bills, saying he'll pay it back with his big winnings… there were never any winnings.

I heard from mom's friend Phil that Mike was borrowing

from Santos Navila. His crew, the Wretched 72 ran the crime syndicate in the area. Probably a stupid move on his part because if you can't repay, they make sure that they never find ALL your body parts, but they will let you find a few.

He wants the money to pay off Santos and keep his body intact. He can't do that without my inheritance.

He might be using Santos and his resources to track me down. This is likely how he keeps finding ways to reach out to me.

And that made me worry. How far was he willing to go? How desperate was he?

Chapter Thirty-Two
Asher aka Wicked

PROTECTED
THE MERCILESS FEW MC: DEVIL'S IGNITED
Briarswood, Mass.

It was nearly 300 miles driven today. As we handed off the last load near the house, my back felt like it was on fire.

"Thanks for getting these transformers here safely. As always, it is a pleasure doing business." Raymond tipped his hard hat as we signed the delivery slip and handed it over. He whistled for the line of forklifts to start picking up the crates from the 18-wheeler.

"No problem. Until next time."

"Yeah, see you soon." He chuckled while handing over a check.

Lucifer turned around, brow raised. "How soon?"

"Maybe five days or so. Since finding this little gem of a port, it's much easier getting supply to where it needs to go. We're clearing out the backlog in Boston faster than anyone else. Once most of our inventory is out, we'll start recommending you to the others."

"Thanks Raymond for, you know, keeping our work at an even pace. Don't want to burn my boys out. We still have the charity event."

I know the girls were already discussing the food options. I don't know how we can top the BBQ and topless bike wash. The way those girls washed and caressed my Stormy was nothing short of erotic. It made me rock hard thinking about it. I would need to take care of this feeling soon. It had been a while since Kitty and with Kynlee in the house and in my room; I have this urge to know everything about her. I have other urges too, but I know that taking my time will reward me with what I want most, a genuine connection.

Her lying in bed with me was the most incredible feeling. She felt comfortable and safe. She even said so. That made me feel like a hero, protecting the damsel in distress.

I relished in it. I wanted to be her Prince.

It's almost dinnertime, but it's still light outside. I saw where Kynlee was and felt that familiar lump in my throat. I always got it when I went over there. I questioned life and fate because it wasn't fair. An innocent life cut short, never seeing her parents and her parents heartbroken and slowly healing from the loss of their daughter.

My beautiful angel niece.

Kynlee was kneeling in front of her memorial. She had some wildflowers she was arranging on Avery's plot.

"Oh sweet darling, I don't know what happened to you, but I see the love they have with these ribbons and beautiful handmade marker. To have you resting so close to home. I wish you so much peace." She placed the last flower across the bed, touching the ribbon with her name beautifully written in script

She looked away and saw me there. "Oh."

"Sorry I interrupted." She pats the ground next to her. I look around and pick this vibrant purple flower. It was the only one around, I call it destiny.

"Avery, the sweetest niece and angel an uncle like me could ever ask for. I wish you were in my arms as much as your parents do. I know you're watching over us. I love you and miss you so much." I sigh, the lump of emotion almost choking me.

"What happened to her?"

"It was horrifying. My sister tragically lost her at the hands of her abusive ex before my brother could rescue them. They're still grieving every day. It hurts, but also gives me some peace to see her here." I sigh and she side hugs me.

"How awful! I'm…so…angry for them!" She clenches her fists.

"Most people are once they hear the story. What are you doing out here?"

She rubbed her face with her hand before running it through her hair. "I just needed some air! Aunt Sam wants me to write testimony against my step dad. To paint him as the heartless predator he is. It got to be too much, reliving the…" She choked up, then cleared her throat. "I wanted to clear my thoughts. The bright colored ribbon drew me over here. Further proving to me that sometimes life's not fair."

"Yeah, but you can't let the past dictate your future."

"If I only had the power to forget it in entirety." She pressed her fingers to her lips, then placed it on the ground. "Rest in peace, little one." She gets up and looks back at me mischievously while walking the path into the thick forest that opens up into a field.

Like a siren's call, I follow. We walk side by side in silence. I feel like I couldn't force her to talk. She would when she was comfortable.

She stopped in the middle of the field, now holding both

my hands. She's looking up at me, on her tiptoes, a spark in her eye. I felt myself slowly lower to meet her.

"Asher…" She whispered, then bit her lip. I have been trying to be a proper gentleman, even more friend than love interest, but at that moment my resolve snapped, lifting her up on my waist, kissing her as we stood in the field. Each kiss left behind a lingering taste of strawberries and the scent of vanilla in the air. I can feel myself react to her hands all over me. I have to admit I've been wanting this for so long.

But I can't.

I separated us and put her down. I had to adjust myself, and I watched her curiosity get the best of her. She looked surprised. Not sure if it was because I stopped us or the adjustment.

"But wha…"

"Listen Kynlee, you're the girl that I want to do right by. And not because you're Sam's niece, but because you genuinely see me for who I am and not the mistakes I made."

"I want this so bad." She leans up again. "Let's seal it with a kiss."

"I know what you're doing, gorgeous. Okay, just one…" She hopped up on me, causing me to lose my balance.

As we tumbled to the ground, the world seemed to blur around me. My focus was on the beautiful girl on top of me. The intense scent of freshly cut grass filled the air, mingling with the earthy aroma of damp soil. I could hear the rustling of leaves and the distant chirping of birds, their melodies blending with the sound of my own ragged breaths. My body felt heavy, every inch of her pressed against me.

"Kyn…Kynlee…I can't breathe." She stopped and looked at me. "Don't call me that. Call me something cute, but not my name!"

"Okay, Peanut." She gasped, and I laughed, then she pouted. I brush her hair behind her ear. "Whatever you want, I'll need to think about it. It should be special, but until then, how about being my baby?" She slammed her lips against mine. A whirlwind of emotions erupted within me. Each kiss was like an electric shock, awakening every nerve in my body, sending shivers down my spine and causing my breath to catch in my throat. The physical effects of her kisses were undeniable.

"Yes! I love it!" She screamed happily, attacking me again.

Then a thought came to mind during this carnal moment and I reluctantly put space between us. "Now that I'm thinking about it, I think I should get your aunt's blessing before we start any relationship. She apologized and seems to be open to us hanging out, but dating is another level." I caught a faint whiff of her perfume as she leaned closer to me. I enjoyed the warmth of her body as she gently pressed against me, before reluctantly pulling away, leaving a lingering tingle on my skin.

"I suppose so." She muttered, but her piercing gaze burned through me like a searing flame, leaving a trail of desire in its wake.

I stand up, brush off the grass bits, and check her as well. Because that wouldn't look suspicious.

I hold out my hand. "Come on, baby." Her smile stretched from ear to ear as she reached for my hand.

Then her phone buzzed, catching her attention. She glanced at the screen, typed something, and quickly put the phone away. I could feel her hand tighten, and a shudder ran through her.

"Is everything okay?"

She smiled, "It is now." I brush her curls, then kiss her forehead.

Dinner was spectacular, as usual. The girls made meatloaf, mashed potatoes, and asparagus. I was very attentive to Kynlee, holding out her chair and fixing her plate before I fixed mine. She kissed my cheek once I sat down and my eyes automatically went to Sam, but instead of disgust, I saw her smirk. Lucifer gave me a nod of approval.

Kynlee held my hand under the table for the entire meal. We discussed our options for the charity event. The bunnies started in on their ideas about what we should do this year. Of course, it involved gratuitous nudity.

"I'm just saying a Merciless Few calendar would sell like hotcakes. One for the guys and one for the bunnies!" Lila suggested. All the guys' faces scrunched up. "Fine, then the bunnies will be the whole calendar. Maybe next year?"

Sam smiles, "It's a thought!"

"Sam, you'd be a babe as Lady Liberty or Mrs. Claus. In a tight, sexy…"

Lucifer holds up his hand. "Ha, cool your jets, babygirl I haven't signed off on the idea yet."

"But Bubba… it's for charity!" He just growled.

"Let's focus on this year, then. I still vote for the car wash. All proceeds from the wash go toward the final donation. We all know sex sells, and these girls could raise a million dollars!" Kynlee looks around to gauge their reaction.

The bunnies whoop and holler. "Damn right! I like her already. Wicked, don't screw this up like last time. Lila signaled she was watching me.

Without a second thought, I gently lifted our joined hands, feeling the warmth of her skin against mine. The softness entices me to press my lips against it, leaving a tender kiss. The sound of her gasp echoes in the air. A public gesture. "I promise, I won't."

Lucifer was stunned, Sam was all smiles, and I was relieved. A blush rose from her cheeks. She had to look away from our intense stare.

Lil clapped her hand, causing everyone to jump. "Well, I can't take credit for this one, but I am happy to see you happy, Wicked."

"I'm surprised Lil, the love doctor, didn't spin this her

way." Reaper added, and she stuck out her tongue. "You're just mad you were my first successful case. And you can keep your mouth shut, case number two!" Fiend just held up his hands.

The table got loud about who saved whose love life and Demon remained quiet because, technically; he was the last man standing. It'll be a winter storm of literal ice on fire in Hell before we see him settled down. I'd no sooner shave my head.

"Alright, quiet down! I'll take all options into consideration and get back to you tomorrow. Fiend and Reaper, you got dish duty before you leave. Send my daughters and the grandbabies my love." They both groan at kitchen duty. Sam sits back laughing. "Thank you, my handsome boys. Kiss my babies for me!"

"Asher?" I turn to see Kynlee yawning and rubbing her eyes. "Can we go to bed?"

"Sure, baby." We stand up, hands still together. "Good night everyone."

"Good night, you two." Sam said cautiously. "Keep it PG, my poor heart still has to process this…"

I feel my doubt creeping up again. My need to bash myself and call myself unworthy.

"But, I can see the joy in your eyes and so…" She gets up and hugs her, kisses her forehead, then I get a kiss on the cheek before her face goes serious. "You hurt her, I'll kill you."

There was no room for misinterpretation. I felt that in my soul. I only nodded.

"Good! Good night, everyone."

Kynlee was so happy that she moved her bag back over to my room. She had little to begin with, but she wanted to lay claim. I thought it was cute.

When Avi and Raven moved into Reaper's space, you could see it brightened his outlook on life. I remember telling him I was glad he was happy now, and he said I'd get my time one day.

And here it was.

She was in the shower when I saw her phone light up in succession, but it was face down. I didn't see the need to look.

I changed out my comforter for a thicker one I use when the temperatures drop at night. I stood back and stole the pillows off Reap's bed to make it cozier. I come back and she slams the phone face down, running her fingers through her hair and sighing. I chose not to address it.

She saw me and looked relieved to see me. "There's so many pillows! I could get lost in them."

She leans back against them and I hover over her, lips dangerously close.

"I promise you, I will keep you tethered to me so you will never get lost."

She smirks. "Careful... Aunt Sam doesn't want to hear us..."

Then our ears tune in, "Oh god Demon, yes! Fuck me like you mean it! Ahh!"

Kynlee looks mortified. "That would be Kitty. She has a crush on him so she can be a little...much. Stroking his ego."

"Among other things!"

"Welcome to life at the clubhouse. I'm going to take my shower. Be right back."

It's hard not to fantasize about her while in the shower, but actually it keeps me from acting on my urges. To back her up against the cold, misted glass shower wall, feeling the droplets of water hit me as I corner her. The sound of rushing water fills the air as I watch it pour off her skin. She locks eyes with me, her breath quickening as my fingers gently trace the curves of her lips. Slowly, I guide them down, feeling her quiver under my touch, overwhelmed with pleasure. She'd hold my wrist as I worked her up to the edge, calling my name with a soft moan until she came.

I traced my hand down my chest, feeling the warmth radiating from my skin. Imagining her soft hands instead of mine. The sight of my raging hard on made my breath catch in my throat. A tingling sensation that sent shivers down my spine accompanied its pulsating. As my fingertips grazed its sensitive surface, a hiss echoed in the quiet room. I'd never been this sensitive before, a testament to the effect she had on me.

But it felt so good. "Fucking hell, baby, yes…" I kept my movements slow to build up the climax, the promise of us and our emotions being entwined. I speed up and place my other hand on the wall. I feel this may be one of those where you temporarily black out or your knees buckle. It'd be hard to explain finding me naked on the shower floor.

My breathing picked up as I moaned her name, but not too loudly, although I'm sure the continued screams of pleasure from Demon's room could cover up a brutal murder.

I focused back on the overwhelming sensation. "Yes, baby, like that…ooh…" A jolt of electricity shot down my back and I was close. I grunted until I couldn't keep quiet. "Ohhh, Kynlee, baby…" I moaned loudly, feeling a surge of pleasure that made me release more than I usually do.

Wow. I sighed in relief and post orgasm clarity. I was sure of my intentions and my outlook on life had a little spark in it and she was lying in my bed. I hurried and dried, put on my clothes and headed back to my room.

I slowly opened the door to find her knocked out. She was sleeping like she hadn't slept in days, indicated by her louder snoring. I slip in on her side for a change, sitting up a bit. She shifted enough to find me and lay against me. I kiss her forehead. "Good night, baby."

"Mmm..ni-night." She muttered, barely cognizant. I inhale the scent of her and I fall peaceably asleep.

bzzz bzzz bzzz bzzz

I'm annoyed by the unnerving sound and realize it's her

phone and not mine. I look and now see a frown on her face. She's squirming a bit.

bzzz bzzz bzzz

Who is texting so much and this late at night? I grab her phone, wanting to put it on silent.

Do you think you can get away with this, huh?

I'll find you and make you pay!

Your aunt can't save you. I know where you are, and once I get you, NO ONE will find you!

What the fuck? The number was unavailable. I check to see if she ever replied; she doesn't, she just blocks the number. There are over 25 different numbers blocked by both messages and phone calls.

Someone's harassing her.

"N-no. You're a monster! Stay away... I said stay away! Ahhh!" She shot up screaming and panting. I turned on the light so she could see where she was and that she was with me.

"Are you okay?"

"Yeah, I'm...fine." She tries to catch her breath. She points at my hand. "What are you doing with my phone?!"

"It was buzzing, and you were tired, so I went to silence it, but then I saw all these threatening messages come in. Who is this?"

"It doesn't matter! It's nothing. Can we go back to sleep?"

"It matters when someone is threatening to hurt you! You just had another nightmare and you want to brush it off as nothing?"

"It is nothing! I don't want to talk about it!"

"I..." I wanted to talk some sense into her, but I was so lost in what to do.

I really wanted to protect her, but she needed to trust me first. Meanwhile, my senses were on high alert.

"Okay. I'm sorry I looked. You should put it on Do Not Disturb, so you can get better sleep." She agreed and put it back face down again before resuming her position on me.

I kissed her forehead and felt the need to whisper, "You're safe with me. I'll always protect you." A smile formed as she sighed. "I know."

Could she actually be running away from someone? If she's in danger, I need to know.

"Go…away…stop…" ***whimper*** Her eyebrows knitted in fear. I need more information about her family life in Oklahoma.

"Who are you running from?"

Chapter Thirty-Three
Sam

PROTECTED
THE MERCILESS FEW MC: DEVIL'S IGNITED
Briarswood, Mass.

"Demon, my niece is in this house! Can you keep your escapades down, please?"

"Please Sam, I'm sure she's been riding the old Wicked express since she got here. Besides, she's an adult, not a child, like when Raven was here."

I didn't want to think about it, but I knew eventually it would happen. I just hope he treats her right, that I raised him right.

Wicked comes in at the tail end of the conversation.

"Wicked, why don't you break the news that you two have been boning so she can get off my back!" He chuckled.

It's almost as if I witnessed the moment his body seized up, heart pounding out of his chest. His hands shot up as if he was involved in a bank robbery. "That is not true! All we've done is kiss. I want to do this right. I see the difference now." I lit up like a proud mama.

"But, eventually, I'll tap that!" Demon laughed out loud, clapping his back. I was horrified!

"I'm kidding. That part of me is long gone. But you know it's inevitable, right?"

"I don't want to talk about my baby girl having sex. Either way, Demon, keep it down, for Christ's sake! Or I'll clear out your little sex dungeon while you're out on a run."

I knew I would hit a nerve, "Aww come on, Sam. Not cool." He walks out of the kitchen.

"Sam, can I ask something serious? About Kynlee?" He looks concerned.

"Of course."

"Do you think she only came here to be with you or save her mother?"

I was unsure what he meant. "Why do you think she's here?"

"I think she's running from someone. She got some text messages that were pretty threatening last night, but she didn't want to talk about it. I let it go, but I could not go back to sleep. I stared at her phone, wondering who would want to hurt her and why. In the past few days, my presence has startled her a couple of times, causing her to put her phone away quickly."

I gasp in revelation, "I've seen that too! I thought she was talking to some boy back home, but when she openly showed interest in you, I was confused. Now I'm worried."

"Maybe she'll talk to you about it?"

"We have to go to the post office this morning to expedite the paperwork to Phil, who's representing us in court on Thursday. I'll see what I can find out, but I hope you're wrong."

I knock on their door. "Hey, you have your statement ready for mailing?" She sets down her pen. "Yeah, just making

THE MERCILESS FEW MC ANTHOLOGY: PROTECTED

sure I mentioned the important stuff." She holds the paper and stuffs the thick packet in an envelope and seals it, handing it to me. I place it in the padded envelope with all my other papers.

"Come hang out with me today. Once we drop this off, we can have a girls' day or something. It'll be fun to get away from the Neanderthals. Remember when you used to do my nails when you were a little girl?"

"Yeah, you said I was the best nail tech you had, even though there was nail polish all over your skin. It's okay. I knew it wasn't my calling."

We hop in the truck. She sputters when I release the brake, "Oof, sounds like she's due a tuneup. Better get one of the boys on it." She agreed, and we were on our way.

I noticed her gazing out the window, mesmerized by the quiet charm of our small town, the distant church steeple silhouetted against the morning sky. I wasn't a church going gal, but I believe in something higher than man.

"Kynlee, I need to ask you something important."

"No, Auntie, we have not had sex." She says so nonchalantly. "I'm looking to change that soon, though." This mischievous smile appears.

"For the love of God, why are you both so comfortable telling me this?! I wasn't talking about that! Please spare your old fragile aunt from your...sex fantasies."

Her eyes reacted to what I said earlier. "Huh, he told you that too? Interesting..." The smile grew wider.

Help me.

She lets out a sigh and says, "For the record, I'd like to remind you that this is a wild, rowdy motorcycle club. We've got alcohol flowing like water and there's always an abundance of exposed tits. Some of them are quite impressive! Makes me think I should get a boob job." She raises her hands to show her point before she proceeds. "Demon's a sex pervert and you and Uncle Rocco make out like horny teenagers. I'm sure eventually I'll be privy to your escapades. Think how traumatized I'll be!"

"Fair point and I understand. Anyway, I need you to be honest with me when I ask you this." I glanced over as I turned onto Main street. "I was already working on getting your mother out way before you trekked across the country. Why did you leave home? Did something else happen?"

I noticed her fidgeting, "There was nothing there! A go nowhere town and if you had no money you're stuck there. I couldn't go to college and my job was a dead end. I wanted to be free, and close to family! You're all that I have left. Once dad was gone, his family was gone, too. I hear from Grandma and Aunt Pam occasionally. But you, I know you care about me. You'd fight the world for me."

"I would, Peanut, and you know you can tell me anything…besides your sex life."

"Haha. Just so you know, I'm not a virgin. He was awful. There, I said it."

"They don't get good until you tell them what to do. Otherwise, you're stuck with mediocre sex for life.

"Noted."

Oh, my god! I just gave her sex advice. I shudder at the thought of her telling Asher what she wants. I remember those teaching years. I guess we all have to go through it. Hopefully hers is shorter than mine. Bubba was the only man I didn't have to guide. He asked me what I wanted, was that good or did he need to go deeper, faster, or after I came, he'd make sure I was okay, then coax at least two more out of me.

I need to cool down. It would be awhile before I was in his arms or grasp.

"Auntie Sam! You zoned out…you were thinking about Uncle Rocco, weren't you?"

"What? No…"

"You were! You're all flushed! It's okay, I was daydreaming myself. I really like Asher. I hope he likes me, too."

"I don't think you have to worry about that. I see past all their manly behavior to know they want happiness too, each in a different way. Asher arrived conceited and smug, assuming all women adored him. His ego got worse while dating the twins. However, being dumped and humiliated in front of everybody taught him a harsh lesson. It deflated that ego and revealed his true self, his vulnerability. He's still a menace, but growing into who he is. Considering your personalities and how well you get along, I suppose it isn't shocking that you two ended up drawn to one another."

"See, he's not so bad. In fact, I was wondering...what you think about...me...becoming a bunny?" Those big, brown eyes, the ones that had melted my heart years ago, were now attempting to work their old magic.

This was different. My hands clenched the steering wheel as I shut my eyes, each shallow breath a desperate attempt to calm the rising anxiety.

"I did not agree to that! Why on Earth do you want to be a bunny?"

"What's wrong with being a bunny? You seem to love all the girls like family, anyway. They get along so well and I can learn so much about the club, all while being near my man."

Oh, brother.

I look at her and see this spark, and although I don't have exact details of what she endured, she seemed to be much more carefree. I assumed that her mother's care, her job, and her friends moving on or away stressed her.

Maybe here she had a choice in what she wanted her path to be and it included being a Merciless Few bunny.

"Let's discuss that more later. It's time for you to answer the tough questions." She didn't respond, but I knew she would open up to her favorite aunt. We walked into the post office and waited in line.

I express mailed the package and texted Phil the receipt with the arrival date.

We arrived at Serenity Spa. I had a beautiful facade, but the inside was even more tranquil and serene.

"Wow, Aunt Sam, I was just expecting a nail salon and some face masks at home, but this is insane!"

"I haven't been here in so long, but they are known for being the best at what they do."

We walk up to the reception desk, "Welcome to Serenity Spa, where we put the ahh in spa. My name is Penelope. How can I help you?"

"Yes, can I do two full body Swedish massages then mani/pedis."

"Absolutely. Do you have a sexual preference for your masseuses?"

I look at Kynlee, "Male." We both said, then burst out laughing. I know Bubba would kill me for having a man touch me, but they get so much deeper into the muscle.

"Okay, I will assign Brett and Tony to you. Please follow me to the changing room.

The massage was what I needed to gather the courage to find out the real reason she was here now. Now we are in spa grade massage chairs with our tootsies in bubbling warm water.

"Alright, truth time. I want you to know you can tell me anything, no matter how tough it is, because you're safe here."

She sighed loudly. "There's so much to unpack."

"Not everything needs to be revealed today. I know we might have to return to court, and I prefer not to be surprised by your testimony.

"Well," I take her hand and squeeze it. "I was running away...from Mike. Everything seemed fine after he had mom committed. He said it was for the best, and I stupidly believed him. How could I ever think he would be a good father figure for anybody! Then, he started neglecting the house, saying it was my responsibility. That's what women were for! Not to mention he was spending money like water and not on essentials. Then one day he told me my paycheck would pay the bills, and he threw this huge stack of overdue bills at me. It was way more than I made and I didn't know how to make up the rest! I paid what I could, requested extensions, and even requested extra hours to earn more."

"What was he spending the money on?"

"What do you think? Hookers, drugs, and his gambling habit. When I would question it, he'd get so angry and threatening! Telling me it was none of my business and that he would shut that smart mouth of mine. He would make these…statements that were creepy and made me super uncomfortable. And then…he started peeking into my room when he thought I was asleep. I wasn't asleep when he did it or the creak of the door awoke me. The first few times he stood at the door."

My mind raced with all the sick possibilities, hoping it wasn't as bad as I hoped. I noticed her grip was tighter.

"One of those times I realized he was watching me and masterbating. He grunted so loud, zipped up his pants and closed the door. Then it became routine, ending with him finishing all over my carpeted floor. I never walked barefoot in my room again. Anyway, I would have my music in my ears, but one day he got bold and sat on my bed. Petrified, I prayed he wouldn't go any further, like grabbing my hand to finish him off. The sound of the belt buckle and zipper indicated he whipped it out, and I squeezed my eyes tightly until it was over.

The culmination was at dinner. He said, 'Since your mom is unable to, it's your job to satisfy my needs.' I knew that was the final straw. I feared the next time, he would not take no for an answer. I still have nightmares where I scream for him to get out of my room. I couldn't risk it. I gathered all my money and took the greyhound here. It was two and a half days but I slept better surrounded by strangers than in my own room. I regret not stopping him from having mom committed! I should have done something!"

Her eyes welled with tears. "Don't. You couldn't have known he was going to do this. I should have known he was a money grubbing son of a bitch who didn't give a damn about my sister. He just saw a vulnerable single mother he could manipulate. I won't let him win! And god help him if I see him on the streets! I'm so sorry you had to endure that nasty man. I am glad you came to me. We have each other and will fight this with everything I have."

She exhaled, "I know."

"Is he the one threatening you on your phone?"

"How did you…"

"Asher and I had a talk this morning and he's concerned about some things he's seen."

"Well, it's none of his business! I told him it was nothing!"

"Kynlee, it's not nothing! We don't know how serious Mike is about his threats. He may be a druggie alcoholic, but denying him the money he thinks he's owed could make him do crazy things, and Asher only wants to protect you! As for Asher, this is the first time I've seen him so concerned about anyone outside the family. Don't be angry he asked me, be understanding that he wants to keep you safe."

"Mike can't get me, he's 1500 miles away!"

"He can still reach you by phone."

I didn't even see the messages, but I know scumbags like Mike like to threaten and intimidate into submission, and if that doesn't work, they go to violence. Even 1500 miles away, I still consider him a threat.

"Aunt Sam?"

"Yeah, Peanut."

"Thank you, I needed this."

I didn't know if she meant the spa treatment or the talk.

"Anytime, sweetie."

Chapter Thirty-Four
Asher aka Wicked

PROTECTED
THE MERCILESS FEW MC: DEVIL'S IGNITED
Briarswood, Mass.

Another day and four separate runs this time, but we bagged almost $8k each! This working legitimately was really paying off. I think I heard Reaper say that Avi wanted her own bike so they could take rides together.

That would be so hot.

Our last drop took us past downtown, and I saw the truck at the spa. A girl's day. I'm sure they both needed it. At the entrance of the paper mill, we rev our engines and the gates open. The trucks were filled with new equipment such as fiber guards, rope cutters, and raggers. Vital pieces of equipment the mill needs to run and highway pirates will rob the truckers to cannibalize the parts. It happens more often than you think, especially among competitive territories. We were the neutral party.

Lucifer signs the manifesto, "Thanks Roc. You don't know

how long we've been waiting for these parts. We can ramp up production to 100% now. These 16-hour days were killing me!"

"Glad to be of service. Get some much needed rest." He claps his back.

"Are you guys doing your annual charity event this year?"

"You know it. We're hashing out ideas right now."

"Make sure to have that car/bike wash. Those girls gave quite the show last year. I don't know how you can be around so much beauty."

"I have my beauty. Besides, those girls are too young for me, but my guys can handle them."

"Now they're all mine." Demon says, effectively confirming my status as taken and unavailable.

I smile, thinking of how soon I can have my arms wrapped around her.

"Well, you look like you can handle them."

"They don't call me Demon for nothing!" Everyone laughs.

"Alright boys, let's head home. Time for a good celebratory meal."

The house was dark when we got home. "I saw the truck at the spa earlier. Maybe they're still there. I asked Sam to ask Kynlee about what happened back home."

"You might be right. Let's switch it up and cook for the ladies, then. Tell Avi and Poppy to come to the house."

"Umm, Poppy's appetite has been limited lately. She only wants tacos or lasagna, sometimes both." Poppy happily revealed that she and Fiend were expecting their rainbow baby after the tragic loss of Avery, his namesake. He's been helicoptering her ever since, super overprotective.

"We have both! No problem, just ask her which one she wants and Papa Rocco will make it for her."

I go to wash my hands and even though I know she's not there; I couldn't help but to check our room, anyway. I loved seeing her presence by her bag or her clothes that she shoved into a drawer.

Forty-five minutes later, we were grilling burgers and setting up a taco and nacho bar. They assigned me to make french fries for the burgers.

We hear a bunch of voices and see the bunnies arrive. Avi and the kids arrived next and Poppy slowly made her way in. Fiend was helping her onto the couch.

"Papa Rocco! Raven screamed as he bent down to hug her and Onyx." The way he lit up with his grandkids would make anyone's heart melt, even Demon. Raven would pick on Uncle Aven. He thought his size would intimidate her and keep her away, but she strolled right up to him and asked his name. She wore him down faster than he bags a woman.

The girls are surprised to find us cooking. "Is this the twilight zone? The men are cooking!"

I was offended by their comment, "Hey, we grill all the time!"

"Yes, but you're in the kitchen…cooking. Grilling is different."

The debate kept going when Sam and Kynlee walked in. I don't know what it was, but she looked more relaxed, even happier. She bee-lined it to me. I put the basket down and wiped my grease splattered hands. She leaned up for a kiss. I hesitated with everyone around, then obliged. "Hey, baby, how was the spa?"

"How did you know?"

"Saw the truck as we delivered a shipment. You're glowing."

"Yes, I had the best massage ever! Brett was a real life…" Her eyes widened. I cornered her, "Brett… that better be a super butch name for a girl, hmm?"

Judging by her blush, it wasn't. I leaned in closer, not caring who was watching. She pursed her lips for a kiss, but not this time. I shook my head, denying her pleasure. "So you let some guy rub all over you before I could? Tsk tsk…" I back away and drain the rest of the fries on a paper towel. I could see her pouting out of the corner of my eye.

"I needed someone to work out all my knots! I was stressed, you know that! Don't be mad."

Ha, she thought I was mad; I wasn't, but I could almost taste the burning desire to erase his touch from her body tonight. A mischievous chuckle escapes my lips as I reach out and grasp her delicate chin, sending a shiver down her spine. With a gentle lift, I tilt her head ever so slightly, locking eyes with her. "Not mad, baby," I whisper, the sound of my voice filled with a mix of anticipation and determination. "But just know I have plans for you later." She was practically melting to my touch.

"Okay." Was all she could squeak out.

Good.

Sam was so shocked to see her boys cooking in the kitchen! She kissed her husband. "Bubba, what are you doing?"

"You needed a break and since you were at the spa, I thought I could help and you can relax. Why don't you pick a movie for us?"

She was smiling ear to ear. "Okay."

We finished, and everyone grabbed their plates before settling into movie night. We ate at the table, then I had my girl laid against me on the living room floor. My arms around her like I'd been dreaming about all day.

I relish feeling her, but it was also causing a problem. I kept trying to put just a tiny bit of space between us, but she scooted back against my dick, doing quick movements that made her ass rub against me. After the third time, she gave me a mischievous smirk. She knew what she was doing.

She'd pay for that soon.

About two-thirds through the movie, half the group was asleep or falling asleep. Reaper gathered his family and went home. Fiend and the mom-to-be also took off. The girls headed to the bunny house and Lucifer picked up his sleeping beauty and went to bed.

Before she could even register what was happening, I slid my hand around her throat. The sound of her gasp pierced the air, mingling with the faint hum of the TV. She exhaled, then moaned, "I know what you were doing earlier." A surge of adrenaline coursed through my veins, heightening my senses.

"Me? I was being completely innocent." She said in that sugary sweet voice, conveying her purity, but nice try. I tightened my grip, feeling the warmth of her hand against mine, as she let out another louder moan that echoed in the room, mingling with the scent of her desire.

"Were you? Or did you think you could tease me without punishment? Your aunt knows about us now, so I can have my way with you. And it starts …in the shower…go…now." I whispered the last part with authority and her body shuddered in excitement. I let go, watching her scramble to the bathroom.

Demon is still there grinning like a jackal. "I taught you well."

I roll my eyes, "Keep your mouth shut."

"You should be worried about keeping her mouth shut." He chuckled before tipping his beer and texting on his phone, heading toward his room.

I hear the shower running and her singing. I slip in and turn off the lights. She gasped, "In the dark, really?" I ripped everything off and opened the shower door. "This is my fantasy, not yours." I growled. I was still adjusting to the dim lighting, but her panting gave her away. She was standing opposite of me, so I cornered her. The water splashing off me. Her hand grabs my face and pulls me down for a kiss. Then I felt her hands on my chest. She rubs the loofah all over. I smelled the scent of ivory soap. Her other hand followed the sponge as it went back across and then lower. I inhaled hard when her hand was stroking my dick, causing me to slam my lips onto hers.

"Fuck, baby. That feels so good…" I massaged and placed kisses all over her breasts. Then I remembered my plan and rinsed us both off. She wrapped herself in the towel and I wrapped my lower half. She peeks out before we both sneak into my room. I pick her up and toss her on the bed.

She sighed as she removed the towel, her fingers tracing down her body to her pussy. "Oh god, finally. I'm so fucking sensitive down there."

I place my finger on my lips to remind her to stay quiet. She nodded while frantically stroking herself, "Ash…Asher, please…" A desperate plea escaping her lips in a hushed whisper. The sound of her rapid breaths filled the air. The scent of arousal hung in the room, growing stronger as she quickened her pace. Her body trembled with anticipation, on the brink of finding release.

Although that would be hot to watch, that was my job. I grab her fingers, putting them in my mouth to taste her. She looked frustrated that I stopped her. "Better keep it down if you don't want your aunt to hear."

Then I exhaled hard, my breath causing her to squirm before I tasted her. She tasted so sweet, like fresh tropical fruit. If she was going to cum, she'd drown me as she struggled not to scream out in pleasure. Her muffled moans challenged me to make her break. I dove deeper, watching her try to squirm away from me with both hands slapped over her mouth. She sat up, "No…stop, I won't be able to…oh my god, right there…there!" She whisper yelled, her breathing labored.

"So is that a yes or stop? Because I can have you shaking so hard and that's just with my tongue. If…you…want it."

"Yes. Oh god…I'm so fucking close. Please, Asher, baby, please. I need it." She begged and two minutes later, I was drowning in her orgasm.

She laid there, panting. "You okay, baby?"

Next thing I know she was straddling me, her hands gently caressing me with a slow, teasing rhythm. The sight of her, her body moving sensually, was enough to drive me wild. She was sliding back and forth, her orgasm making her movement easier.

"Baby…"

"Shhh… you wouldn't want anyone to come knocking, do you?" She shook her head. I had been dreaming about this moment for so long, the instant chemistry telling me it was okay to fantasize about her since I met her.

"You're a lot bigger than I imagined."

I slide my hands up to her breasts, squeezing them, coaxing another moan out of her. "Really?"

"Mmm…mhmm." She slid back until she was bumping against it, then she lifted herself, lined up, and slowly slid down.

With that grip, no way I'm going to last.

I muffled a grunt with a pillow until she took it away and tossed it. "No fair, that's cheating. Now, let's see how quiet you can be now. Hmm?"

Her panting replaced her moans to stay quiet, but I was fisting the sheets and being deliciously tortured by the grip her pussy had on my dick. I thought she'd take it slow and build up her next orgasm, but I guess my sheer size and filling her up caused her to rock hard and fast.

"I just need to get this one out of the way. Ooh, I promise baby I'll take care of you…. just let me…let me…cum…"

Who was I to deny her what she was begging me for, another mind blowing orgasm?

I sit up and she grabs my shoulders to rock even deeper. My hands grip her ass. She was perfectly pounding herself onto me with no help, and I enjoyed feeling it.

"Does it feel good, baby?" I said smugly.

"Ohhh… yes, so, so good. I'm so close." I took my cue to

lick my thumb and gently circle her clit while sucking on her nipples, taking moments to gently bite them. She slapped her hands over her mouth and slammed her legs together, quivering and cumming all over me. Then she collapsed on top of me, breathing hard.

I pushed her hair away from her face. "You okay?" She nodded. "That was the most amazing series of orgasms ever."

"No need to inflate my ego, as long as you're satisfied." I kiss her forehead, threading my fingers through her hair.

"No ego boosting, promise. I never felt that way before. Oh...but you're not satisfied...let me take care of that." She said so innocently, but before I could contest, she slid down, blowing her cool breath on the tip. My dick jumped, and she smiled. Instead of sliding her hand around my still throbbing cock, she ran her fingernails up and down.

I hissed, then moaned. I never felt that type of sensation before and the pulsing got worse. Then she switches to stroking me.

"Tell me, Asher, do you want to cum? Tell your baby what you want."

"Yes, yes baby, I want to cum, so bad." She had me begging while trying to keep quiet.

I needed her to go faster. I'd cum all over her hand in no time.

"Watch me." She says.

I'm not sure why... oh...

My eyes rolled to the back of my head as I slid flat against the bed. I looked up to confirm I saw her sliding those pretty little lips over my dick. I tried to stay quiet, but was failing miserably. Seeing her try her damndest to get me all down her throat, and then she started humming against me. It pulsed against the vein and I lost control.

Witchcraft! As I shot everything I had down her throat. I conceded to screaming into another pillow. Once my breathing calmed, I removed it to see her smiling. "You lost, spectacularly."

"W-worth it. Fuck, I've never reacted so fast. You're dangerous."

She kissed my dick in its soft state, and it still jumped. She chuckled. "That I am." I pull her up to lie against me. She sighs and I kiss her forehead.

"Just know, one of my other fantasies is to blow you while you're sleeping."

"Oh, shit."

"Yeah."

"Dangerous. Maybe I should do the same...all's fair..."

When I opened my eyes, I noticed she was staring at me. "Thank you for wanting to protect me. Aunt Sam told me how concerned you were."

"I assume you told her about the texts?"

"I did, and now I'm ready to tell you about what led to it and the nightmares."

What she revealed had my blood boiling. I understood how my brothers felt when their significant others were in danger and felt that black out rage. NOW I was ready to do time, so he would never threaten her again. What a sick pervert! She did right by leaving in the middle of the night. There was no one there who could protect her, not like I can or will!

She tensed up as she revealed the days that led up to the escape. I couldn't hold her tighter or kiss her enough, giving her words of encouragement. "I'm your protector."

"I know. Oh, and guess what? I'm going to be your bunny!" She said excitedly.

"What?" I got flashbacks to when the twins told me the same, but I wasn't excited about it.

"No, Kynlee, it didn't work out for me last time. I don't need my girlfriend to be a Merciless Few bunny." I separated us and she looked shocked.

"Well, I'm not them, alright?! I want to be a bunny, not because you're in it. That's just a bonus. Don't punish me for something they did. I'm being genuine!"

She was right; there was no justification for the comparisons made between her and them, nor the backlash she received for a sweet gesture intended to make me happy. The possibility of losing her sent me into a panic. I pulled her to come lay back down, but she didn't budge.

"I'm sorry."

"Are you? Because you just freaked out on me! After such amazing sex." She pouted.

"It was amazing. You're amazing. I'd be proud to have you as my dedicated girl. Will you...be my girlfriend and my bunny?" I was laying it on thick, but judging by the megawatt smile I could see even in the dark, I had made her night.

"Oh my god, yes! Yes!" She wraps herself around me."

And although we were just talking and her agreeing, I realized what this could sound like from the other side of the door.

"I can't breathe, teddy bear!"

She showered me with kisses, exclaiming, "I love my nickname!"

"I told you it would take time to find the perfect one. Good night, my teddy bear."

"Goodnight, my handsome boyfriend."

And all was right in the world.

I woke up the next morning with her cuddled up to me. That's why I call her my teddy bear. I was elated that we finally had our moment last night. I discreetly lifted the blanket to glimpse at both of our naked bodies. The sight of her breasts reignited my excitement.

"Slow and steady, Asher." I remind myself. I shift a bit and she slides off me to lie facing away from me. She placed her arm above her head before drifting back to sleep.

I remember what she said last night about her fantasy.

Let's turn those tables, shall we?

The only problem is that there's a lingering possibility she won't stay quiet, her voice echoing through the walls, shattering the silence that envelops the house on this early morning.

You know what, worth the risk. She was officially my girlfriend, and I'd do anything to keep her happy.

Quietly, I slipped from the bed, the soft fabric of the sheets brushing against my skin as I knelt down and pulled back the covers to ease myself under. I lifted my head up to see the rise and fall of her breasts and heard some light snoring. Good.

I positioned myself above her pussy and was able to bend one leg away for easier access to my prize. I slid down and realized my feet were dangling off the bed. Probably about time to upgrade my bed.

She sighed, and I waited, hoping she wouldn't turn over because then I'd have to flip her back and devour her without warning.

She had only switched her bent leg to the other one and her hand landed on her breast and she moaned. Maybe she was having a dream about last night.

I laid on my side, inhaling the very familiar scent of her while stroking myself. I had this insatiable need to devour her, and I did. She woke up with a gasp and a moan. "Oh, ohhh! Ash, Asher?"

I lift my head, but she can't see me. "Yes, now shut up while I enjoy my breakfast." I encircle my arms around her trembling legs. Savoring every inch of her with fervent licks, the taste flooding my mouth with pleasure all while stroking myself. Doing both felt so damn good.

"Oh, baby, yes..." Her hands instinctively found their way under the sheets and on top of my head, trying to shove me deeper. The sensation sent a surge of electricity coursing through my entire body, creating an exhilarating sting that traveled down my spine. "Grrr...that's right baby, I want you to cum all over me."

"Yeah, yeah, yeah...gonna...gonna, right there, right there!"

And she did, screaming my name.

"Oh, Asher, yes!"

Now I'm sure I can never leave my room. I'll have to die in here or Sam may kill me. She might send Lucifer to kill me now that everyone knows I've defiled their niece.

Despite that, I was still able to reach orgasm while listening to the sound of her panting. She throws the cover off, "You sneaky bastard, that was my fantasy."

I kiss her pussy after licking my fingers. "I could do this every morning."

"And you should. Come on, let's get dressed. Sam wants me to talk to the bunnies about bunny life."

And it made me think, would I take it a step further? Would I want her to be my ol' lady? It's a prestigious title among biker couples.

Although I have witnessed some badass catfights.

I got dressed for today's activities. Supposedly Lucifer was going to give his final decision on this year's event.

Now that Kynlee wants to be a bunny, it puts perspective on the whole topless carwash idea. I just got to see her tits. I don't want everyone else to!

Chapter Thirty-Five
Sam

PROTECTED
THE MERCILESS FEW MC: DEVIL'S IGNITED
Briarswood, Mass.

"Alright girlies, the men are away and we can finalize our top three options to raise money for our charity B.A.C.A., which stands for Bikers Against Child Abuse, if I didn't tell you." Kynlee nodded.

"Also, before I forget, Kynlee wants to dedicate herself as a bunny, so show her the ropes and tell her all the rules. No special treatment." Everyone giggles.

"Oh, she's definitely Wicked's bunny." Lila smiles.

"I am, but it's official, too. I'm his girlfriend!" She squealed in delight.

I had an inkling after hearing her call out his name this morning. It still makes me feel woozy.

"Well, I guess you'll be the only bunny to call him by his name. It's club rule, you know. Until he makes you his ol' lady."

"Which is what I am." I interjected.

She nodded. "I know about that rule and I will adhere to house rules outside of our room. Inside might be quite different."

"So, I've heard." She gasped at my comment. I walked away before I heard any details about last night.

The girls gave her all the insights of the club, the history, and juicy not-so-legal stories, including their jail time. By lunch, she was all caught up.

Around noon, I got a call from Phil. "Hey, Phil. Please tell me you have some good news."

There was this long, tense pause before he sighed and I knew my world was about to crumble.

"I'm sorry. She's gone, Samantha. Chelsea had a heart attack and they couldn't revive her. I got the call ten minutes ago. I'm still in shock."

My world went black.

Heart attack.

Heart attack.

Couldn't revive.

Couldn't revive her.

Gone.

Gone.

What am I going to tell Kynlee?

I woke up to the guttural screams of my niece. She had crumpled to the floor with my phone in her hand. No doubt she asked Phil what was going on. I see Lila on her phone, frantically trying to get in touch with someone.

"Keep her awake, I got a hold of Fiend, they're turning around right now. Sam, stay with us!"

But I couldn't. The weight of guilt settled heavy on my shoulders, causing my muscles to fail and ache. Each breath was a struggle, as if carrying the burden of the world within my chest. My heart, once full of hope, now thudded painfully, a constant reminder of my failure.

I had failed my sister. Waves of sorrow crashed over me, threatening to engulf me in their depths. Tears welled up in my eyes, blurring my vision. The rawness of my emotions manifested as a lump in my throat, making it difficult to speak or even swallow.

The world around me seemed to lose its color and vibrancy, as if a dark cloud had descended upon my existence. Every sound muffled, every touch dulled, as if trapped within a cocoon of my own anguish. The heaviness in my heart seemed to pull me down, making it difficult to find any refuge from the overwhelming sadness that consumed me.

I failed everyone and now I had to find the strength to pick up the broken pieces of my niece. I had to be there for her, to offer solace and support as we share this unspeakable grief.

My sister was dead.

Chapter Thirty-Six

Kynlee

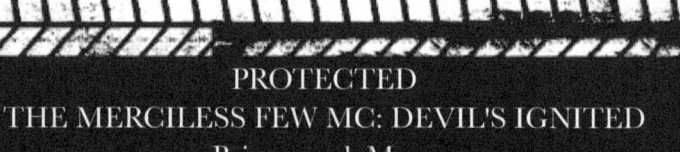

PROTECTED
THE MERCILESS FEW MC: DEVIL'S IGNITED
Briarswood, Mass.

"Aunt Sam!" She collapses to the floor, the color draining from her face. Kitty tries to hold her up, propping her against her legs. I'm almost hyperventilating, calling her name, but she's not waking up completely.

I'm frantic, looking around. I see her cell and can hear someone call her name.

"Sam? Sam!"

I crawl over and pick it up. "Who is this?! Answer me! What did you tell her?"

I heard a loud sigh. "Kynlee, it's Phil." He paused.

"Okay." Another long pause.

"I'm so sorry, sweetie, but your mom had a heart attack… she…she didn't make it."

"Wha…"

I opened my mouth to speak, instead a wave of silence

washed over me, leaving my voice trapped in my throat. I saw the world around me blur and dim, as if a hazy filter covered my vision. The phone slipped from my trembling hand, hitting the ground with a dull thud. I could feel my body growing unsteady, like a marionette with its strings cut. With every step I took backwards, an icy shiver ran down my spine. I heard the voices…echoing, calling my name, but I was stuck in a dark void.

No. No. No.

All I felt was pain, a physical stab in my chest. The tears blinding as I finally found my voice. It's like I inhaled for such a long time and let out a soul-crushing scream until I started coughing. But that didn't keep me from shrieking. I crumpled into a ball, a darkness surrounding me, knowing that I would never see my mother again. It had already been so long. He made sure I couldn't visit her. He took her from me!

I felt hands cover me and try to pull me from being bent over in anguish, but I couldn't. I experienced so much bad luck that it caused me to lose all hope and break down completely.

I was broken.

And although I knew they were trying to help, I only wanted Asher. He was my protection.

He would help me through this.

Chapter Thirty-Seven

Sam

PROTECTED
THE MERCILESS FEW MC: DEVIL'S IGNITED
Briarswood, Mass.

I finally got the strength to open my eyes. All I know is that it's nighttime and I'm in my bedroom. I hear the voices and know that my husband put me here. I know he doesn't know what to do and neither do I.

I have an inner fight between soul crushing guilt and uncontrollable rage. I couldn't wallow in pity. I have to pick myself up and bring my sister home. I know I can't have her buried next to Avery, but she can find peace at Vineyard Hills cemetery, not too far from here.

I throw the covers off and rub my eyes, still feeling weak from the shock of the news. Rocco walks in with a tray of food.

"Samantha Ann, back to bed. I will not argue with you on this. We will deal with all this in the morning."

I felt the sting of the tears as they fell. "She was my sister!"

I fell back and sobbed, so hard I couldn't breathe. He scoops me up into his arms. "I know babygirl, I know and we will do everything we can to have her buried here. I found your phone and called Phil and we have a plan. We can plead for post-mortem rights and gain the rights to her body, if we can prove abandonment, given her husband's absence, for at least a week. Phil said Kynlee is the legal beneficiary, so she'll inherit after the court case concludes. He said he'll put in all the other paperwork on your behalf and will call you in a couple of days."

Some glimmers of hope in what he said. The fact that no one at the hospital had seen Mike in a week made me curious.

He brings the tray closer. "I need you to eat something." Food was the furthest thing from my mind. "Where's Kynlee? I need to see her."

He blocks me and I feel that rage return. "Get out of my way!" He doesn't budge and I wail on him and his chest until I'm a sobbing wreck.

"I know…let it out. I promise you, Asher is taking care of her."

I know he is.

PROTECTED
THE MERCILESS FEW MC: DEVIL'S IGNITED
Briarswood, Mass.

I was completely unprepared for the chaos that awaited me as soon as Fiend screamed out we needed to get home ASAP. That Sam and Kynlee had just received some devastating news, and to make matters worse, Sam was unconscious on the floor! Lucifer never moved so fast, and I was right behind him.

We rode our bikes up to the door instead of parking them and immediately heard someone screaming. This prompted us to hurry inside, and upon entering, we found Sam lying on the ground, flickering in and out of consciousness. The girls frantically try to keep her awake.

Kynlee, my poor girl, lay on the floor, shattered and screaming for her mother. Desperate for answers, I searched for someone to explain the situation.

"Sam was on the phone and then she passed out! Kynlee

took the phone and collapsed! She's been screaming nonstop and she won't tell us what's wrong!"

Lucifer picked up Sam's phone. "Hello, who is this?! Uh huh…oh…no. Yeah, no, she's in a bad way, but we'll take care of both of them and I'll call you back later for details. Thanks, we got it from here."

Telling us that her sister died almost broke Boss Man. Our family had taken a devastating blow.

I approached Kynlee, my heart breaking as I heard her cry out in pain. It seemed like she couldn't catch a break. I lifted her up, and once she knew it was me, she clung so tightly. "I'm here, teddy bear. I'm right here."

Her excessive crying overheated her entire body, flushed her face red, and soaked her clothes with a mix of sweat and tears.

I removed all her clothes except her underwear to prevent her from getting sick, and then I put her to bed.

"Please, don't leave me!" She cried out while reaching for me. I pulled her to me, her body shaking, wracked with sobs. I wiped the tears away, but they kept coming.

I wanted to reassure her, to tell her everything would be alright, but what right did I have? I still had both parents and could only imagine what I would do if I got that call.

I'd be utterly inconsolable. She's stronger than I would be.

My priority, at this moment, is her well-being; ensuring she knows she's cared for.

After what seemed like hours, I glanced down and noticed she was fast asleep. It wasn't a peaceful slumber, though; it was more of a 'nothing left to give' exhaustive sleep.

I gently laid her down without waking her. With a heavy sigh, I eased the door open; the hinges creaking softly as I slipped out.

The atmosphere in the clubhouse was incredibly somber, and I couldn't help but feel sorry for the girls who were present and unsure of how to react. Wanting to offer some comfort, I give each of the girls a warm hug. "You guys did the right thing. Are you okay?"

Lila shook her head. "It gave Kitty and I bad flashbacks to when our parents died. I never want anyone to feel that type of earth-shattering pain, but unfortunately, we all will have to." This even affected our resident bad girl as she wiped the tears away, holding herself for comfort.

Kitty cleared her throat. "Kynlee's reaction was exactly like mine. I wailed for hours, so much that I couldn't talk for a week. I had literally damaged my vocal chords. I wouldn't wish this feeling on anyone. Don't let her go comatose or mute, Wicked. Talk her through it, no matter how tough it is. She needs you."

As I looked into their eyes, I could sense the pain that they both carried. It was a pain that my brother Fiend understood all too well. He, too, had lost his mother, and I could see a similar turmoil within him. He chose not to express it, but nodded silently to validate their shared understanding. It's a battle he continues to face, even to this very day.

Lucifer poked his head from the kitchen. "Hey, I'm making soup for Sam. Do you want me to split the pot?"

"Yes, please. Thank you." I was so lost at what to do, but I heed their words. Just be there.

"Asher? Asher!" I hear her scream with so much fear in her voice. I burst into my room to see her sat up with the blanket pulled up to her neck. Her eyes were wide. "I woke up, and… and… and you weren't here! I thought you were gone!"

"What?! No, I was getting you something to eat and drink. I was coming back."

She slumped back. "I'm not hungry. My life just went to shit! Both my parents are gone. I'm all alone." She whimpered.

I lean against the bed, and she immediately wraps her arms around me. "You were never alone. You have Sam and

Rocco and now a whole new family here. And you have me and I'm not going anywhere, teddy bear."

"I feel so numb, like, is it real? Is she really gone? A heart attack! I don't believe them! I put nothing past Mike. And…if he…. I'll…"

Overwhelmed with emotion, she struggled to explain her anger and threats towards her stepfather.

knock knock

Rocco walks in with a tray filled with soup, a plate of bread, a glass of water and a shot glass full of some brown liquor.

He kisses her forehead. "Hey sweetie, the shot is to calm your nerves. I want you to eat something, just a little for strength. I don't want to force you, but I need you and your auntie to get better so we can deal with the planning and details."

Tears welled in her eyes as she looked up, her lip quivering to the unbearable weight of grief. "How is she?"

"Not well, sweetie. But I'm going to do my best to nurse her back to health. Just like Asher will do with you. Get some rest, both of you."

He appeared extremely fatigued, deeply concerned about his wife. There was a flicker of hopelessness on his face, revealing that her condition might be more serious. I have never witnessed him losing his composure before.

Kynlee sighs. "She's taking this worse because she blames herself. I remember when I could visit mom she would tell me, 'One day you'll see your auntie again and I want you to tell her, no matter what happens, this was not her fault. I'm at peace and I am completely lucid. You hear me Kynlee Marie?' I knew she was. She loved to call me by my first and middle name to show she was in her right mind. And she was right, none of this is her fault or mine, it's…his and if I ever see him again I am going to bathe in his blood, do you hear me?! I want him to suffer because he did something or paid someone to make it look like a heart attack. She was in perfect health, minus her mental state. That fucking rat bastard is going to pay!"

And she meant it, her breaths coming in ragged gasps, her chest heaving so violently I thought she might faint. "Easy killer...I can't have you committing felonies. Let the legal system deal with him and then hopefully some prison justice."

"Aww, come on Asher, we all know the justice system is a dumpster fire of corrupted bullshit. If I do it, at least I'll be fucking thorough!"

"I know you want to exact revenge, but would she want you in prison for that scumbag? No. We'll all get together and create a plan, but right now, I need you to eat."

Tears replaced the smile she tried to muster as she looked up at me. "Thank you for caring."

I kissed her forehead and then, lifting her chin, gently kissed her lips, whispering, "Always."

She gave me hope she was on her way to healing by eating some soup and all her bread. She joked that she never turns down carbs. It was a glimmer to the silly girl I knew.

The way she held me was a different type of intimacy, and I knew I would be her peace. I adored this woman striving to live her life despite the obstacles.

"You're such a beautiful soul. I'm so lucky to have you in my life. I fall more and more every day." I nestled into her and drifted to sleep.

The next morning, everyone was pitching in on all the housework and cooking. To my surprise, I saw Kynlee wasn't in bed, so I went to find her and found her outside on the swing. The wind blowing her hair gently.

"Good morning. Are you okay?"

She didn't look my way. "Morning. I wouldn't say it was good. But earlier, an overwhelming sense of peace hit me. It felt as if I could hear my mom's voice, encouraging me to embrace the tranquility of outside. I know she's no longer in pain or in her mental prison. I even hope she's up there meeting baby Avery and anyone else from this family. Welcoming her with open arms. I think I'm going to be okay. She made sure of it."

I sit next to her and lace our fingers together, kissing her hand. "Uncle Rocco and Phil have been working all morning to figure out the next steps since we have that injunction on her will and policy. To tell you the truth, I don't even want the money, but I damn sure don't want Mike to have it. If I have to go back to testify, then so be it. He no longer has power over me. I won't live in fear anymore."

"Damn right, baby, because you have all of us." Another kiss to her hand. The sudden opening of the door startled me, and I saw Sam standing there. The utter despair etched on her face brought me to my feet. I placed my hands on her arms and pulled her into a tight hug. She sighed, "Thank you, my dear sweet boy. I need to talk to her alone, please."

"Absolutely. I love you."

She gave me a forced smile, but I knew what those words meant to her.

She is the heartbeat of this family and we were going to walk through the darkness with her.

Chapter Thirty-Nine

Sam

PROTECTED
THE MERCILESS FEW MC: DEVIL'S IGNITED
Briarswood, Mass.

The love and adoration I have from this family and what they've shown me in less than 24 hours proves how blessed I am. I fought my husband tooth and nail. I didn't want to eat or talk but the knucklehead, frustrated on how to help me, shed tears and it broke me.

He said that he was here for whatever I needed. He would drive me across the country back to Oklahoma if that's what I wanted him to do. He said I looked like I was ready to give up on life.

For a split moment, he was right. What right did I have to live when my sister died alone? Wondering where we were. I should have been there! I repeated and he let me cry in his arms but he countered with all those stories I told him about Chelsea and I. From our adventures in dad's car and rides to the quarry, sneaking into the movie theater because her boyfriend worked there, seeing movies we definitely weren't supposed to see.

"Your sister is alive through your memories and her daughter. "The special connection you and Kynlee share will see you both through this." I signal for a kiss and he happily obliges.

In the morning, after finally getting some sleep, I walked out to everyone pitching in and my heart was full.

Everyone gave me a small smile. "Thank you guys. I'm okay, I promise." That seemed to lighten the mood in the house. I didn't see Kynlee in all the activities. I looked out the window to see her talking to Asher.

She looked better and I can see he was being so attentive. Listening and assuring her with constant touch.

But she and I needed to talk. Rocco gave me the quick rundown of his talk with Phil. Seems like Phil put in the guardianship paperwork on my behalf, citing spousal abandonment and witness statements. He also pulled the electric bill to show no activity had been recorded in at least seven days, but it was more like weeks. There was a good chance she and I would need to go back to Tulsa and fight to not only bring Chelsea home but to make sure her insurance and will provisions go to her daughter and not that bastard.

When my son told me he loved me before he left, I truly felt it. I sat next to her, and she took my hand in hers. The sniffles start when I pat her hand. "You look so much like Chelsea, more so now than ever. I wanted you to know that we may have to go back."

"I know. But what if he shows up to contest?"

"He has no right! This whole situation is his fault! I would love for him to show his face, if you know what I mean."

"I do. Asher told me that mom wouldn't appreciate me going to prison and I will say the same to you."

I groan. I really wanted him dead. "Fine, for your sake. I'll call Phil to get the exact court date and we'll go."

"Auntie, I have a really sensitive question to ask you. Something I've been thinking about all morning."

"Alright?"

"Do you think… after being locked away for so long that mom would want to be confined in another box?"

I sat there for a moment to really digest those words. As a child, Chelsea was a free spirit. She was the tire swing, flipping into the lake, riding down the hill without protection, girl. A true tomboy at heart. Her spirit needed to soar, and her child knew that.

I nodded in an unspoken agreement.

Kynlee and I spent the next week and a half gathering everything we could or would need to fight any stipulations put into place. We already overturned him being the sole beneficiary. We would go to the circuit or probate court to get the official decree before contacting my sister's bank and insurance company. We'd transfer the funds to a local bank here in Briarswood.

"Auntie, it's time to go! Flight's in four hours." I grab my duffel bag and see everyone in the living room.

"Well, wish us luck. Take care of each other." I hug everyone.

"We will. You bring your sister home so we can honor her memory." Demon hugs me super tight. My wild child being affectionate? That's quite unexpected, but I appreciate his kind words.

Asher held Kynlee tightly, giving her kisses like a reserve. When she told him she and I would go alone, he and Bubba flipped! We explained it was only for a couple of days and we'd be with Phil the whole time. Our flight was early enough to get stuff done when we landed, attend the hearing, have dinner, and be on our way back the next afternoon.

I hear Asher try his last pleads, "But baby, I just don't like the circumstances! I'd feel much better if I were there to protect you."

She kissed him quickly to short circuit his argument. "It's two days, today and tomorrow. I'll be fine, I promise. If you're good, I'll treat you to…" And she whispered in his ear. He squeezed her sides, and she jumped while squealing. I know what she offered. It's the same thing I had to promise Bubba, so he would let me go. He demanded to drive us to the airport, and I agreed.

The flight was uneventful, but stepping outside of the airport, I felt a looming sense of dread. Everything about this town was full of negativity and bad energy. My best memories now live in my head.

I took a deep breath, then shivered. "Now I remember why I left."

"I told you." She said.

A blue SUV pulls up in front and Phill steps out, hugging us both. "Samantha, Kynlee, so glad you made it safely. I'm sorry it wasn't under better circumstances. You both have my deepest sympathies."

"Thank you Phil. We couldn't have done this without you. We don't have much time, so what's the first task?"

"Depends on how strong you feel." He stayed quiet. I knew what he meant, and so did Kynlee. Her breathing hitched, but then she squared her shoulders.

"Let's go get mom."

A 20-minute ride and we're parked outside the Pasadena Villa Outpatient Center. The once pristine pictures of a gleaming, modern facility were now replaced with a disheveled and dilapidated institution. The sight of it alone evoked images of decaying asylums depicted in bone-chilling horror movies, sending shivers down my spine. Anger surged through me, fueled by the realization of the suffering my sister endured within these walls, subjected to inept staff and subpar treatments.

"I ought to burn this piece of shit facility to the ground! Phil, I want you to file a complaint with the state board about this place. There's no way they are compliant. No…my sister suffered here." I clenched my hands into fists. "Let's get her out of here."

I was even more infuriated by how right I was. Mike chose this inferior facility as another form of punishment and control. The sounds of screaming, bloodcurdling screaming echoed through the hallways. The air carries a musty, stale odor, as if the place has been abandoned for years, except the areas that smell strongly of urine. I could hear the creaking of the worn-out floorboards under my feet, a haunting symphony of neglect.

I demanded to speak to the facilitator, and I laid into him and was just shy of coming across that desk of his. Phil caught me, but I told him I would plaster his face and this facility across the news, have his license revoked, and to expect to hear from the state board. I left him pissing in his pants like his patients.

He will pay for my sister and all the other families that had to bury their family members unexpectedly.

We went down to the chilly space of the morgue. Luckily, they followed our instructions, placing her in a beautiful maroon and gold urn that I paid Phil to buy. Kynlee sobbed while smiling, finally able to hold her mother again even in the most heartbreaking of circumstances.

She hugged it so tight. "Hi mom, I'm here to take you home. I-I miss you so much. I'm sorry, sorry I didn't do everything I could!" The same guilt she told me not to feel fell on her like a torrential rain.

"Hey, no…like you told me, this is not your fault. She wouldn't want you to feel this way. We have her now and we're going home. Now let's head to the courthouse."

"Okay."

I truly believe our physical presence helped our case. The urn was a grim and stark reminder of what the court allowed to happen to her. Like a true coward, Mike didn't show, and we found out some things the facility turned in as testimony. Like he actually had not physically been to the hospital in six months! It was mandatory that he check in with the facility once a week for a report out. It was originally a physical requirement, but he created some cock and bull story he was traveling for business and they compromised with telephone calls. The calls only lasted about two to three minutes and they called that sufficient.

The fact is, Mike hadn't been in the home for weeks, at least! Phil searched his usual spots, the bars, the strip club, that seedy motel right outside of town. No one had seen him except this hooker named Iris. She said he said something about taking care of business and paying off his debts soon with a windfall.

We stepped into the house and the stale, gross smell confirmed all the claims. Kynlee went to grab some of her things that she couldn't in haste, including several pictures of her and her mom and a mini photo album with pictures of all of us.

Then she stomped her foot. "That bastard stole my jewelry! Including the pearl earrings you gave me when I was five. Thank goodness mom put her jewelry in a safe at the bank. And yet still! ARGH!"

He had stolen everything valuable out of the house to pay off his debt to keep himself alive.

She put what she had in her bag. "Let's close this chapter of my life, please."

I pulled out my lighter and flicked a beautiful flame that could wipe away the abuse and pain, but it was missing his half-dead, bloodily beaten body in the middle of the living room.

I smiled at her. "Absolutely."

I went to turn off the lights but remember he didn't pay the bill, so I shut the door.

The next day, we transferred the bank funds to Kynlee's

new account, collected her mother's belongings from the safe deposit box, and stopped by the insurance office to give them the information they needed for the payout.

By 3 pm we were heading back to the airport. A chapter closed for my niece and onward to endless possibilities for her.

All my family was coming home.

Chapter Forty

Kynlee

PROTECTED
THE MERCILESS FEW MC: DEVIL'S IGNITED
Briarswood, Mass.

I didn't want to scare Aunt Sam, but I saw a piece of paper in mom's room. I recognized his poor handwriting. It looked like a checklist.

Have her committed
Stage accident to collect insurance money
Make sure will has my name on it, not daughter
If all else fails, kill the daughter, claim familial grievance as sole heir
Pay off debt
Move to the Bahamas

Kill, he was going to kill me had I not ran in the cover of night! Now all those threatening texts from so far away didn't seem so ridiculous. This piece of paper literally said it.

Hearing her move around, possibly closer to the room, I shoved it in my pocket.

Maybe I wasn't as safe as I thought I was in Massachusetts. And that means that everyone was in danger.

Including Asher.

Chapter Forty-One
Asher aka Wicked

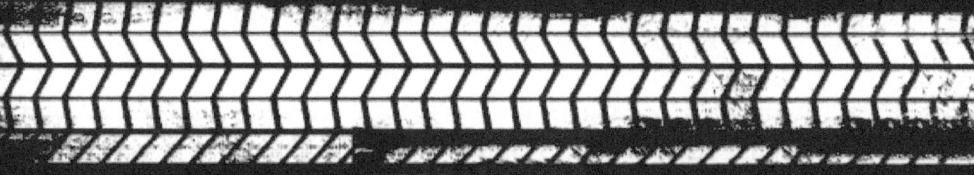

PROTECTED
THE MERCILESS FEW MC: DEVIL'S IGNITED
Briarswood, Mass.

I slept horribly without the warmth of my teddy bear. She reassured me with texts and calls goodnight, but I never felt she was 100% safe. Something always felt off.

Lucifer went to go pick them up. I hated that the truck only legally fit three people. It's not like we haven't broken that rule before when Reap and Fiend brought Avi and Raven home from the hospital, but that was a few minutes' drive, not two hours. I offered to ride behind him, but he countered that it would put an extreme amount of stress on my body. He was right. Even now, I can only comfortably ride for an hour or less. On long rides, we take multiple breaks to break up the tension.

So here I am, pouting until she's in my arms again.

"Let's talk, baby brother, because it's inevitable and you're just drawing it out." Demon says, passing me a beer.

"What are you talking about?"

"It's the same story written in a different font, every single time. Reaper with Avi, Fiend with Poppy, look my stomach can't take all these emotions."

I laugh hard. He looks nauseated even talking about emotion. "You lost me, bro."

"I see the way you look at her. It started on day one when you were cooking together. It was so innocent, but I saw the spark. You all get the spark and god willing, that spark never finds me. You never once had that spark or look with the twins. That was truly carnal pleasure, but Kynlee, there's so much emotion. I'm no Lila, the love doctor, but I'd like to get one up on her by saying, brother, you have fallen in love."

I damn near choked on my beer. I wouldn't dare spit it out, so I forced it down. "This is such an uncomfortable conversation to have with all people, you."

"Am I wrong though?" He arrogantly sips, waiting for my answer.

I spent the two days holed up in my room thinking about that. I didn't want to hang out, go drinking, and damn sure didn't want to go to Throttle to get my fix. I wanted to watch movies, or sit at the lake, or just lie in bed together and listen to her talk, or even better, watch her sleep. Sleep so comfortably in my arms.

He was right; I was in love.

I looked up, and he was grinning like a Cheshire cat. "Alright, Doctor Demon, I admit it. I love her. Now what do I do?" I regret asking that question to him, but he holds his hand up.

"I know I'm the last person to ask that to, but I think I can try. I am your big brother and all."

"Oh, brother."

"You see, she's vulnerable right now after losing her mom. Her emotions are all over the place and even though she has been living here, today marks the first official day of her life in

Briarswood. You commit to helping her every step of the way and she will grow. You got a big heart, knucklehead." He punches me in the arm. A form of affection that isn't sadistic or masochistic. I decided to return the wisdom.

"Remember those words next time Kitty is around and really pay attention." His eyes went wide before he rolled them. "Yeah, sure." He waves me off. I know when he falls, he's going to fall like a mighty oak.

I glance at my watch. They should have landed and are on their way home. Now that I had something to confess, I wanted to make the moment special.

"I have a phone call to make."

Two hours later, and with some tidying, I was ready. I heard the old truck backfire. I stepped out of my room, trying to keep my cool, but I was nervous.

Lucifer came in with Sam's bag and I think Kynlee's as well. Sam was holding an urn, and I realized it was her sister. She smiled when she saw us, but it didn't quite meet. She was trying to be strong.

I couldn't wait and met Kynlee outside. I picked her up and slid her down enough to kiss her, then set her down. "I missed you, teddy bear."

"I missed you, too!"

"I have a surprise for you. Do you want to see it?"

She playfully pushed me. "What a silly question, of course I do."

I lace our fingers and walk inside. The music was on, but not full blast. Boss Man had taken residence in his lay-z-boy with Sam nestled into him. No words, just simple touches like rubbing her thigh and her tugging on his beard as they shared kisses, and that spoke volumes about how much they missed each other.

Leading the way, I walked us to our door and then stopped. "This pretty much sums up how much you mean to me. You didn't judge and saw the real me, not that egotistical bullshit. I never had someone so caring, so sweet. Someone, no matter what she's been through, only wants to make the world shine. You've brightened my world and, beyond this door, tells it all. I hope you like it. Open it."

She kissed my cheek. "Okay."

She stepped in and gasped at what she saw.

"Oh my goodness, Asher. It's beautiful!"

I kiss her temple. "You're beautiful."

I watched her take everything in, including the six dozen Dublin bay and black ice red roses I had expressed delivered. I set the vases on every flat surface and broke a few down to spread the petals everywhere. With the roses, I bought four balloons that all relayed the same message.

She gasps again. "You love me?"

When I turn her to face me, I see tears of joy, not the sadness she had been enduring.

"Asher?" She waited for confirmation.

I brush my hand against her face before gripping her chin. "I do. I love you Kynlee Marie."

She gasped. "Oh! Wait! I don't know your middle name." Her eyes pleading.

"Ugh, Thomas."

"And I love you Asher Thomas!" She slams her lips against mine. I groaned to my middle name, but it quickly turned into a moan when she jumped and wrapped her legs around me. I grip her ass, trying to keep my balance. I take a few steps and fall backwards on the bed, the petals flying everywhere. A couple tangled in her hair. I gently picked them out.

She sits up, straddling my lap. "Mmm, tell me again." I saw that spark, that playfulness in her eyes.

I sat up to pull her shirt off. She responds by pulling mine off. "I love you." Giving her what she wanted to hear.

That seemed to rev her engine as she lifted up to fiddle with my belt behind her, but I flipped her and laid her on the bed. "No need to rush. We have the whole night."

I slipped her bra off to feel the warmth of her breasts pinching her nipples. "Yesssss…" She whimpered.

The friction was driving me mad. I hadn't felt the touch of her skin, heard her sweet gasps and moans in days, and it was this moment that made me realize how much I needed her. Our connection was like a drug.

I can see lust in her eyes. The room, dimly lit, cast a soft glow on our bodies. The air filled with the sound of our breaths intertwining, caught in a whirlwind of desire. Her motions increased and her breathing quickly picked up.

She's chasing her orgasm already, but I guide her hips to go slower, to take control. "Slow down, my little teddy bear… were you going to rub yourself to pleasure without my help? Did you miss me that much? Did you fantasize about this, touching yourself to my voice, whispering in your ear, telling you how good you taste, baby? Or did you imagine my lips on yours, my hands exploring every inch of you?"

"There's that arrogance."

I kiss her hand. "Never arrogant. I'm confident the woman that I love loves me and life is that much sweeter." She leans forward. "I do love you. In my toughest moments, you were there."

I lean up, her hands on my chest, "Always. Now, for your punishment for letting another man's wandering hands all over you…lay down."

She looked so confused. "But… it was Aunt Sam's idea!"

The haunting reality is she had just brought her mother home in an urn. I wanted to comfort her.

Her head must be a torrent of emotions she doesn't know how to express, but she knows sex would convey some sort of outlet.

"But baby, I was ready…" She whined as I guided her off my lap and onto the bed.

"You're always ready. Let me treat you to my world famous massage." I grab the gel lotion from my dresser.

She settled in. "World famous, huh? How many others have been privy to this massage?"

Now that she mentioned it, I realize..."None, actually. You're my first."

"Then how can it be world famous?" She giggled.

"Because you'll be the one to tell everyone just how good I am."

She got comfortable, laying her head down. I rub my hands so they're warm before putting the gel in my hands. I start at her feet and she jumps, giggling but fisting her hands. She's ticklish. She endures as I make my way up her legs. I could see her physically relaxing and eventually once I was massaging her lower back, her hands fell open. My face was hovering above her ass, and I noticed she was soaking wet. I inhaled the scent of her and she wiggled in response. I raise up and tag her ass. "Don't tempt me. Patience."

She huffed and shrugged her shoulders. "Worth a shot."

She'd get what she wanted; she just didn't know when. After massaging her neck and shoulders, I pretended as if I was going to continue the massage down her back to her feet, but that wasn't my intention. Once I slid backward past the hump of her ass, I rubbed my hard erection before sliding myself forward, filling her like she had been begging me for. I held her wrists down, giving me the advantage of getting balls deep.

"That's it, baby. Is that what you wanted? Hmm? Answer me."

I could tell by her moans, but I needed her to focus elsewhere and stop squeezing me so hard because I wouldn't be able to hold on much longer.

"Yes, I missed feeling you inside me so much. It feels... ohh...so good. Please...please..." She begged.

I released my grip on one wrist, allowing my fingers to weave through the strands of her hair. As I pulled her closer, the taste of her lips mingled with the faint scent of her perfume, heightening my senses. I flipped her over and positioned myself. She was even wetter, sending shivers down my spine. She came hard and fast, gripping the sheets, pulling them to her mouth to scream into them. I felt the warmth enveloping me as she toppled over in pleasure. Giving her no time to relax, I pulled out, diving face first into her pussy, savoring the intoxicating taste of her orgasm, a guilty pleasure that worked me to climax in my hand as she was about to cum again.

"Mmm…more…" I anxiously listened for those anticipated words to escape her lips. "I'm so close… again, please..." The air was heavy with anticipation. I positioned myself swiftly, the sheets rustling beneath me. As I entered her, the friction was almost unbearable, sending shivers down my spine. My pace was deliberate, almost agonizingly slow, teasing her senses. Her walls clenched and released, a rhythmic dance of pleasure mingling with the soft sighs and moans that escaped her lips. I resisted the urge to speed up, determined to synchronize our climax. Her moans grew more urgent, enticing me to go faster, but I maintained the steady rhythm. I could feel my body responding, the throbbing, the telltale signs of my impending release. Her pleasure teetered on the edge, aching to topple over into bliss.

"You ready, baby? Cum with me." With a gentle touch, I caressed her, feeling her beneath my fingertips. Now the room filled with the intoxicating scent of passion and desire, mingling with the determination of climax.

"There, right there!" Her body accepted her fate.

"Cum for me, baby. Squeeze my dick, just like that… yeah…" As she came, her body trembled with an intensity that ignited a fire within me, giving me one of my strongest orgasms. In that moment of shared pleasure, our connection deepened.

"Oh god!" She curled up into the fetal position, panting

heavily. I leaned back and pulled her towards me, noticing her hand resting between her legs.

"Why is your hand on your pussy?"

"It's still trembling. In-internal orgas-orgasm. I think you broke it." We both laugh. Never had that happen before. The old chauvinistic me would wear that as a badge of honor. Immediately bragging to the guys of my accomplishment.

Now, I was proud I brought her pleasure and it'll be my goal to do it every time. "Well...I can kiss it and make it better."

"That's what got me here in the first place! You've done quite enough. Just hold me, it'll stop."

I did as she asked, and she sighed. "Scratch my scalp, please." She mumbled, her head tilted back in expectation. I lightly rake my nails on her scalp.

Chapter Forty-Two
Kynlee

PROTECTED
THE MERCILESS FEW MC: DEVIL'S IGNITED
Briarswood, Mass.

All my pain and suffering with Mike means nothing now that I know I have a man who loves me.

I thought it was silly to think Mike could touch me. I was safe and deeply in love with my bad boy biker. He's actually a big teddy bear, even though he claims me as his own. Maybe I should give him a nickname too!

"Hey."

My gaze drifted back to meet his. "The bike ride is in five days. Do you want to ride with me?"

"Are you kidding me?! To be your backpack! Absolutely."

He chuckles, and I was curious why. "Oh, that's actually Fiend's nickname for Poppy. Odd, but suits them perfectly."

"I'll have to get the perfect outfit. I'm thinking leather…or maybe lace? Definitely fishnets." I caught his breathing hitch.

He was thinking about the possibilities. He squeezed me, causing me to yelp.

"All that sounds sexy. Just make sure you wear high-top sneakers or boots so you don't get burned accidentally by the exhaust. These long rides increase the chances."

"Yes, sir…" I purr while rocking against him to tease.

He growled, then nibbled on my ear. "Careful. Your pussy just stopped quivering." His hand traced between my breasts, down my stomach as I anticipated him, but he left his hand on my hip.

Tease.

I swallowed hard and my pussy throbbed like his voice commanded it to. He was dangerous.

Then I changed the subject. "So, what is the decided charity event this year?"

"I think we're just sticking to the car/bike wash and providing food again. Lucifer doesn't want to overwhelm Sam too much. He knows you two are still dealing with the loss."

"It will be a much-needed distraction for us. Keep my mind off of the will and insurance payout fiasco. If Phil hadn't found out about mom's safe deposit box at the bank, we would have never known he altered everything to make himself sole beneficiary. Now we have the original copy and I think Aunt Sam's going to talk to the police on pressing charges for forgery, among other things. Oh, and we found out something very interesting, not surprising though because he's a low down slimy snake. It turns out Mike has pulled this con three times before!"

He looked confused. "Done what before?"

"Find vulnerable women to manipulate. He would do whatever it takes to get access to their money and bleed them dry. But my mom was the only one he actually married. It was because he found her insurance and will paperwork and he saw the amount. My mom would be his golden ticket. He would live the life and never have to work again. Not like he worked anyway!" She huffed.

"Her mental issues were the cherry on top. To push the 'she isn't well' agenda. The concerned husband looking out for his wife's wellbeing. What a crock of shit!"

He rubbed my arm, and I relaxed again. "Sorry. I don't want to talk about him anymore. He's gone. Everything my mom earned now goes to me, and I have a plan to honor her memory."

I could see he was curious. "What do you want to do with the money?"

"That's a good question. It really is. I have some thoughts, but nothing set in stone."

"That's okay. You have nothing but time. Now, get some rest." He kissed my forehead, and I felt at peace.

Later, my phone buzzed, causing me to open one eye. An icy chill ran down my back. Asher was lying on his back, giving me space to reach for it. The space between us seemed to disappear, and the devil was at my door. Or on my phone.

I sit up a bit, readying my response to leave me alone or else and I would mean it!

I am temporarily blinded by the bright screen. My eyes finally adjust to see:

Hey, it's Cathy. Just checking in on you. Please let me know if you are safe.

I sighed in relief. I almost forgot about Cathy, my old coworker. She was a sweet, older lady. We ran into her when we were in town. I let her know I had moved to Massachusetts to be with my family. I sent a quick response, realizing I forgot to set my phone to Do Not Disturb. But before I could, I saw the voicemail icon. Even if you block the number, they can still leave voicemails. I click the icon and see it's 26 seconds long. It's him, it's definitely him. I get this uneasy feeling as I press play.

"I see you've become quite the whore now. You thought I

wouldn't find you? I'm going to make sure you never see a dime of what's mine! Maybe I'll gut your little boyfriend, too. The next time I call, you better answer for instructions or people will die. You wouldn't want that for your precious family now, do you?"

And the click to end the call. I clutch my chest because he knows where I am. He knows about Asher and everyone else.

No one is safe.

I unintentionally put everyone in danger. I felt trapped but desperate for my happiness here in Briarswood.

I felt like I was being watched and I didn't sleep a wink, clutching my phone just in case he called.

I couldn't miss it.

Chapter Forty-Three
Sam

PROTECTED
THE MERCILESS FEW MC: DEVIL'S IGNITED
Briarswood, Mass.

I busied myself, burying myself in the details and a to-do list for the after rally celebration. I gathered up the buckets and hoses and tons of soap for the car/bike wash. We even made signs where to get washed and where to park so they dry. Although I am not lathering up my tits for a good cause, I am dressed for it, wearing shorts as a compromise to Bubba.

We decided to repeat last year's BBQ to take things easy on me and Kynlee after our loss. I explained we were okay, but everybody insisted. I promised next time would be an absolute blowout with all the bells and whistles.

I checked the deep freezer to make a note of everything we already had. I gave the boys a much shorter list than last year. You should have seen the relief on their faces. It should only take one trip.

The bunnies, Kynlee included, were cutting and chopping

potatoes for fries and potato salad, onions, lettuce, and tomatoes for the burgers. The guys had every cut of meat available to bbq to perfection. After being told to relax again, I sent Demon and Reaper out to grab six sheet cakes and 12 pies and let them choose the flavors. I gave Reaper the responsibility. I did not trust Demon. He'd pick something awful like banana flavored.

I fill two pots with water and ask Wicked to put the heavy stockpots on the stove. "Thank you, my strong, handsome man!" He kissed his biceps. "Of course." This was not the same boy that I saw years ago, so excited to be a part of this organization. No, after living the bachelor life and having his heart broken unexpectedly, he really took his relationship with Kynlee to another level. He treasured and valued her, and I saw a younger version of Rocco and me in them. Caring and attentive, I could not be happier.

The morning of the ride, I checked myself out in the mirror. I decided not to go too overboard. A plain black t-shirt under my cut and the agreed upon shorts with my boots. I wore my bikini top underneath as a surprise.

Kynlee, though, was being an absolute menace! She had dressed and left their room before he could see her. She had on a bikini top and cropped blue jean jacket, leather shorts, fishnets, and motorcycle boots. A perfect outfit to tease him and show that we had some of the most beautiful girls in the Merciless Few organization. "I'm going to take pictures with Stormy. I'll be right back!"

"Alright!"

Chapter Forty-Four
Kynlee

PROTECTED
THE MERCILESS FEW MC: DEVIL'S IGNITED
Briarswood, Mass.

I hope to make Asher proud. I know it wasn't a competition, but he was a handsome specimen and they needed to know he was off limits. Lil taught me that.

I slipped out of our room when he went to take a shower, but everyone else saw me.

"Hot damn Kynlee! Are you trying to kill the man?" Demon said while staring a little too long.

"Now that's a Merciless Few bunny! Hot as fuck!" Lil said while smacking my ass. I look to see what Aunt Sam thought. "Looking good, but you were always beautiful to me."

Suddenly I heard the shower stop, my plan!

"I'm going to take pictures with Stormy. I'll be right back!"

I ran out toward the barn. She was beautiful as the rays of sunlight poked through the cracks of the roof. "Well, Stormy, I

219

hope I did you justice." I did a little turn for approval. I smile, "I think so, too. Us together is going to blow his mind. Then...maybe I'll blow him while he's leaning against you? Sounds like a plan since he took my other fantasy." I position myself on her and begin taking selfies, making sure they're as sexy as possible. I even take a few pics flashing him before quickly covering up.

I remembered how he stated that being with the twins was a threesome every night. I was going to give him a different kind of tryst with me riding him while he lays across Stormy. No girl got more attention than the other and we both got time with him. I bit my lip, fantasizing.

Tonight might be fun.

Chapter Forty-Five
Asher aka Wicked

PROTECTED
THE MERCILESS FEW MC: DEVIL'S IGNITED
Briarswood, Mass.

It's the day of the ride and I am super excited. There's something about leading the hundreds of brothers and sisters in attendance. Plus, I got my girl riding behind me.

Even though it's my usual outfit, today it seems more badass. I threw on my cologne and the chain my mom got me for my 18th birthday. I called to check in and when I told her about the ride; she sounded excited for me but she couldn't help but to tell me to be careful.

The house is way louder than usual. We were the last available bathroom before the ride, so the early arrivals were taking advantage. I brush past my brothers from the New Jersey chapter. On their cuts they have this huge blazing Phoenix on fire, easy to spot them. I see my group in the kitchen hanging out. The calm before the roar of freedom!

I see Kynlee, who already locked eyes on me. They were

full of mischief. I approach her slowly. She has her hands behind her back, swaying, causing her tits to move in that barely legal bikini top. I really take in the outfit. She's a 20 out of ten on the sexy meter.

"Fucking hell, baby." I take her hand to spin her, realizing that this is in fact her outfit for the carwash. I growl and she laughs.

"It's for charity, baby. I promise you that later I have a special treat for you."

My brows raise, caging her in and stealing kisses.

"Oh brother, get a room!" I look over to see Avi and Poppy giggling like schoolgirls. I see Lil is with them, so no doubt she spilled all the tea about us. At least I knew Kynlee has a strong group of girls as friends and family.

She slips from my grasp. "Later." She joins the girls. I resign to pull Stormy out and set her behind Prez's fiery red beauty.

There are a good number of groups I recognize. Like the New York chapter, those crazy bastards. The only chapter to have a drive-by happen during festivities. I hope they kept that back home. Then there's Boston, Philly, hmm, even the Detroit chapter. Didn't know if they would show after one of their members died in an accident. In memory of him, they display his biker name on their vests.

I know HQ is coming, but there's still a few hours for them to show. I see Everett and his group, formerly known as The Ace of Spades, he renamed The Wild Aces to start fresh. He came by last week to ask for permission to ride, one because Lil was a Merciless Few bunny and two to mend the wounds his leader made. Fiend was understandably suspicious as Hell. He screamed about what he lost, what they both lost and the physical and emotional scars she has because of his President. He was damn near in tears, but it was a cleanse he needed. Everett took the brunt of his hatred but also reminded him that everyone present was not involved, or even in town. He

THE MERCILESS FEW MC ANTHOLOGY: PROTECTED

apologized profusely for what his former President did and he did not condone it. He also gave his word as a man that he would never hurt Lil. Her loyalty is with us and he respected her decision.

He's an all-around great guy.

"Everett. Wait, did you finally pick out club names? Because calling you by your government name is weird."

"Yeah, it's Maverick, Tex, Duke, and Austin. Are you ready for the run?"

"Those are bad ass names! As always, now you can see how the big boys roll. I'm glad you guys are here...Maverick."

I see him beam with pride when he looks at his guys. What a President should be.

"There's so many chapters! We're just sitting here trying to guess what they're like, their persona."

"What do you mean?"

He points at a group under the tree. I squint and see they are the Maine chapter. I know all about them.

"I can tell, those bastards are crazy! They look like they shoot first, then ask questions. The guy licking the knife only proves my point. Who the hell does that?" He shuddered, and they laughed.

"Good eye, Maine is a 1% club of down right psychos, however if you respect them they might let you live. Might." They all went silent, and Everett swallowed hard. "Fuck."

"Yeah, but in peaceful times, they're cool people. Anyone else you think you got figured out?"

He looks around and points to a group chilling near the tree line. "Now they seem like a new chapter, the way they are looking around and observing. They look nervous. They're probably new because they don't have any patches.

I observed them. None of them were actually sitting on their bikes, which was weird. They were leaning against the tree. "Hmm, must be new. The next newsletter comes out next week. Maybe HQ will introduce them then." I shrug. I noticed they're all looking our way while still talking. I did not feel the need to walk over there and introduce myself.

I head toward the barn to pull out my Stormy. I turn the corner and…

She's not there! What the fuck! I was not in the mood for any pranks, especially when it came to my bike! Now I'm pissed! I'm going to kill Demon!

I look around, and I see her at the back of the barn near the other exit.

Now that I know she's here, I chuckle. I go to retrieve her but slow my stride as I get closer I notice a flaw, an imperfection in the form of a long scratch mark across her beautiful paint job.

"What the actual fuck?!" I was hot! Somebody vandalized my beautiful girl!

I turned to go find who did this…

bam

I'm fading in and out of consciousness.

"Bring the van back here and load him up."

"How do you know this will work?"

"She'll sign anything over to save his pathetic life. Now let's go! Leave the note for her to find. She won't let him die. I'll get that money and her."

Chapter Forty-Six

Kynlee

PROTECTED
THE MERCILESS FEW MC: DEVIL'S IGNITED
Briarswood, Mass.

I asked Demon to use the mirror in his room to check my outfit one more time because the bathroom line was nothing short of chaos.

I walked in casually but stopped short. He has a literal dungeon in here! I thought it was just talk. Is that a St. Andrew's Cross?! I never saw one in real life before!

I wonder if he'll let us rent it? On second thought, even if we clean it…it'll never be clean. It needs holy water. I laugh to myself. There's a full-length mirror in the corner opposite the lower bed. Of course he watched himself!

I straighten my bikini and make sure my girls are safe. Can't give them a free show. I pull my lipstick out to freshen it up. I was ready for my inaugural Merciless Few charity ride!

When I go to the kitchen, nobody's in there, so I make my way outside. Everyone's talking and getting ready. Some people are showing off their bikes, revving them, the mating call of the truly depraved. It gave me goosebumps. Uncle Rocco is talking to the group from Maryland, easily identified by their state flag. It was…colorful.

Wicked isn't with him. Poppy and Avi are filling the buckets with soap and water. Of course, Poppy is sitting down with the hose. She's absolutely beautiful and glowing. I'm glad she's been blessed with another baby after Avery.

Hmm, no Wicked, where was he?

I make my way through the crowd. The further I went, the more I felt dread. I was halfway from the house and barn when my phone rang. Not a text message, but a phone call from an unknown number and I knew…

I didn't speak when I hit answer.

"Hello Kynlee, long time no hear." His voice instantly made me nauseous.

I felt the tears forming along with the lump in my throat.

"You know why I'm calling. Go into the barn, now!"

I cautiously stepped in, fearing he would be standing there, waiting.

"Go to the back."

I walk to the back to see a switch blade stabbed into the seat. And poor Stormy, someone used that blade to scratch her across her beautiful custom paint job!

I know Asher is pissed!

I remembered I was on the call. "You don't deserve a fucking penny after what you did to my mom! You can threaten me all you want, but I'll never give you a dime! You should be dead!"

He tsked. "Careful who you wish dead, darling. You will give me the money or some very bad guys are going to hurt your little boy toy. Isn't that right?"

My ears tune in to muffled noises. Then someone screamed. "Kynlee, baby, don't! Oof!" Then he grunts and groans a few times…he's trying not to cry out in pain, but they're tormenting him!

"Stop! Please!"

"He can really take a punch, but how many more? Is his life worth more than money?"

"Yes! Please stop hurting him!" I'm sobbing at this point. I fell to my knees, defeated.

"You're going to meet me at the location I just sent. And you're going to come alone…or else! You have 30 minutes! If you're followed, I'll make sure he suffers an excruciating death."

Then he hung up, giving me no time to respond. I sat there for a few moments in shock, trying to absorb what happened. I check my messages and see an unread message. It's the old candy factory outside of town. We've driven past a few times. It's also in the middle of nowhere. How can I get out of here without being seen?

I pull my hair in frustration. I checked my watch. I wasted three minutes! Screw it! I didn't have time! I storm out, pushing through the crowd and grabbing the truck keys. I angrily wipe the tears away as I aggressively start her up. People quickly clear a path for me.

I can hear my name, but I don't have time to explain.

I have to save him!

Chapter Forty-Seven
Sam

PROTECTED
THE MERCILESS FEW MC: DEVIL'S IGNITED
Briarswood, Mass.

"Kynlee! Kynlee!" But she kept going, into the truck, then she peeled out of here! Did she and Asher have a fight? I look all around for him to get some answers. Bubba comes to me, the boys follow. "What was that about?"

"I-I don't know! Asher, did you guys have a…" I stopped noticing that Asher wasn't with us. "Asher? Have you guys seen him?"

"I thought he went to grab his bike for the lineup." Reaper said, and they nodded. I lead the way toward the barn and through it. I stop in my tracks when I see his bike seat has a giant knife stabbed into the seat!

"Bubba!" He rushes up to me and I point to it. He pulls the knife from the seat, looking around. The boys started looking around the barn.

He looks at me. I already know what he's going to say. "Don't you dare tell me to be calm right now!"

"Babygirl, you're no help if you panic. We don't know what's going on."

But I do. It screams this bastard's M.O.

"Are you fucking kidding me? It's Mike! He has them, or he has Asher and threatened her to come wherever they are. He wants that money and he followed her back here to get it! And you know she will! She loves that boy so much and doesn't want to see him hurt!" Just the thought of him suffering causes me to break down. My boy's in trouble and we don't know where he is.

"Hey, is this her phone?"

I look to see Fiend with her phone, covered in dirt and dust. I knew from the heart sticker where she crudely scribbled their initials on it. She must have dropped it! I grab it and am relieved she doesn't have screen lock. I go into the messages and see an unsaved number.

The last message is where she's going.

Bubba leans forward. "I know that place. It's an old factory. But wait, let me confirm…"

He pulls out his phone and logs into an app. A black and green grid map opens up and four green dots are blinking close to each other. He zooms out further and further until he locates another dot. He presses it and it gives coordinates.

"I knew it wasn't that easy. That is not the factory, he's somewhere else. Kynlee's headed into a trap."

"Let's go!" I screamed.

"No way, sweetness. We will handle this…"

"Rocco Samuel Perez, I will not stand here and wait! That motherfucker killed my sister and now has my niece and is going to do god knows what! If anyone causes his last breath, it's going to be me!"

I am seething and all I can see is red! The boys have never seen me like this.

"Boss Man, let's take her with us. She's right, she needs to see this to the end."

I look to see all my boys agreeing. My husband, not so much.

He growls in frustration, "Fine, but you stay behind me. We need to pass off the lead for the ride to HQ and give them a short rundown. They'll all want to help and that could hinder. Let's go."

In 15 minutes, we had notified HQ what was happening and that the event could go on as planned. They volunteered some of their guys to stay back and guard the house and start the grills. The girls are absolutely horrified when we tell them what is happening, especially Poppy seeing that she has gone through something similar. Fiend comforted her, and she gave him a hopeful smile.

"To the basement, strap up. Make it heavy, we're not going 1%. We're going 0.1%"

I know that first term. He's only announced that one other time with the Ace of Spades fiasco, but 0.1%? That's a threshold I never thought I would see my boys shift into. It's so rare it's almost unheard of.

"Come on babygirl, you're strapping up."

It was an exception that I'm allowed to go down there. I am amazed at the arsenal located just below our feet. Holy shit!

He hands me a holster; I put it on and he hands me his vintage chrome twin 9mms.

"These are your prized possessions!"

He tilted my chin. "No, you... are my prized possession. I know you can handle your own, but please, Samantha, don't let emotion override logic."

He kisses me, and it calms the rage momentarily. "Okay, Bubba."

Once everyone loaded up, he laid out a plan.

"Kynlee is on her way to the factory, but Wicked is here."

"How did you do that anyway?" Demon asked.

"I put trackers in all of your cuts for this exact reason. There's also one on your bikes as backup. We've been through too much for me not to take precautions." He sighed in frustration and I squeezed his shoulder.

We're going to get my family back.

Chapter Forty-Eight

Kynlee

PROTECTED
THE MERCILESS FEW MC: DEVIL'S IGNITED
Briarswood, Mass.

I made it to the factory in 15 minutes, 24 minutes total, since the call ended. I hopped out and stared at this massive, dark building. I hesitated, but then remembered hearing those brutal thuds of their fists against his body or his face!

What if he's…

No, we can't think like that.

"You can do this." I lean so I have to take the next steps forward toward the giant opening where the doors would be. I noticed a faint glimmer of light toward the back. I also memorize the layout and how to make my way back to the exit or any closer exit.

The dust, or possibly asbestos, makes me cough, echoing off the walls. A closed door is where the source of light was coming from. I wasn't stupid. This could very well be an ambush I'm walking into. If it was, I would just call…

I reach for my phone and realize that it's not there! In my rush, I must have dropped it, thinking I had slipped it into my pocket. Now I have no way of letting them know!

Fuck!

Then I heard a click and something pressed against my back, no doubt a gun.

"Move it!" The voice bellowed as he pushed the gun further into my back. When I glanced behind me, I saw this huge guy in a black suit before he shoves me forward.

"Go!"

Instinctively, I raise my hands and step forward. As I push open the double doors, a sleek and modern office comes into view, a stark contrast to the eerie atmosphere of the abandoned asylum outside.

How long have they been here to do this?

"My humblest apologies, Bruno can be very ruthless when it comes to my orders. He forgets his manners. Especially when it comes to beautiful girls such as yourself."

My stomach churns in disgust as I close my jacket to try to cover up.

I look up to see a Hispanic man in a very nice suit. Who knew a tailored suit could fit slime so well? Besides Bruno, there was another henchman near a different door.

"Santos Navila."

"I know who you are." I spat.

"Good, you should know who I am. You should also fear for your life if you do not follow my instructions clearly. Bring him in!" The other guard goes into the room behind the door.

I was so happy! I needed to see if my love was okay!

The back door opened, and he threw a body onto the floor; they landed with a thud, covered in dust. Finally, they let out a cough.

They stood up and turned around and I should have known; he was too scrawny. It was the Devil himself. I guess because he seems to work for or owes money to Santos, he's more like the Devil's advocate.

Judging by his black eye and busted lip, he's had better days. He stands awkwardly beside Santos's chair, as if injured on one side. They must have really worked him over.

Good. I would have paid to see that.

"Where's Asher?!"

The bodyguard in the background pours a cup of coffee. Santos sips, "Cream please." He shoos him away. "Anyway, business first. Mike tells me you have money that belongs to him. And he owes me a significant amount of money, don't you?" He points a gun to Mike, who flinches but doesn't respond.

"He doesn't have a dime! Mom left that to me!" I screamed, looking directly at him as Santos sips his upgraded coffee.

"Ahh, he said you would say that. That's why we kidnapped your *amour*."

The tears gathered. "Where is he? Please…" My heart physically aches to see him.

"Ahh, young love. Do not fret, if you look at the screen, you'll see a CCTV feed and look, there he is. A little bloodied and battered, but breathing. For now." He chuckled at my reaction to the grainy feed. I could still make out the bruises, black eye and bruised cheek.

But what injuries couldn't I see?

"A-Asher."

He clicks off the TV and my heart sinks. "Let's talk business. Tell her!" He yells at Mike, who flinches.

What a fucking sniveling coward.

"Transfer the money to his offshore account or he's going to kill me!" He pleaded.

I couldn't help but laugh. "Did he think you were some great father figure that I'd save out of love? I don't know what he told you but I'd rather watch your live autopsy than pay whatever you owe him!"

Mike looked absolutely baffled, but he couldn't believe I would save a vile human being who's been harassing me with violence, saying all those disgusting things threatening to assault me.

Santos looks at Mike like he better convince me or else.

Chapter Forty-Nine
Asher aka Wicked

PROTECTED
THE MERCILESS FEW MC: DEVIL'S IGNITED
Briarswood, Mass.

I regained consciousness to see a tall, lanky man in front of me. He appears confident and arrogant, despite his disheveled look, black eye, and busted lip. I can't help but laugh. This can't be him.

"What's so fucking funny?" He demanded, causing me to laugh again. He was no real danger. No, there had to be someone more powerful. He was nothing more than a boot licking lackey.

"You must be Mike, the boy who threatens women like a goddamn coward. You're pathetic."

"That's tough talk for someone who's tied up." That bruised my ego. He had a point.

"No matter, she's going to give them money willingly, and it's all because of you. I don't even have to threaten her. Love makes people stupid! That's how I conned all those women. They thought I loved them, but I loved their money!"

Then he pulled a gun from his jacket and aimed it at my head. "Maybe I should kill you to teach her a lesson."

The bodyguard comes barreling my way, shoving Mike to the ground, his gun sliding away from him. "That's not the boss's plan. Remember the rules, we shoot him if boss sends the signal and only then! Sam goes for you!" Mike jumped up like he was going to do something, but the guy had his hand in his jacket. His eyes grew wide before he calmed down.

The guard sounded like he had more power over this situation. The weasel chuckles nervously before retrieving his gun.

"Whatever. I'm headed back, so you can get paid and I can finally get that blow job she owes me. Maybe we'll broadcast it. The feed goes both ways. Enjoy!"

I struggle against the ropes that bind me to this chair. "I'll fucking kill you if you touch her!" I scream. But a part of me worries. I'm not sure my family knows she's there or even where I am. I can only hope.

Chapter Fifty

Sam

PROTECTED
THE MERCILESS FEW MC: DEVIL'S IGNITED
Briarswood, Mass.

We ride together until Demon and Fiend peel off to head to the location that has Wicked. I know they can get the job done.

But it doesn't dull the black out rage fueling me right now. A squeeze on my thigh brings me out of my thoughts.

"Hey, we're here." I noticed we're on a dirt road, hidden in the untamed brush behind this massive old factory. I hopped off, getting ready to storm toward it, guns blazing, when his arm stopped me.

He looked at me, a few seconds of silence, and I understood he was trying to get me to focus and think and not go thermonuclear. I inhaled and exhaled hard and nodded.

A quick kiss and he leads the way through the bushes. It was almost as tall as me. We made it to the door. He looks through the clouded windows to see if there was any movement. "All clear." He lets me know before he tugs on the door until it opens loudly with a creak. "Draw your weapon."

He's right, the noise could have tipped them.

Chapter Fifty-One
Kynlee

PROTECTED
THE MERCILESS FEW MC: DEVIL'S IGNITED
Briarswood, Mass.

Knowing I wouldn't help him and would rather watch him die mercilessly, Mike storms towards me. He raises his hand and smacks me, causing me to fall to my knees. I hold my cheek with one hand and check my mouth with the other, spitting out blood.

I laugh, I know my blood filled smile only pissed him off more. He yanks me up by my hair. "The camera goes both ways, sweetheart. How about I shove my dick down your throat so your boyfriend can see the whore you are! Then we pass you around?"

I guess he thought that was a threat. "You put it near me I'll bite it the fuck off! Do you want to risk it, asshole?"

I glance over to see Asher screaming out something as Mike still has his hands in my hair, pulling tightly.

He pushes me away, then adjusts himself. "Fucking bitch."

"Likewise."

Santos slams his gun on the desk. "Enough! I'm tired of the distractions. I want what you owe me! Now, what's it going to be, cupcake? All I have to do is send a message and they'll splatter his brains all over that camera!"

He texts something and turns the screen in time for me to see him getting punched in the stomach. "Oof! Uhhhh!" He grunted out. Then the guard looked down at his phone again, then pointed his gun at Asher's head.

I can't...I can't lose him! "Stop! I'll pay just please stop hurting him. The money doesn't matter. It...doesn't...matter." I fell to the ground, sobbing. I was so tired of my life being centered around money! I didn't need a dime as long as I had Asher. His love was what I needed. It was worth more than gold.

I can hear Mike laughing at my misfortune, "Told you she'd fold. Bitches always fold over good dick." He cackled.

I sneered at him. "I guess no one's folded over you then, have they?"

I didn't care anymore. I would not stand in fear. If I had to fight him, I would.

bang

It rang out loudly, causing me to scream. My ears were ringing, my vision wavering. I don't know which one of us he was aiming for!

"Enough Mr. Thomas, don't forget you owe me $150k and if I don't get it in this transaction, you die an excruciating death. And no one will find ALL of you."

Mike went pale and swallowed hard, nodding.

I scoff, then smirk. "I'd rather not pay and watch you die!"

"But remember, your boyfriend dies, too. So let's get this transfer started, hmm?" He presses a button and I catch them punching him in the face!

What choice did I have?

Chapter Fifty-Two

Sam

PROTECTED
THE MERCILESS FEW MC: DEVIL'S IGNITED
Briarswood, Mass.

"Do you see her?"

I try to look over his shoulder. "Yes, now stop making noise. Hold on…"

He pulls his phone, types something and puts it back.

"What did you do?"

"We got ten minutes." He looks, then pulls his gun. He lets me step in front of him to see. When I peer in, some guy's got a gun pointed at her and she's typing on the computer.

"He's forcing her to transfer the money! It's always been about my sister's money that was never his. He forged her signature, we proved it!"

She pauses, looking at a TV screen. We can't see what she sees.

She screams, "No! Please stop…I'll do it! I'll do it! Stop!"

"That seems to be the only way you continue." This other

242

guy says. He looks like evil in a nice suit. They always wear suits…Frankie then Sébastien, now this guy! They're all the fucking same!

What's obvious is the guy definitely has authority over Mike or… what makes more sense is that Mike owes this sleazebag.

She's typing away frantically, obviously making mistakes because she can't think straight.

"Ready babygirl? You take Mike and I'll take the bodyguard and suit. I'll circle back if you need help."

"I won't need any help." He nods and bursts through the door.

It all happened so fast that it was like slow motion. After he kicks the door, everyone looks our way.

I run behind the crates that are in the room before the bullets fly. The boxes look like leftover inventory from when this place was a bustling candy manufacturer. The bodyguard was reaching for his piece, but since we already had ours out, Bubba was able to shoot the guard, two in the chest. He recoiled before he fell into a pile of packaging.

Meanwhile, I decided a quick death was way too easy. He is so focused on my husband that he doesn't realize I'm determined to kill him. He was shooting at my husband and when I heard the click of an empty clip; I aimed at Mike's upper leg.

bang bang

I hear, then see him fall hard. Seeing the blood spurt out makes me happy. I purposefully avoided the femoral artery, but I was close.

bang

A bullet whizzes past me, and Bubba loses it. Emptying the rest of his clip into the suit. Must have been six or seven bullets. He fell back into his chair, wheezing. He was still alive, but not for long.

"Aunt Sam!" Kynlee jumps up from her hiding place and runs to me, hugging me so tightly we both begin bawling.

I pull her away, "Thank God you're safe! Did he touch you?"

I stare daggers as he writhes on the ground. We both walk up to him and he's laughing like an idiot. He may have suffered significant blood loss. Then he blew a kiss at Kynlee, still laughing like he won.

Kynlee laughs too while she pulls the other pistol. Aiming quickly before firing, sending a bullet into his groin. Not his leg, thigh, or even inner thigh. The hole and the blood started pouring from the center. He was in so much shock, there was a delay in his reaction. He grabbed his crotch, shaking uncontrollably from the shock.

"And you will never threaten anyone with your useless dick again, but I hope you get fucked in prison! Good luck, prison bitch!" Then she spat on him.

He pulls back his trembling hands, covered in blood, as he finally screams bloody murder, and that is more satisfying than him being dead.

Then we heard a strained grunt as we saw the suit press a button on his phone.

"No! Asher!" Kynlee screams out, then we hear a gunshot from the television screen, but there's no feed! Kynlee knew... something happened as she fell to her knees.

bang*

Bubba shot him point blank in the chest. There was smoke billowing from the hole. I hear the faint sound of sirens.

I sigh, "The Sheriff?"

"You know it. I'd rather turn myself in and give my statement than have state police snooping in our business.

I pull Kynlee up as he makes a call. The blue and red lights bounce off the building.

"You need to go, both of you."

"And leave you? No!"

"Samantha! Asher's been shot! I called Fiend after the sound. He said it looks bad." He tried to whisper the last part, but Kynlee heard and collapsed again.

"Goddamnit!" He helped me pick her up. "Sam, get to the hospital! You know how to ride Ruby. Go! Now!"

I pull Kynlee out of the building. We make it to the bike as I see Bubba step out with his hands up. The cops quickly take him into custody.

"Help me push the bike, Kynlee! If you want to see Asher, you have to help me!" That seemed to knock some life back into her, but she was still whimpering and I understand. It's the not knowing that's killing her.

"I killed him! I was supposed to love him, but I…"

"You stop that! He's going to be fine. Now hop on, we're far enough away to start it."

She does, but I can feel her sobbing.

Please let him be okay!

Chapter Fifty-Three
Asher aka Wicked

PROTECTED
THE MERCILESS FEW MC: DEVIL'S IGNITED
Briarswood, Mass.

I squeeze my eyes before prying them open. It's super bright in here.

"Ugh…mmm…" My throat is super dry, forcing me to cough. I notice something, someone laying on my side.

I realize I'm in a hospital gown. What the hell happened?

I vaguely remember being tied up by her step-dad and that big ass bodyguard guy. I heard someone come in and gunfire. I remember Reaper trying to untie me…he yelled something. I felt a burning pain at the same time I heard a pop and then everything went black.

I got shot! I run my hand over my body to try to find the wound.

"Mmm…" I'm distracted by the faint sound. I look and know those beautiful locks anywhere. She was uncomfortably leaned over from the chair that sat beside me. She looked worried and exhausted. She didn't even stir when I started coughing. How long had she been here? How long had I?

"Kynlee… Kyn…" It hurt to call her, but I had to try. I take a few deep breaths, clutching the bandage I found on my left side.

Feeling a surge of energy, I tried one last time. "Wake up, ted-teddy bear."

She slowly sat up, her hair a mess as she tried to push it out of her face.

"Asher?"

"Yes." I smiled. Trying to keep my responses short.

"Oh my god! I'm so sorry! It's all my fault you got shot!"

I point. "Remote please." I raise the bed up so I'm not lying completely flat.

I graze her cheek and the tears fall. "I'm fine. See?!"

"But I…"

"Kynlee Marie." I say sternly, causing her to laugh through the tears.

"Do you still love me? How could you love me after all this trouble I caused?" I saw the guilt she harbored, but it is nothing to the guilt I would have felt if something happened to her.

"Not only do I love you, I'd be so proud to call you my ol' lady."

"What?"

I took her hand. "You heard me and I know you know what that means."

She jumps up and hugs me around the neck, causing me to cough again. "I do! I do! Yes, yes, yes!" Her smile could light my darkest days. She's already brightened it so much.

"Ahh!" She screamed in sheer joy, but then handed me a cup of water to help with my coughing.

knock knock

I see Sam peek in. She looked relieved to lay eyes on me.

"Come in. I know you're all here." I joked, but they all filed in as expected.

"You know, we got to stop meeting like this." I chuckled, but no one laughed. Kynlee cried immediately.

"Baby, I'm sorry. I didn't mean to joke about it."

"You could have died…you did die!"

Well, that's a shocker. I think they saw it on my face.

"You flatlined because of the bullet clipping a few capillaries, but they found the damage and stopped the bleeding." Sam said somberly. "But another problem arose, they needed blood for transfusion and you are O-. You can give to any blood type, but you can only receive blood from another O- donor!" She got choked up and looked away.

Lil ruffled my hair. She looked no worse for the wear. "The problem was the hospital didn't have enough on hand and started calling other hospitals. They didn't have time. You were already on the operating table!"

Reaper stepped forward. "While they were calling around, they asked for volunteers to get tested for your blood type, and we all did."

Everyone showed their cartoon themed bandaid. I chuckled at the sight.

"And it was a miracle. One of us was a match!"

"Don't keep me in suspense! Who saved my life?" I look at my family, trying to find my guardian angel.

Then I felt her squeeze my hand. Tears filled her eyes. "It was me. I was your perfect match."

I kissed her hand. I should have known my angel saved my life. I couldn't love her more.

"You've been my perfect match since I met you. Thank you, my sweet girl. You saved me. I love you."

The entire group gasped at my declaration. The girls beaming. I see Fiend and Reaper hand Demon twenty each, and he nods at me, waving the money.

Did they bet on me? What the hell?

The room went quiet. Kynlee kind of laid on my chest as I sat closer to the edge of the bed.

"Well, someone tell me what happened."

Lucifer stepped forward. "I turned myself in and gave all the details, citing self defense and telling them to pull the feeds from the TVs at both locations. I still have to go in for next steps and you and Kynlee will need to make a statement. All the bad guys are dead except for Mike. The girls here made his life much more difficult. He'd probably rather be dead than in his current condition." All the guys grimace, then laugh. It seems like they already knew.

"He didn't deserve to die so easily. Aunt Sam shot him in the thigh."

"Nice!"

"You think that's good? Your girl shot him in the dick!"

"I hope I blew his balls off! He'll be a eunuch for the rest of his life and a fleshlight for other prisoners!" She sounded so proud of what she did. Sadistically proud.

"Damn, remind me never to piss you off! I'd like to keep all my bits." I cover myself.

She leaned over to whisper, "I'd never do that. I'd rather feel you deep inside me." She leaned back, grinning.

Now I had to think of anything else to not pop a boner in front of everyone. Thank goodness I was already covering so my hands can keep it down.

I find myself lost in her eyes and somebody groans.

"Alright, looks like everything is good here. Let's go, we could all use some rest. Kynlee, I brought some more clothes and snacks. I'll take your dirty laundry."

She points to the corner. "Thank you, auntie."

And they all file out.

"Umm, how long have I been here? Have you been here the whole time?"

She sets the new bag by this recliner chair and it answers my question.

"I agreed to give the blood if I could stay in your room while you healed. I had to be monitored after the draw, anyway. The chair is comfier than it looks, besides it's only been three days."

There was a light knock on my door. "Mr. Benedict, good to see you finally awake. I'm Dr. Hill. I am your primary physician. How do you feel? Scale of one being terrible and ten being perfect."

He sits me up further, checking my vitals.

"Honestly? Solid seven, doctor."

"That's good to hear. A couple more days, you should be able to go home. I'd like to monitor that wound for a little longer. These types are prone to infection. That's why you're on an antibiotic drip." He taps the IV bag with his pen.

"I understand."

"I hear you're a motorcycle rider. Well, let's get the bad news out of the way. No riding for six months and I want you to start slow when you do."

The single worst thing you can tell a die hard rider, but it made sense because of the location of the incision. I don't want to pop a stitch. They bandaged me tightly, but I still felt the wound. Riding would be a bitch in the beginning.

"Alright, everything looks on track. I'll have the nurse bring you dinner. Miss, would you like dinner as well?"

She shuddered, trying not to laugh. "Um, no thank you, I'll hit up the cafeteria for...anything else."

"Alright. You're on strict food options, Mr. Benedict."

Well, there goes my dream of a double cheeseburger and fries. The nurse punctuated my sorrow with the beige tray full of mashed potatoes, jello, fruit cup, and a side salad. I forced a smile and thanked her.

Once she left, I twisted my face up.

"Hey, it's temporary. When we get home, I'll make you whatever you want."

"Pasta salad." I smiled hard.

THE MERCILESS FEW MC ANTHOLOGY: PROTECTED

She feeds me to encourage me to eat. She snacks on chips while holding my hand and watching TV, occasionally passing me a chip or two. I knew my baby wouldn't let me suffer.

The night nurse offers to bring in another bed so she can sleep next to me. She lit up for the chance to snuggle up to me again and be my teddy bear.

She showered while I brushed my teeth, gargled, and spit it back in the cup. If she was going to be laid up on me, I would not miss the chance to kiss her every moment I had.

The bathroom light clicked off, and she came out, her hair wrapped in a towel. She wore a t-shirt and shorts. She got a little closer before I realized, "Hey, is that my black t-shirt?"

"You mean one of twenty that you own? Yes, I stole some to be closer to you. They all smell so good, like you. It comforted me while you were unconscious." Her face fell thinking about the uncertainty while I was healing.

"Come here. I missed my little teddy bear." She hops up on the other bed and climbs over to lie on my uninjured side. The warmth of her body against mine is comforting and tempting. My hand automatically squeezes her ass, causing her to look up at me while rubbing her leg on mine. She bit her lip.

"Fucking hell, don't do that, baby."

I am pent up. It has been so long. Even unconsciously, my fantasies ran rampant. Dreaming of hiking her up around my waist, bringing her soft lips to mine before I bit them softly and pulled back. Our tongues would wrestle for dominance, but ultimately, I would overpower her. She'd gasp in fake surprise.

With each touch, the sensation of her sweat kissed skin against mine ignited a fiery connection, sending shivers down my spine. A tingling warmth spreads through our bodies and amplifies our pleasure. I'd pin her hands against the wall with one hand and rip off her top with the other and reveal this salacious red lace bra that pushed her tits up, teasing and tempting my need even further. Then the dream flashed to us, entangled in silk sheets. I rocked her against me as she tried to catch her breath. Our bodies entwine, lost in the moment, consumed by the physical effects of our emotions. Every touch, every kiss, every gasp for air was a testament to the power of desire, leaving her breathless, yet craving more. She felt like she was constantly in an orgasm as her pussy squeezed me dry.

And then I woke up.

"Asher." I look down, and she's peacefully asleep, whispering my name. Was she dreaming of me, about me, the same erotic intertwining of our bodies? I noticed she was rocking with her hand between her legs. Then it wandered over to my leg and higher… higher…

I grab her hand before I blow my load from her touch alone. "Teddy bear?"

"Hmm?" She didn't open her eyes.

"Were you having spicy dreams about us?" Her hand rested on my chest, rubbing across the thin fabric of the gown.

"Mmm…may…be." She giggled against me. I took her hand and kissed it. "Guess we both were, but you're causing a problem, baby. I'm pretty sure if I'm not cleared for riding, I'm not cleared for sex."

She sat up, and for a moment we stared at each other in silence. "I'm sorry." She said, and I nodded. Her hand sliding slowly down my chest. She glanced at her hand and smirked as it slipped under the blanket.

"Kyn…"

"Shhh… the next shift doesn't come in for another 90 minutes. I've always wanted to sneak a hand job in a public place, and what better time than now?"

She pulls back her hand and licks her palm before returning to my dick, sliding slowly. I groan loudly until she shushes me. I'm panting while watching her hand stroke me up and down.

I felt myself get close, and I realized something. I pull the blankets away. I did not want to explain that to the nurse.

"Baby... I'm so fucking close... I'm going to cum...going to..." I lift and move my gown over to one side to avoid staining it. She gave me sensual kisses and alternated between those and moaning in my ear.

"Cum for me, baby. I know you want to. Please..." She moaned the last part, and I lost it.

"Shit!" She milked me dry, then laughed. "Wow, you were really pent up!"

I grabbed her face, kissing her passionately, catching her off guard. I left her panting.

She hopped up to the bathroom, washed her hands, and came back with a warm towel. The initial touch of the towel makes me hiss, then sigh.

She tosses it and lies on me. I kiss her forehead. "Thank you, baby, but I won't be satisfied until I'm devouring you in our room."

Chapter Fifty-Four
Kynlee

PROTECTED
THE MERCILESS FEW MC: DEVIL'S IGNITED
Briarswood, Mass.

"Speaking of our room, what do you think about remodeling it?"

He cocked a brow. "You don't want to move out like the other couples? Buy a house?"

"Nah…one we have plenty of time for that and two, I wouldn't mind living with Aunt Sam and Uncle Rocco. They're the only family I have left. I enjoy being in the same house, if you don't mind?"

The way he looked at me, I knew he understood.

"Of course, whatever you want. Maybe we should kick Demon out of his room and tear down the wall?"

"That room needs Holy water and an exorcism to be clean! No, I love our space. It just needs some rearranging and new furniture and, with the extra money, we can do whatever. I want to honor my mom's memory, like a tattoo."

"Or…I have a less invasive idea. I want you to talk to

Fiend, I mean Jett. He had a beautiful tribute to his mother and I think you should consider.

I agreed, and we went to sleep hand in hand.

The next morning, I had Asher call Jett to the hospital.

knock knock

"Are you kids dressed?" He says before coming in with his eyes covered. "Hey bro, how are you feeling?"

"Better. Should be home tomorrow or the next day."

"Good! So Kynlee, I haven't told you personally, but I'm sorry about your mom. I went through something similar, and Asher wanted me to tell you what my family did to honor my mother. My sisters had memorial jewelry made with our mother's ashes. Mine is this necklace, besides in the shower I never take it off. I thought it should be an option for you and Sam. They do any type of jewelry you can imagine and that way a piece of her is always with you."

His necklace fit him perfectly. It was a motorcycle shaped with wings, manly and rugged, but also a reflection of a boy who cherished his mother. That's perfect for the first part of my plan.

"Jett, I need something from you, a favor." Asher looked confused because I hadn't discussed this part with him.

"Umm, sure?"

"My mom spent her life wasting away in a small room, strapped down against her will. The reason I had her cremated was to give her wings to fly. Once I get the amount needed for the jewelry, I would love to spread her ashes at the lake. I never felt a peace like that before. It'd be the perfect place to set her free." I wiped away a stray tear.

"Oh, I am honored to let you do that. Poppy says the same thing about an overwhelming calm. Let's all come together and honor her memory much like we did with…Avery."

I saw him wince. Even after all this time, it's still like a fresh wound. I lean over and squeeze his hand. "Hey, she's always in your heart." He nods.

"And now we have our miracle coming soon."

"I can't wait! If you'll both excuse me, I have some calls to make.

Chapter Fifty-Five
Asher aka Wicked

PROTECTED
THE MERCILESS FEW MC: DEVIL'S IGNITED
Briarswood, Mass.

Three days later, they finally released me! The Sheriff's Office came by for my statement, having gotten Kynlee's a few days ago. Unfortunately, they charged Lucifer with a couple misdemeanors but no jail time because of his upstanding reputation.

The court charged Kynlee with first-degree assault with a deadly weapon for castrating Mike. She pleaded self defense and because of the evidence including all those threatening messages; they gave her a year's probation.

"You're dating a dangerous criminal now." She joked. I cornered her in our room. "Baby, I was a convicted criminal long before you. I did actual time in the big house."

"Mmm…that's kind of sexy."

"It is, isn't it?" I lean in ever closer, smelling the peppermint on her breath.

"Don't even. I need to get dressed. Today's a special day!" She touches her new necklace before going into the closet. I switch out my usual black to a white t-shirt and jeans. Since I can't ride Stormy, I head to the truck.

I have not gone back into the barn since I saw Stormy's damage. It turns my stomach and I don't have the heart to see her like that.

I turn her on to warm it up. I get back out and grab the urn and throw a seat belt over it to make sure it doesn't move. "Miss Chelsea, I hope you're comfortable. Soon you will be free and I promise you I will protect your daughter for the rest of my life. She's the best part of me."

Kynlee comes out in a beautiful white sundress. She smiles at me before hopping in. "Hey mom. Are you ready to fly high? Let's set her free."

The guys follow us to Jett's house. There are white balloons and streamers everywhere. Poppy is waving while rubbing her stomach. She's starting to show and is absolutely glowing. Everyone gathered at the fireplace, with Sam holding her sister.

"Thank you guys for being here and thank you to Jett and Poppy for letting us use this beautiful lake to release my sister's ashes."

They nod. We walked to the east side of the lake because of the wind.

Lucifer wrapped his arm around Sam, "My dear sweet Chelsea…I love you so much and although I couldn't save you, I know you're free now. I have my small piece of you I'll never take off. I'm going to take good care of Kynlee. She will make you proud. I love you so much."

She hands the urn to Kynlee. "Oh mom, I know I can't change what happened but I can give you wings to soar, fly high. Don't worry, Asher's going to take care of me. I love you to the moon and back, mom."

I kiss her temple. "I'll always be your protector."

She sighs, she and Sam walk to the edge of the lake. Kynlee takes off the top. They both look down, whispering something. Then they tip the urn and slowly a cloud of dust blows into the wind. We release rose petals at the same time. The released petals meet the ashes, swirling together in a beautiful symphony.

We ended up back at the firepit. Demon and Fiend grill some burgers and Sam puts together tacos for Poppy's strict pregnancy craving. Fiend said she has literally cried until he made it for her. Loving her role as grandma, Sam was going to spoil her daughter and future grand baby.

Kynlee jumped into my arms, kissing me deeply. "I'm so happy she's free now."

"Absolutely. Are you okay?"

"Uhhh…yeah. I feel lighter."

"Happier?"

"Always when I'm with you."

Three months later

I finally got cleared to ride. But first, I need to survey the damage and get her fixed. I know she's going to be pissed I all but abandoned her. Well, it was now or never. I only had a couple of hours of sunlight left.

I gather the strength and make my way to the barn. I imagine this is going to cost me a few thousand bucks. I inhale hard and exhale to round the corner.

"Stormy baby, I am so sor…"

I stop and stare. Stormy is fixed! She even has a new paint job! "Stormy, girl…I can't believe it! You look good as new! But how?"

I ran my fingers across her body where I remember that gnarly scratch, but it wasn't there! She was like new, like it never happened.

I slowly put one leg over and groan as I sit, and she settles to my weight. I start her up and rev her engine, listening for signs of any maintenance needs.

Suddenly Kynlee straddles Stormy but facing me. "I had all her maintenance work done after she was repainted. If you hadn't openly avoided her because of the damage, I'd never get her fixed." She leaned back, her midriff showing off her new belly button piercing. Her skirt teased me with her upper thigh.

I lace my fingers behind her waist and pull her to me. "You fixed her?"

My eyes focused on the fullness of her lips. I steal several kisses before she places her hand on my chest. "I had the money to, besides having her fixed was a part of an even bigger plan."

"Oh, it was?" She stood, then hopped off and grabbed our helmets. "Yes, now take me here." She showed me on her phone and I knew exactly where it was.

It was the southernmost of the Grotto Lakes, about 30 minutes from the house. A beautiful pristine lake, the fishing was not so great. This was the runoff, the end point for all the lakes, but that didn't make it any less gorgeous. It was more secluded than the others that had picnic areas, docks, and other things for people to do.

She guided me to a semi private spot away from the main road. She hops off, then takes hers and mine's helmets and sets them on the ground. She has mastered taking off her helmet without tipping over.

"Slide back." She tells me as she straddles Stormy, facing me again. I swallow hard. Infinite possibilities play in my head. She sits up straight. "You know, when you told me about your nightly threesome with the twins, I was jealous. I wanted to be the girl that fulfills all your fantasies, but since they beat me to one of them, I am going to recreate it, but with a twist. Because I'd never share you with anyone else."

I was confused. "Is that right? Is my girl jealous? What do you mean by recreate…" I grab her by the waist.

"I mean, you, me…and Stormy. We had quite the girl talk about logistics, making sure we both get equal time with our man."

I laugh. "You and Stormy figured this out? When did this happen and where was I?"

"You were in the shower getting ready for the ride. I slipped out before you saw me in the kitchen. She and I took some…photos together. Oh, that's right, I never got to show you."

She pulls her phone and presses some buttons.

"There you go."

I feel my phone buzz, showing a text message from her. I smiled, seeing 'my love,' pop up as her title.

As I click the notification, "You looked damn sexy when I saw you in the kitchen, so I know these are…holy fuck! Oh baby, this has got to be illegal."

"Must be the topless photo. There's more than one so enjoy. Anyway, I had my own fantasy that works alongside yours. Stand and lean up against Stormy, please." She orders me. I do as I'm told, but these pictures are fucking hot! I'm panting and not focused on her at the moment.

Until she leans in, lips grazing just barely until she smirks. That mischievous smirk that turns my world upside-down. And this time is no different. Her fingers slip between my shirt and my jeans. She pulls my shirt out, unbuttons, then unzips my pants. Her tongue glides across her plump, glistening lips, tasting the remnants of a sweet, fruity lip balm. I've tasted it many times.

"Before we delve into my fantasy, I want to say how much you mean to me. You are my strength, my protector, and you gave me so much hope after mom died. With you and Sam, I can do anything. I love you so much, Asher Thomas."

Confirmation of receiving the best gift ever after being

humbled. I didn't have to gloat or brag about how amazing I was. I just had to be me. She loved me.

Last year, the idea of me being settled down would have seemed completely far-fetched. I was all about the fast-paced lifestyle. Booze, bikes, and...well, you know. My life is a million times better with you...and only you. I love and adore you, my teddy bear." She completes the much anticipated kiss but also frees me from my jeans. The combination of her icy hands from the ride and breeze cause me to hiss. And that's all I could get out before she dropped to her knees in front of me and Stormy.

I had to plant my feet and lean against Stormy for leverage. "Oh, baby...like that..." The vibration of her laugh made her constrict and flicker against my already sensitive skin. I look down to see her watching me. "Such a dirty fucking girl, sucking me off in public. What if a sweet, older couple ventured over here and saw you choking on my dick?" I growled.

She stood up. "They wouldn't...they'd see so much more..." She straddled Stormy, propping one leg on the footpad, revealing her lack of underwear under her skirt. My mouth fell open before rubbing my chin and licking my lips. "My my my...no underwear. Seems like my little teddy bear wants to get fucked on my bike? Am I right?"

She rocks, her pussy rubbing against Stormy, sliding her hand under her crop top, squeezing her tits.

I growl, that's my job, but I'm in awe watching my girls touch each other so intimately. I never told her I fantasized about this and somehow it became her fantasy, too. She was the one to grant my most carnal desires.

"Yessss..." She finally answered me in between her moans.

Whatever you want.

I position myself opposite of her. As I face her, I watch intently, taking in the sight of her teasing herself with one hand. The air carries the faint scent of anticipation, mingling with the sound of my own steady breaths.

"Such a tease. Keep going…I'll tell you when to stop."

Almost where I wanted her while I stroked myself.

"Ash…Asher…"

I smile. "Yes."

"We're waiting." She licked her fingers that were previously deliciously inside her. "Mmmmm…"

That fucking did it.

I leaned forward, feeling the soft brush of her hair against my face. With a firm grip on her waist, I pulled her closer, and the sound of our breaths quickened in anticipation. As our bodies met, a surge of electricity ran through me. We lined up perfectly.

"Oh! Mmm…"

"Fuck baby, you're so wet…ready for me. Ooooh…"

She answers by rocking against me. She's getting closer.

"Turn over so I can watch you bounce against me. Cum all over me, leave your mark on me and Stormy. You girls are going to be the death of me."

She flips over and speeds up, bouncing back and forth, chasing her orgasm. Her ass is mesmerizing.

"Oh…I'm gonna…gonna…cu…cu…ohhhh!" She's trembling, trying to slam her legs together, but she can't in this position. I need her to cum, for her to squirt all over me and Stormy. She collapsed, laying flat, as I pounded into her.

"So good, baby. Cum for me." She sat up on her elbows, licking her lips lasciviously while her tits bounced to the motion. Losing myself in the rhythm, the feeling and the love of the woman who loves me.

"Oh, baby… you feel so damn good." I feel the all knowing signs of an orgasm and somehow I want to see her cum again.

She gasped when my fingers reached around. "What are you…"

S. COURTNEY

"Just one more for me. It's so fucking hot watching you come undone all over my dick. Can you do that for me?"

I squeeze her tits, pinching her nipples. "Uh huh, uh huh...there...there!"

I firmly grasp her hips, feeling the heat radiating from her skin, punctuated by her breathless moans. I grip her hips and slam into her, harder, faster.

"Oh, Fuck! Yes!" She shot up, holding onto me as I came hard. "Goddamn baby, shit!" I fell on top of her, breathing hard.

She wiggles her ass while I'm still inside and I feel him jump. I smack her ass. "Watch it." I leaned all the way back, looking for my clothes to put myself back together.

She slid forward and winced at my dick slipping out. "Oh, I am. I couldn't even if I wanted to. Let's go home."

"Whatever my ol' lady wants."

She puts all her clothes on. "I love hearing that so much. You know what I can't wait to hear next?" She says, leaning against Stormy while making sure everything is in the right place.

I slip my cut on reaching in my pocket. Now she's sitting, waiting for me to jump on and take us home.

"Calling you the future Mrs. Benedict. What do you say, Kynlee Marie? Will you marry me, my sweet teddy bear?"

"Wha...are you serious? You're serious! Oh, my god!" She slaps her hand against her mouth, the tears start.

And now she's hyperventilating.

"Breathe, teddy bear, breathe. Take your time."

She snatches the ring and puts it on, "Oh my god, yes, yes, yes! I'll marry you." And she attacks me with kisses.

Now that I think about it, I definitely can't tell the proposal story as it happened. Can't say, yeah, I fucked her senseless on my bike, my dream threesome, then asked her to marry me.

264

We'll need to revise the story to risk not giving Sam a heart attack.

She's holding her hand up, marveling at the sparkling ring, her eyes widening with delight. The soft twinkling of the ring's diamonds catches the final moments of sunlight.

"You know I'm supposed to put the ring on…"

"Oh my gosh, I'm sorry! Here!" As she hands it back, she chuckles and smiles widely, wiggling her fingers. I slide it back on and gently kiss her hand.

"So, is that a yes?"

"To go from bunny to ol' lady to wife? You bet your ass! Merciless Few forever, baby."

No sweeter words have been spoken.

THE END

Epilogue
Asher aka Wicked

PROTECTED
THE MERCILESS FEW MC: DEVIL'S IGNITED
Briarswood, Mass.

One year later

"Mrs. Benedict, can we go now? We're almost there, a few miles from realizing your dream and mine."

Kynlee insists on getting a souvenir from every state, attraction, or monument we visit. Now we were 15 miles from Berkeley, California, where there was the famous grove of giant Sequoias. She gets to touch these mammoths and I complete my cross-country trek with my two girls.

The door bells ring signaling her exit from the seashell shop. "Alright, alright. I want our display case to be epic, so I got these pretty shells, see? I want to tell the most amazing stories about our trip."

"Do we tell them about how I've fucked you in every state on the way over here? Or how we eloped in Vegas and this is now essentially our honeymoon?" I kiss her hand intertwined in mine. The gold band was a recent addition to my hand.

"Mmm, I don't think that's a detail that they need to know, though I loved moaning your name in every single state. Can't wait until tonight." She squeezes me after getting settled on the bike. She sits more forward than usual because of the two bags strapped to the back. She leans back enough to put on her helmet.

"Ready, teddy bear?" She held out a thumbs up and squeezed her thighs. I loved being able to reach back and rest my hand on her thigh on long stretches of road.

The highway wound and curved, revealing some breathtaking views, including the California coastline. The ocean seemed more lively, more active as it crashed upon the cliffs. We found a scenic point to sit and bask in the sounds and serenity.

"Five miles to go. Are you excited?"

She sighs as she laid against me on the picnic table, watching the birds dive for dinner and boats skim the horizon. I wonder if any of them are on their way to our dock.

"I am! I know the pictures do not do them justice. Thank you for doing this for me." She looked back and kissed me, then straddled me, my hands cradling her, making sure she didn't fall backward.

"Anything for my wife."

She squealed, holding out her hand. "Oh, I can't believe it!"

"Believe it, Mrs. Benedict. Let's go."

She was right. There are no words to describe these majestic beauties in all their glory. Riding my bike through the trunk made me feel small, like an ant. There were towering branches reaching towards the sky and sunlight filtering through them, creating a soft, magical glow. The sounds of rustling leaves and chirping birds filled the air, creating a symphony of nature. The smell of damp earth and fresh foliage enveloped me, invigorating my senses..

We parked close to one and watching her run toward it to touch it was funny. She seemed to have shrunk compared to the massive tree. "It's so beautiful!" She craned her head up while touching it. When I walked up to her, she had tears in her eyes. "While living in Oklahoma, when times were bad, I imagined coming out here and being amongst the trees, my safety, my refuge. And because of you, I fulfilled that. Now we can spend our time making new memories, the sky's the limit! You don't know how much you've changed my life and how happy you've made me."

I also touched the rough bark that filled me with a sense of ancient wisdom and strength. I couldn't help but smile at her.

"Excuse me, do you want a picture together?" A young girl asks.

"Yes, I can show off my ring!" I hold her by the waist, she holds up her ring and kisses my cheek and I saw the flash go off a few times. They may have caught me smiling. How could I not be when I had the most beautiful, sinful girl as my wife.

My ol' lady, my wife. Wow.

She hands us back her phone. "Congratulations!"

"Thank you! He's my husband now!" She happily declared.

"So, Mrs. Benedict, what do you want to do now? We have a long trip back."

She pondered for a moment. "Let's find a different route home to see how many more states you can defile me in."

She sauntered away, leaving me with my fantasies...and a problem. I growl and pick her up, headed toward Stormy.

Life is good.

Merciless Few Forever.

About the Author

Thank you for taking the time to read Protected. I hope you enjoyed the book and would love if you could leave a review on any retailer or Goodreads.

If you would like to hear more from me about new releases and sales, you can visit my website.

Website: https://www.scourtneybooks.com/